RUSSIAN
AND SOVIET Story

K. Paustovsky

IN THE HEART OF RUSSIA AND OTHER STORIES

Raduga Publishers Moscow

Translated from the Russian
Designed by *Andrei Nikulin*

КОНСТАНТИН ПАУСТОВСКИЙ

Во глубине России

Рассказы

На английском языке

Printed in the Union of Soviet Socialist Republics

П $\frac{4702010200-135}{031(05)-86}$ 018−86

ISBN 5-05-000651-1

CONTENTS

Some Random Reflections*

It is useless expecting a writer to explain his own work. "Read my books — it's all there" is what Chekhov used to say on such occasions. And this represents my views entirely.

So I shall limit myself here to a few general reflections on my writing and a brief outline of my life. There is little point in giving a detailed autobiography as this is already the subject of my work *Story of a Life*. Six volumes covering some forty years from early childhood up to the beginning of the thirties have already been published, and I am still working on the later periods.

I was born in Moscow on May 31, 1892, in the family of a railway statistician.

My father was a descendant of the Zaporozhye Cossacks who fled to the banks of the

* These notes by Paustovsky, which are reproduced here in slightly abridged form, provided the introduction to an eight-volume collection of his works published by *Khudozhestven-naya Literatura*, Vol. 1, Moscow, 1967.

River Ros near Belaya Tserkov after the suppression of the *Sich*. This was where my grandfather, who had formerly served in the ranks of Nicholas I's army, lived with my Turkish grandmother.

In spite of his profession which called for a sober assessment of things my father was incurably romantic and nonconformist with the result that he never stayed for long in any one place. After Moscow we moved to Vilno, Pskov and finally to Kiev where we settled more or less permanently.

My mother, the daughter of a sugar factory clerk, was a strict, overbearing woman.

Our family was a large one, composed of highly different individuals but all artistically inclined. We liked singing, playing the piano, debating and were passionately interested in the theatre.

I went to the lst Kiev grammar school.

The family broke up when I was thirteen and after that I had to find a way of earning my own living and paying for my education. I managed to struggle along by coaching, a rather arduous job.

In my last year at school I wrote my first short story which was published in the Kiev literary magazine *Ogni*. This was in 1911 as far as I remember.

After leaving school I studied for two years at Kiev University and then got myself transferred to Moscow University and came to live in Moscow.

At the beginning of the First World War I worked as a tram driver and conductor in Moscow and later as a medical orderly on trains for the wounded both in the rear and at the front.

In 1915 I moved to an army medical unit and worked with it during the long retreat from Lublin in Poland to the town of Nesvizh in Byelorussia.

Then I happened to get hold of an old newspaper which reported that both my brothers had been killed on the same day in different parts of the front. I went home to my mother who was living in Moscow at the time, but found it impossible to settle down there for long and set off on my wanderings again. First I went to Yekaterinoslav and worked at a metal factory, then at the Novorossiisky factory in Yuzovka, and after that in a boiler factory in Taganrog. I left the boiler factory in the autumn of 1916 and found work in a fishing artel on the Azov Sea.

It was in Taganrog that I began writing my first novel *Romantics* in my spare time.

After that, shortly before the February Revolution I returned to Moscow and became a journalist.

My character both as a writer and person developed in Soviet times and it was this factor which determined the whole course of my life.

I was in Moscow during the October Revolution and saw many historic events between 1917-19, hearing Lenin speak on several occasions and living the hectic life of a newspaper correspondent.

But the itch to move soon got me again and I went back to my mother who was now living in the Ukraine again; I saw some turbulent events in Kiev and then left for Odessa. It was there that I came into contact for the first time with a group of young writers: Ilf, Babel, Bagritsky, Shengeli, Lev Slavin and others.

But my "wanderlust" would not let me be and after spending two years in Odessa I went to Sukhum and then to Batum and Tiflis. From Tiflis I travelled to Armenia and even got as far as northern Persia.

I returned to Moscow in 1923 and worked for a few years as an editor in the Russian Telegraph Agency. During this period my work was beginning to appear in print.

My first "real" book was a collection of short stories entitled *Meetings in the Open Sea* (1928).

In the summer of 1932 I began writing *Kara-Bugaz*. After the publication of *Kara-Bugaz* I gave up all my other jobs and ever since then writing has been my single all-consuming, and sometimes agonising profession, but one which I love with all my heart.

I continued to travel a lot, even more than before.

During the Great Patriotic War I worked as a war correspondent at the Southern Front and also moved around a good deal. After the war I again travelled extensively. In the fifties and early sixties I visited Czechoslovakia, lived for a while in Bulgaria in the delightful small fishing towns of Nesebur and Sozopol, travelled all over Poland from Crakow to Gdansk, sailed round Europe, visited Istanbul, Athens, Rotterdam, Stockholm, Italy (Rome, Turin, Milan, Naples and the Italian Alps), France, particularly Provence, and England where I went to Oxford and visited Shakespeare's birthplace, Stratford-on-Avon. In 1965 due to my chronic asthma I spent a fairly long time on the island of Capri — that enormous rock set in the warm crystal-clear waters of the Mediterranean.

My impressions of all these journeys and the people that I met, all very different and all interesting in their own way, have provided material for many of my stories and travel sketches.

I have written a fair amount in my time, but I still feel that I have a lot more to do and that certain aspects of life can only be fully understood and described by a writer when he has reached a ripe old age.

In my youth I had a passion for the exotic.

In the dull Kiev flat where my childhood was spent I was constantly surrounded by the whispers of an exotic world conjured up by the force of my own young imagination.

These whispers carried the scent of a yew forest, the foam of Atlantic breakers, the rumble of tropical storms and the ripple of an Aeolian harp.

But this brightly coloured exotic world

was simply the figment of my imagination. I had never seen a dark yew forest (with the exception of a few yew trees in the Nikitsky Botanical Gardens), or the Atlantic ocean, or the tropics, and I had certainly never heard an Aeolian harp. I did not even know what it looked like. It was not until years later that I read about it in the memoirs of the explorer Miklukho-Maklai. He built a harp frame out of bamboo around his hut in New Guinea. The wind made a blood-curdling howl down the hollow bamboo and terrified the superstitious local natives so much that they never interfered with his work.

My favourite subject at school was geography. It provided objective confirmation of the fact that there were exotic, far-away countries. I knew that my poor, unsettled life of those days would never give me the opportunity of seeing them. My dreams would obviously never come true, but I went on nourishing them all the same.

My state of mind could be described quite simply as a mixture of delight in the world of my imagination and sorrow that I could not see it. These were the two sentiments that predominated in my early poetry and first immature attempts at prose.

With time I abandoned my love of the exotic with all its titillating, extravagant glamour and indifference to simple, ordinary people. But its golden threads continued to weave at random in and out of my stories for many years to come.

We often make the mistake of confusing two different concepts, the so-called exotic and romantic. We substitute the purely exotic for the romantic, forgetting that the former is only one of the external forms of the latter and has no independent content of its own.

The exotic as such is divorced from real life, whereas the romantic is firmly rooted in life and feeds on its rich sap. I abandoned the exotic, but I did not abandon the romantic and never will. I will never renounce its purifying fire, its compulsion for human warmth and spiritual generosity, and its constant quest.

A person with a romantic disposition will never be false, ignorant, cowardly or cruel. The romantic element is an ennobling one. There are no reasonable grounds for renouncing it in our struggle for the future good of mankind or even in our everyday life...

I think that one of the most distinctive features of my prose is a tendency towards romanticism.

This reflects my character, of course. It is ridiculous to expect anyone, least of all a writer, to renounce this tendency. Anyone who makes such a demand does so through ignorance.

With a few rare exceptions the seeds of romanticism are planted deep in all spheres of reality and human activity.

They may be ignored or crushed, or else given the opportunity to grow, embellish and ennoble man's inner world with their blooms.

Romanticism is inherent in everything particularly in learning and knowledge. The more a person knows, the fuller is his perception of reality, the closer he is surrounded by poetry and the happier he becomes.

Ignorance, on the other hand, makes a person indifferent to the world, and indifference is like a cancerous growth in that it develops slowly but surely. For the indifferent person life soon becomes bleached and faded, vast layers of it withering away, until in the end he is left alone with his ignorance and pitiful sense of well-being.

True happiness is above all the lot of those eager for knowledge, the dreamers...

My life as a writer began, as I have already mentioned, with the desire to know and see everything. And it looks as though it will end on this note as well.

The poetry of travel blended with unadorned reality has produced the best possible fusion for writing books. Traces of my wanderings can be found in almost all my stories.

At first it was the South. *Romantics, Glittering Clouds, Kara-Bugaz, Colchis, The Black Sea* and a number of short stories.

My first visit to the North—to Leningrad, Karelia and the Kola Peninsula—completely overwhelmed me.

I came to understand its deep fascination.

My first experience of the white nights over the Neva did more to deepen my understanding of Russian poetry than dozens of books and many hours of reflection on them.

I realised that the concept of the North stands for more than just the quiet beauty of its landscape. It is also Pushkin's poem *Friend of My Hard Days* written in the solitude of the Pskov forests. It is the brooding cathedrals of Novgorod and Pskov, the slender magnificence of Leningrad, the Neva seen through the windows of the Hermitage, the chanted epics, the calm gaze of the women, the black conifers, the sparkling mica of the lakes, the white foam of the bird-cherry trees, the smell of bark, the blows of the woodcutters' axes, the rustle of pages read at night when the dawn is already rising over the Gulf of Finland and Blok's works are ringing in one's mind:

> *...One dawn*
> *Has stretched its hand to another*
> *And, sisters of two heavens, they weave*
> *A mist, now pink, now blue,*
> *And in the sea a dark drowning cloud*
> *Shoots from its eyes in angry death throes*
> *Flashes of light, now red, now purple.*

I could cover many a page with these vague associations which give such a clear picture of the North. The North captivated me more strongly than the South.

The North inspired such books as *The Northern Story, Charles Lonceville's Fate, The*

Lake Front, and short stories.

But it was central Russia which turned out to have the most productive and beneficial influence on me. This happened fairly later on when I was nearly thirty. Of course I had been to these parts before, but my visits had always been brief, passing ones.

It occasionally happens that you see a path across the fields or a little village on a hillside and all of a sudden you know that you have seen it somewhere before long ago, perhaps even in a dream, and it became overwhelmingly precious to you.

This is what happened to me with Central Russia. I fell under its spell immediately for the rest of my life. I became aware of it as my true native land and felt a Russian to the very core of my being.

Since then I have known nothing closer to me than simple Russian people and nothing more beautiful than our land.

I would not exchange Central Russia for any of the most famous, fantastically beautiful spots in the whole world. Now I remember with a smile my youthful dreams of yew forests and tropical storms. I would give all the splendour of the Bay of Naples, with its riot of colour for a willow bush wet from the rain on the sandy bank of the River Oka or the winding little River Taruska on whose quiet banks I often live for long spells.

My life is now deeply bound up with this bush and the cloudy sky blinking with rain, the smoke curling up from the villages and the damp meadow wind.

I have returned to my own people,
My gentle, brooding land...

I found the greatest feeling of simple, ingenuous happiness in the forests of Meshchora. The happiness of being close to one's native soil, of inner freedom and concentration, of hard work and sweet contemplation.

I owe most of my works to Central Russia. It would take too long to list them all, so I shall mention only the main ones such as "Meshchora Country", "Isaak Levitan", "The Tale of Forests" and the cycle of stories "Summer Days", "The Old Boat", "A Night in October", "The Telegram", "The Rainy Sunrise", "Cordon 273", "In the Heart of Russia", "Alone with Autumn" and "Ilyinsky Waters".

It was in Meshchora that I found the pure unadulterated language of Russian country people. I do not wish to repeat myself, so I will not dwell on the subject here. I have described my views on the Russian language in *The Golden Rose* in the chapter entitled "Diamond Language".

The reader may find it strange that the author of this article is concentrating on the external surroundings in which the action of his works takes place, without saying hardly anything about his characters.

It is impossible for me to evaluate my characters objectively and therefore I find it difficult to discuss them. Let the reader judge them for himself.

I have always been at the side of my favourite characters, sharing their joys and sorrows, their conflicts and worries, their success and failure. And as strongly as I loved all that was truly humane in the most insignificant and mediocre characters, I hated stupidity, ignorance and baseness in people.

Each of my books contains a collection of many people of different ages, nationalities, occupations, temperaments and actions.

I used to be interested in the lives of famous people and tried to find features which they had in common, those features which made them stand out as the leading representatives of mankind.

Apart from separate works on Levitan, Kiprensky and Taras Shevchenko I have written stories, sketches and chapters in novels on Lenin, Gorky, Tchaikovsky, Chekhov, Victor Hugo, Pushkin, Hans Christian Andersen, Maupassant, Grieg, Flaubert, Lermontov, Mozart, and many others.

But most of the time I have been happy writing about simple unknown people, artisans, shepherds, ferrymen, forest wardens, buoy keepers, watchmen and village children—my bosom friends.

I owe a great deal in my work to poets, writers, artists and scholars belonging to various ages and lands. I will not attempt to mention them here but they range from the unknown author of *The Lay of Igor's Host* and Michelangelo to Stendhal and Chekhov and there are many of them.

But most of all I am indebted to life itself in all its simplicity and significance. I was happy enough to witness and take part in it.

In conclusion I should like to repeat that my development as a writer and a person took place in Soviet times.

My country, my people and the new truly socialist society which they have created are the noble masters which I have served and continue to serve with each fresh word.

KONSTANTIN PAUSTOVSKY

PRECIOUS CARGO

Stern had read in some book or other that eccentrics add a colourful touch to our lives, but nevertheless nobody liked the one who had appeared on his boat. He wore excessively baggy, yellow check trousers. Their colour irritated Stern intensely, perhaps because everything around, the water in the Gulf of Finland and the sides of his boat, the *Borei*, was a soft grey. The *Borei* was the colour of wet linen, except for a few spots of vermilion where the paint had been scratched off. The eccentric thought it very pretty, but the skipper considered that it was high time for the boat to be given a fresh coat of paint.

The eccentric walked with the gait of an ostrich around the deck piled high with crates. In his deep-blue jacket, green cap and russet-brown tie he looked like a long-legged, tropical bird with bright plumage. His luggage consisted of a suitcase and a violin.

He was on his way to Great Britain with a cargo of toys. Loading the boat with timber, leather or sacks of grain was one thing, but carrying toys was downright humiliating. The old captains from the boats moored nearby simply shrugged their shoulders.

The eccentric had demanded that the greatest precautions should be taken in handling the toys, and they were lowered into the hold as if they were high explosive.

The first mate, Chokh, a superstitious soul with a grudge against life, expressed the view that these "wretched playthings will lead to no good". When Stern asked him what he meant, Chokh mumbled that the cargo was too light to be firmly strapped down in the hold and if there were a storm — you know yourself — the crates would slide over to one side, the *Borei* would list and that would be that. Having expressed his considered opinion Chokh went ashore for some cigarettes.

"Keep your opinions to yourself," Stern shouted after him. "You're ordered to load pigs' trotters, you load it. What difference does it make?"

The irritation on board did not abate. In the morning as they were leaving port a sailor from the *Land of the Soviets* hailed them through the megaphone:

"Everything in order with the cargo of teddy bears?"

Stern felt relieved that there was a mist at sea, as if it would conceal his frivolous cargo.

He imagined being greeted with the polite enquiry from passing ships at sea:

"Where are you bound for and what is your cargo?"

"Toys to Belfast," the watch would reply.

This would create a great stir on the passing ships and their decks would be lined with the grinning faces of the sailors. A chorus of jeers would greet the crew of the *Borei*. "Ma-ma" the other sailors would cry mockingly and their captain would shout from the bridge:

"Safe voyage with the dollies."

Chokh called the eccentric a clown and it was true that he commanded little respect. Sailors are normally indifferent to their passengers and cargo, but now their pride had been hurt. They would openly make fun of him by pointing at his red, sharply pointed shoes and asking him:

"What did you pay for those pumps?"

And the more impertinent ones phrased the question differently:

"How much are those clod-hoppers?"

The eccentric never took offence answering readily that he had paid twenty rubles in the big Moscow department store GUM.

He was in an ecstatic mood. Marvellous things would happen as evening approached. Clouds loomed up like gigantic balls of pink cotton-wool, lighthouses winked through the dark sea mist, and the shores of Denmark seemed to smell of fresh herring and whipped cream. The eccentric would go below to the messroom and announce to Stern:

"I'm most satisfied."

Stern would raise his eyebrows at this, for there was little cause for satisfaction. They were entering the North Sea and the barometer was falling steadily like the weights on a clock.

"Storm rising," he replied and went off to his cabin.

On the fifth day after dinner in the mess the eccentric tapped his glass of mineral water with a knife and asked for permission to speak. A grey drizzle was falling outside and the lamps in the mess were burning brightly. The lamps and the eccentric were reflected in all the four mirrors at once. Stern was watching the eccentric's reflection and could see his profile with the crooked pince-nez on the soft, good-natured nose.

The request put Stern in an awkward position. As captain he could stop the eccentric by telling him that speeches were out of keeping with strict sea customs. He could remind him that sailors were men of few words who despised verbosity (unless a fellow had had one over the eight of course). But he disregarded the displeased glances of the mates with a resigned wave of his hand:

"Let him speak."

The eccentric addressed them as follows:

"An annoying misunderstanding has taken place. The cargo which I am accompanying has given you a lot of trouble for the simple reason that you know very little about toys.

Your professional pride has been hurt. Of course, taking part in an expedition to the North Pole is much more impressive than carrying a cargo of toys. I had not realised that sailors were so fond of the spectacular and so thoughtlessly hostile to things about which they are simply ignorant."

These words rang out like a declaration of war. The eccentric proceeded to get down to the heart of the matter. He argued that the art of toymaking was just as noble as the art of navigation. He stunned Chokh by announcing that a certain German toymaker had become a millionaire through making tin soldiers. He declared that Soviet toys were the best in the world and that the *Borei* was at this moment carrying the best of the best to an exhibition in Belfast. He infuriated Stern by mentioning casually that he had noticed a small canary coloured sailing boat in the captain's cabin. Toys were a precious cargo. The only people with the right to break them were children, certainly not the dockers or the crew. He challengingly described Chokh's fears as sheer rubbish. Ask any sailor whether a ship could keel over from a cargo of toys and he would laugh in your face.

Chokh protested. He recalled an incident in Leningrad when a porter had been crushed by a bale of cotton-wool. He countered the attack by asking whether the eccentric would get a laugh in the face if he went up to someone and told him that a man had been crushed to death by cotton-wool. The argument got heated, until Stern stopped it by asking with barely concealed curiosity:

"What sort of toys are they?"

"Two classes," the eccentric replied.

He dragged his case into the mess and tipped a pile of red-cheeked matryoshkas, sailing boats, rabbits and teddy bears onto the table.

"This is the second class," he explained. "The English customs officials will have a pleasant surprise when they open the cargo of Bolshevik toys and hundreds of dolls with beautifully arched brows and bright artificial smiles tumble out to greet them. These smiles will conceal the real cargo, the first class toys. Here they are."

He shook the case and there was a shower of papier-maché Komsomol dolls and Pioneers, Budyonny on a grey horse, Red Army soldiers with ruddy cheeks, blacksmiths hammering ploughs, policemen with comical faces, spinners at the wheel, miners doubled up in the shafts, crowds of children on May Day floats and, finally, a comical king with white eyes, who gave a hoarse bark at the slightest touch.

The toys were passed round from hand to hand. The junior mate sat a policeman on the sugar bowl, gave him a flick on the nose and stuck a cigarette into his mouth. The policeman swivelled his wicked beady eye angrily. Stern started to argue with Chokh about the model sailing boats. Chokh said that they were tea clippers, but Stern angrily insisted that they were brigs. They got out a book on old ships. Then the wireless operator sat down at the piano and a Pioneer doll began to do a tap-dance under the expert guidance of the mechanic.

The sailors kept popping their heads through the door with a grin. The bosun came to report on the speed, picked up a toy whistle and piped all the songs of the nightingale.

The excitement spread to the crew's quarters. The helmsman Shiryaev boasted that he could carve a torpedo boat with masts, funnels and a conning-tower out of a single piece of bark. Nobody believed him. He gave his word of honour and demanded a piece of bark, but there was none to be found on the *Borei.* The air rang with the names of famous ship model builders from Hamburg, Odessa and London.

Chokh remained true to his superstitious beliefs, regarding the toys, especially the fluffy teddy bears, as a protection against acts of fate.

Stern told them how he had seen workers' children in Le Havre playing in the deserted, refuse-filled spots in the harbour where the port watchmen did not bother to chase them away. Their toys were simple. They used planks of wood for boats and rusty nails for anchors. They played very quietly and there was something very sad about their pleasure because it was so fearful.

The eccentric interrupted him to say that a lot of skill and affection goes into toys, possibly because their makers had an unhappy childhood. A child without toys has nothing but the stuffy adult world around him. He cannot talk to steam trains and rabbits, or have the wonderful experience of unscrewing a policeman's head and looking inside into the hollow plaster ball.

"I quite understand how insulting it must be to carry a load of dolls in lace knickerbockers," he continued. "But our cargo's quite different. You can see for yourselves. We are transporting toys for those parts of the town where the children play with old tins and dried herring tails. It is difficult to imagine how much tears and laughter lie in those crates in the *Borei's* hold, which you hate so much. But you wouldn't mind taking a cargo of salted tripe, would you?"

The noise did not die down until midnight when four bells sounded particularly melodiously in the dark, windless night.

Stern went up onto the bridge. The *Borei* was sailing round the Scottish coast. He took a look at the barometer and cursed. There was a storm approaching from the Atlantic. The stars were blinking in confusion through long trails of mist.

The tender strains of a voilin floated up from the eccentric's cabin. Stern listened. The sound of a violin on the ship at night was as unusual as the cargo lying in the holds. He lifted his whistle to his lips, hesitated and then blew. A sailor came running up.

"Tell Chokh to make sure the cargo is secure," he ordered. "There's a storm approaching."

"Aye, aye, sir," said the sailor, running off.

When Stern went below there were lamps covered with thick nets shining in the hold and Chokh was shouting:

"Careful there! It's not soap, you know."

They were hard at it until morning, but the cargo was secured beautifully, as only Chokh could secure it when he was in good spirits.

The eccentric went on playing the violin until the early hours.

A thick gloom struck against the ship's lanterns and crept behind the stern. The barometer was falling in leaps and bounds.

The eccentric had dropped off to sleep with a book on his chest — *David Copperfield* by Dickens. He dreamt about old England with its yellow post chaises, pale-faced young girls, attorneys with check frock coats, and glasses of grog drunk on an empty stomach...

His sleep was unexpectedly interrupted at six in the morning, when the book slipped to the floor and the *Borei* dived into the abyss.

The eccentric woke up and grabbed his pince-nez to find out what was happening. He could see nothing except a yellowish fog and a raincoat hanging perpendicularly on the wall and flapping against his face. A black monster crawled out slowly from under the bed and began to slither round the room—it was his old leather suitcase.

It felt as if the *Borei* was in an enormous

bottle and someone was blowing into it as hard as he could.

He did not realise immediately that there was a storm. At first he thought that the *Borei* was tossing about like a chip of wood at the bottom of a giant waterfall. The nails creaked in the overdry timber and the iron hinges screeched, but the worst sound of all was the steady, clear howl of the hurricane outside in the rigging.

He threw on a few clothes quickly and went to the mess where he was greeted by the dawn. The scene reminded him of a winter's day in an army hospital: the forgotten lamps were burning with an egg-like flame and the unpleasant light oozed in to form puddles by the windows.

He opened the door and went out on deck. The green, turbid morning was roaring and tossing at the ship's sides. The ocean moved like a wall and the moaning in the rigging made his flesh creep. He crawled his way up to the bridge, but the view here was even gloomier. Here you could see the *Borei* twirling like a potato in an icy cauldron.

Stern's oilskins were soaked through, and so were the junior mate's. Stern gave the eccentric a wry smile and pointed downwards. The eccentric's blood ran cold. This must mean that the *Borei* was about to sink at any minute now. Then he realised that he was being politely requested to go below to his cabin. He shook his head stubbornly and stayed on the bridge.

Stern ceased to pay attention to him. He was staring ahead, frequently pulling the handle of the ship's engine-room telegraph. Torrents of water bore down on the boat, whipping up gigantic mounds of foam before them. There was one moment when the eccentric was certain that the *Borei* was finished. The boat had plunged into the waves and for a few munutes there was nothing but the red funnel and the bridge with Stern sticking out of the lathery ocean. Then the boat rose up reluctantly and water streamed from its deck as if it were pouring out of a bucket with holes in it. The eccentric could see from Stern's taut back that the moment had been a very dangerous one.

He was sobered up by an angry shout through the megaphone, which was almost drowned by the storm. Stern's voice croaked:

"How about the toys in the hold, Chokh?"

"So far so good," replied the echo from the brass tube.

Stern grabbed the eccentric by the collar and shouted in his ear:

"We've got to break through into the North Channel! "

The eccentric nodded in reply, but thought privately that breaking through was out of the question. The *Borei* was jerking like a man whose face is being hit, first right, then left, by a mob of lynchers. He was struck by the fact that the prow did not seek to avoid the blows, but sailed head-on into the most towering waves. This was either the courage of despair or sheer insolence.

Stern opened his lips wide as if they were made of rubber and shouted hoarsely:

"Force eleven! Can you hear me? Yes. At night. We'll deliver the cargo all right. Down, down..."

His lips stretched into a smile.

The eccentric crawled below. A steward was lying on a divan in the messroom. He was upset because the galley was out of order and they would have to serve cold food. The very idea of eating seemed absurd, and the eccentric put the man's words down to an unbalanced state of mind.

At three o'clock the horn sounded gloomily above deck. The eccentric pressed his nose against the icy porthole and saw a rusty boat with its stern rearing out of the water and scraps of a flag flying on its mast. The boat dived into the water and disappeared in the rain. Although he was not a sailor, the eccentric noticed one strange thing: the *Borei*'s flag was on its stern, but on the other boat it was at half-mast. He asked the steward about this.

"What's strange about that," replied the steward annoyed. "They're asking for help."

Even the eccentric realised that asking for help was pointless to say the least. The other boat was carried away in a swirl of foam. After that there were only a few glimpses of its red hull in the breaks between the waves.

The eccentric was shaking. He had lost faith in the soundness of the *Borei* and the omnipotence of Stern. The radio operator picked up two SOS calls. The ocean was like a raving lunatic.

The storm grew. Night was approaching but sleep was out of the question. The only thing to do was smoke and wait. Wait for what? The eccentric avoided thinking about the possibility of death, but then the *Borei* keeled violently over on its side and plunged down, its decks pounded by thousands of tons of water.

A desperate whistle came from the bridge. The white-faced steward cried to the eccentric:

"We're passing the Rock! On deck! "

The eccentric jumped out and recoiled at the sight of white death roaring ahead of him. He did not notice the cliffs, only the powerful jets of water spurting high into the sky. Faint with nausea he crawled onto the bridge. The *Borei* was keeling violently from side to side, water pouring over its deck. It was sailing parallel with the breakers.

"What? What's up?" shouted the eccentric to Stern, but the wind stopped up his mouth like a cork and whistled like a flute on his teeth.

Stern did not even give him a glance. His eyes were fixed on the blindingly white jets, all the more terrifying because the dense gloom of night was advancing rapidly from the east.

The junior mate looked at the eccentric with his tired eyes, seized his hand and traced these words on his palm:

"We're passing the Rock."

The eccentric realised that the most difficult moment had come. The *Borei* was fighting with all the remaining strength it could muster. It was being swept past the cliffs. The turbid waves were as steep as the cliffs themselves.

The eccentric squatted down and closed his eyes holding on tightly to the rail. He was suddenly seized with the overwhelming desire to go deaf and blind. Then he felt a tug at his shoulders, got soaked to the skin and jumped up: a swirling wave had passed just below the bridge sweeping the lifeboat from the deck, which now bobbed about in the water with its keel sticking up. The *Borei* lifted its bows sharply and then plunged down past the last cliff. Waves beat against the stern and the engines gave a light shudder.

Stern wiped his face on his sleeve and spat. He turned heavily to the eccentric, squeezed his elbow and took him down to the messroom. There he sat in silence and the eccentric did not dare to ask him anything.

"Yours is a lucky cargo," said the skipper at last. "It's almost impossible to pass the Rock in this weather. All the boats crash on it. But we had no choice. We'll be protected by the shore in an hour's time."

The eccentric asked why they had needed to pass the Rock. He knew that in heavy storms boats sail against the wind and waves until the weather has calmed down, and never change course so as not to expose themselves to mortal peril.

"If I'd been carrying a cargo of salted tripe, I would never have changed course," Stern muttered. "Now go to bed."

The eccentric meekly went off to his cabin, changed his clothes and lay down. The swell had become regular and pleasant. He got warm and fell asleep.

He dreamed of a town where the snow was falling thickly and quietly, covering the tiles of the houses and the bridges of the ships.

The wintry air off the sea was as fresh as spring and quite unforgettable. Millions of lights were flickering in the dusk.

Stern came out onto the bridge in a new jacket with gold chevrons. His clean-shaved face looked young.

The *Borei* gave a solemn hoot. Huge torches were lit and they began to unload. A smell of fresh paint wafted from the crates of toys.

The eccentric went ashore and roamed around the alleys soft with snow. He met old men like characters out of Jules Verne and savoured the strong smoke from their pipes.

The town smelt of old ships. In the streets jolly, rosy-cheeked nannies told their children how the *Borei* had fought its way through a storm as frightening as the end of the world and as cold as any icy compress, to bring them toys. The children's eyes shone with delight and inexplicable tears.

The snow and flames from the open hearths evoked magical scenes from Hans Christian Andersen. The eccentric noticed the dainty footprints of Cinderella. She had very warm tiny feet and the snow melted as she trod on it. He followed the footprints and they led him to the *Borei*. Cinderella was standing on the boat talking to Stern, whose face was wreathed in smiles.

The eccentric stepped back a pace as she turned to him. Her eyes shone and her face was radiant with joy. Small snowflakes nestled in her dark hair and her dress, the colour of sea water, shone with changing colours in the light of the fireworks shooting up over the town. The fireworks were to mark the beginning of a big winter festival.

The eccentric woke up. It was quiet. He went on deck and before him in the silent light of dawn lay Belfast—an old city with its lights still burning, tucked away in a thistledown mist. There was a scent of autumn grass. The *Borei* steamed along, rocking gently on the water in a slow greeting to the town.

1929

A MOSCOW SUMMER *

I

A halt had been announced. The skis were stuck into the snow. The sun was reflected in their broad curves like amber fruit. The wind and fine clouds were flying over very low, only just above the fir-trees. The fire-lane was being snowed up, and the sun was changing into a damp stain.

Hofman, the architect, nicknamed "the pocket skier" because of his diminutive height, was wiping a ski with his mitten. He was polishing it to mirror smoothness. The wood was warmed by the vigorous rubbing, and the shine was turning into a smell of varnish and fir-needles.

Lelya held the compass on the palm of her hand. The timid needle trembled for a long time. The instrument had become confused in the sparse woods and on the open ground. Then it firmly aimed its white point southwards, somewhat to the left of the sun. Bear Mountain lay in that direction. Hofman checked it with the map. In a faded green patch that indicated forests there was an inscription in black: "Monastery burned down by French." The compass needle was true.

Beyond the monastery, over a gully bristling with firs, on Bear Mountain, stood the unfinished building of The Fifth Day Rest House. It was easily approachable from the Bryansk road, but the skiers were coming from the north, from Golitsyno, through dense forest. The house was being built by Hofman.

Of the five skiers, only one, the journalist Mett, had a practical aim in view. He wanted to do a write-up of The Fifth Day. The others had come on the trip for the snow and the winter forests.

Mett had only known about The Fifth Day from the brief notes in the newspapers. They said that a well-known French architect considered Hofman's a project of genius. Disputes had arisen among the post-graduates of the Communist Academy over The Fifth Day. They reported that the building was cylindrical and built almost entirely of glass. In answer to Mett's questions, Hofman replied tersely and off the point; he cursed the new Moscow houses, calling them "American junk" and invited Mett to go to The Fifth Day on skis.

Mett thought about The Fifth Day in the suburban-line railway-carriage. But he forgot about it in the forest. He could breathe. As if spring had passed over the snows. Mett stuck

his sticks into the ice-crust and looked round;
the snows were exuding a clean, sharp odour.
It was the tang of the wind, of ice when it
melts in your mouth; it was the tang of youth.

Mighty layers of oceanic air had settled on
the countryside round Moscow. When he lit a
cigarette, the match in Mett's fingers was a long
time going out. The flame did not even tremble
in the wind.

Luzgin glided up from behind, his skis swishing rhythmically.

"Ho, ho! " he shouted, frightening the hares
and bearing down on Mett's skis. He wanted to
say something, but Mett could not hear.

He took off his leather helmet and finally
heard Luzgin's words; they were like shouts.

"...Six o'clock in the morning ... dark ... went
to the railway station, and they were turning
off block after block in front of me."

"What do you mean, turning them off?"

"They were turning off the lamps. One—and
the whole ring of boulevards was plunged into
darkness! Two—and out went the whole of
Tverskaya Street to the Triumphal Gates!
Amazing! "

There were little snow-caps on the bushes.
Lelya stopped, took off her glove and touched
them delicately with her cold fingers.

"Just like white sparrows! "

Lelya's husband, Danilov, the reporter, silent and short-sighted, had been lagging behind
all the way.

Luzgin counted the trails of the hares. Fleeing

from the skiers, they were weaving complex loops in the snow.

A low sun shone through the frozen branches. Transparent shadows were cast onto snow untouched by anything, untouched even by the wind. You had to look hard to see them.

It was getting dark. The forest went broadly downwards, towards the gully. Hofman looked round and shouted.

"Bear Mountain! "

They stopped. The mountain, overgrown with scrub, rose up solemnly beyond the gully, like a nugget of old silver.

Lelya cried out. She was the first to spot The Fifth Day on the mountain. The moon was hovering over a wall of transparent trees. It looked like a pink cloud raised to a vertiginous height.

2

Mett thought a moment, peered briefly through the window outside, where the stars and snowy branches were creating a picturesque winter's night, and then he struck the keys hard. Stunned, the grand piano boomed hollowly. Mett hit the keyboard again, a second time, and then a third, and the piano sang at last in full voice:

> *High is the honour and fair is the name—*
> *Granada's a province that's famous in Spain!*

When the wind attacked, Mett frowned. The noise was penetrating into the house and drowning the music. It was coming freely in through the walls and going out again. As in a room with Venetian blinds. A gust of wind fills them with fresh air to the very edges, like water filling a tumbler, and the tobacco smoke is drawn up in an even stream.

Hofman was dozing over a cold glass of tea. When Mett frenziedly banged the keys, he opened his eyes, looked at Mett in astonishment and dozed off again. Lelya was asleep beside him, sitting at the table.

Danilov drew the paraffin lamp up to his nose and wrote near-sightedly, re-reading with one eye what he had written down.

"A cylindrical house. All the walls filled with convex windows of unbreakable glass (no frames). Rooms semicircular. The main hall is round. The walls are very thin and admit sounds in from outside. They have narrow louvres which are automatically closed with laths of polished pine. These louvres can be set at any angle.

Three floors are joined by a broad limestone spiral staircase. The staircase runs near the walls. It sections off floors and ceilings in an unexpected way. There is no lighting yet. All the lamps will be of tungsten glass, which does not filter out the ultraviolet rays. Hofman claims that it will be permanent summer inside, the climate of Algeria. In winter, holidaymakers will be able to sunbathe, as at the seaside in summer.

The centre of the house from foundations to roof is pierced by a round stone column resembling a mast. Generally, there is something of a lighthouse about the building. Hofman grew up by the sea. In youth, he says, he even sailed on schooners carrying Kherson cherries. As watchman for The Fifth Day he has taken for the winter a young Communist, Grishin, demobilised from the Baltic Fleet.

Yet there is something dead about the house, something of the crematorium. It has not been furnished and is not quite completed.

The house is not fenced off. It stands in a grove of trees over a gully. Below is forest and a frozen woodland stream. It is called, strangely, the 'Darinka'."

Danilov wrote "Darinka", "Darinka", "Dar"... and dozed off. The stars flew past the windows, scoring them with green traces.

Mett played more and more quietly, plucking at the keys as if they were strings.

Luzgin went downstairs to the boiler-room for matches. He wanted a smoke. Grishin wasn't there, he had left for Moscow. The boilerman Nikifor was old; he had rheumy eyes.

"Well, Dad, used to this house?" asked Luzgin.

Nikifor thought and peered down into one of his felt boots.

"It's a roundish house, of course. The wind ventilates it all sorts of ways, there's no blockage. A practical thing."

Nikifor was convinced that houses begin to collapse at the corners. He was used to the house. He was preoccupied with something else.

"That Grishin," he said, livening up. "Fired a revolver at a hare the other day. I've never seen that before, though I'm a hunter myself. Can you shoot a hare with a revolver?"

Luzgin said you could.

"The house—it's just beautiful! " sighed Nikifor, as if forgetting about the hare. "When they were building it, there was orders not to break a single little bush round it. You look outside now, there's a road, but they made it narrow so as not to fell too much timber. And what was it like before? They used to tear up the trees by the roots whole dessyatines at a time, they dried up the rivers, they wiped out the game. Some animals made for Meshchovsk, others for Rzhev. The forests were empty. The last time Hofman arrived, we got talking. 'We,' says he, 'are going to make this whole area a nature reserve, or else what rest will people get? Let it all grow and flower without hindrance.' "

Luzgin went back upstairs again. All were already asleep. Lelya had curled up on the divan. Mett and Danilov were sleeping on the floor. Hofman was lying on a camp-bed with his face upwards, like the body of a military leader. His sharp nose threw a gigantic shadow on the wall.

Luzgin admired the shadow, put out the lamp and lay down next to Mett. Dreams float-

ed up as a distant roar—he heard the whistling
of railway engines, the noise of the wind over
the gullies. The piano shuddered and began singing quietly. Luzgin fell asleep.

Only Nikifor in the boiler-room was awake,
reflecting over his felt boots as they dried out.

Mett opened his eyes. He could feel a warm
freshness; his head was amazingly clear. He had
slept enough. Outside, the snow was falling.
Mett did not see it. He only noticed distinct
snowflakes flying away from the glass.

"Beautiful! " said Mett loudly and he lit a
cigarette. He shone the glow from his cigarette
on his watch—it was half past four.

"What's beautiful?" asked Hofman from his
bed. He had woken up earlier than Mett.

Mett was silent for a moment.

"I want to write about this house. You'll
weep with delight at yourself. Not an architect
in the world has deserved such an article. We'll
arrange an interview."

"Oh, to hell with you," muttered Hofman.
"Ask away."

"Tell me yourself."

Hofman thought for a moment.

"The house will, of couse, be written about
by experts. That's important for me, but not
necessary for all the rest. I suppose that The
Fifth Day would best be described by a downright ignoramus in architecture; someone like,
say, you or Danilov. This will be like the opinion
of the lay reader of a literary novelty."

"Thanks," said Mett.

"Cities have outlived their time. If you, citizen Mett, think that's not true, Engels thought otherwise. Each state system has its innate forms of accommodating people. Socialism doesn't need cities. Cities are created by human limitations, the inability to deploy raw materials, labour products and cultural values. All these are piled into a heap and millions of people are collected round it."

"Weak! You're denying the collective principle."

"The radio, telephone, air-flights and the transmission of images at a distance make it possible to forego the necessity of assembling millions in one place. Collectives will be numerically smaller, that's all."

"We'll assume so."

"What is a house? To a man, it's the same thing as its shell to a tortoise or a snail. It must be arranged so as to lighten both the biological and the psychological in our life, giving it a medium in which to flourish. A house must be rational, must conform strictly to its function and delight the eye. The contemplation of beautiful objects enhances the creative mood. This is a powerful factor in the matter of socialist construction and the creation of a full personality."

"That's being denied."

"Who's denying it? The half-baked! " said Hofman angrily. "Who said that only an idiot can't love Pushkin?"

Mett didn't answer.

"You're a layabout, not a writer. I said, didn't I, that a house must correspond to its function. You don't go to Moscow for a rest, you go into the forest for that. Am I right? Which means a rest centre must be inseparable from nature. Hence, form. Relaxing lines are needed. The most relaxing line is the circle, not the acute angle. Hence, round rooms. The walls admit sound, and you were frowning while you played the piano. That was done on purpose. The noise of the forest and the wind are as much master in the house as outside it. Instead of external walls, glass. You are woken not by the slamming of front doors, but by the rising of the sun.

"There are interstices in the walls. The louvres have to be set at a certain angle, the whole house is filled with air, and at the same time there is complete calm indoors. The roof has been divided up by screens according to the points of the compass. You can sleep on it, sheltered from any wind. The ceilings are not high. The louvres in the walls make high ceilings unnecessary. The height of the rooms should correspond to the average height of people, otherwise the room becomes revolting, like a thin man of gigantic stature. Is that enough?"

"For the time being."

Mett looked out of the window for a long time, hoping to see the light tinge of blue that heralds the approach of morning, but he waited in vain and dozed off.

As soon as dawn began breaking, Luzgin woke

up Danilov. Both had to return to Moscow in the morning. They skied as far as Aprelcyka on the Bryansk road. Night turned from black to dark-blue, then grey. The rime-clad tree-tops shone with a yellow glow; the sun rose behind the forest.

Dense steam poured from the stations, the engines and the carriages. The rooks cawed desperately. The smoky, stuffy, weather-beaten trains ran to Moscow which, like a beast of the forest, had breathed a dark patch in the deep hollow snows. Smoke and steam were also bellowing from Moscow, but the Moscow smoke was sombre and majestic. It was, as it were, the smoke of history, of revolutions, the smoke of eternity. So thought Danilov, who had a penchant for poetic metaphors and was slightly overstrung.

"I didn't like Hofman's house," he said in the buffet at Bryansk railway station, where they were drinking tea. "Calculation in every trifle. Is such extreme purposefulness necessary?"

"You just been born or what?" snapped Luzgin glumly. "What nonsense you're talking! "

Danilov was insistent.

"Each house," he continued, "ought to have a certain reserve of useless objects. In each house there ought to be at least one mistake."

"What for?"

"To give it life. Smooth talk without any mistakes is sheer boredom. A mistake is a sign of life, infallibility is death. Hofman's house is dead."

Luzgin shrugged his shoulders.

"Mistakes vary," he said, putting on his rucksack. "A Tatar oil-prospector built a palace in Baku. The architect slipped up and didn't build a W. C. indoors. The guests and their hosts had to go into the yard when they needed it. I don't think they shared your views."

Lelya, Hofman and Mett returned to Moscow in the evening. In the tram, a button was torn off Lelya's fur coat in the crush. The passengers crowded and pushed one another intolerably. Lorries bowled along Pyatnitskaya Street, erupting curses.

Danilov was not at home. Primus stoves hummed in the kitchen. Lelya sat at the table and, slowly drawing a glove off her hand, burst into tears... In reply, a tram, as battered and evil as a dog, growled malignantly outside the window.

3

Luzgin arrived at the factory two hours before work began, as was his habit; he always arrived early. He used to relax at the factory. He would walk about the workshops, stand for a long time near the lathes and swap jokes with the workers.

He was angered by talk that factories are unpicturesque and furnish no material for

artists. Even now, through the hollow March
mist, the windows of the forge shop breathed a
ragged flames; the violet, intolerable stars of
autogenous burners droned in the yard, in the
empty workshops the black portal cranes moved
high up in a pale-blue smoke of electric light
that was refracted in the thick lenses of safety
goggles; steel machines, champing drowsily,
were cutting up the dull gold of brass.

In spite of warning notices in the welding shop
about looking at the flame, it was a great temptation to do so. It evoked the memory of a sea
never before seen, of a smoking, almost lilac
sun, of cities scattered with mounds of street-
lamps in the deep maritime nights, like the
sparks being showered into the darkness by
T-girders as they were cut into with a cruel
grating noise. Luzgin used to stand near the
welders longer than anywhere else.

The factory roared day and night, but Luzgin's ears, accustomed to the roar, detected a
growing, ever-rising note in that noise. The factory was gathering momentum to compensate
for the failure of the winter plan. The factory
lived in calm haste, with crack workers en-
grossed in their jobs.

The teams worked silently, without shouting,
without jokes. It wasn't at all like what the
smart young men in knitted cardigans wrote
up so snappily in the newspapers about this
factory. They stuffed their write-ups with much
verbiage and a hail-fellow-well-met attitude to
the teams. And the men didn't like it. What

stuck out in the notes was an impractical, un-
workmanlike, somewhat pompous approach to
the work; but the teams bore with it; let them
write, we'll get on with our job.

Luzgin used to curse the reporters. He tried
to drive it home to them that work in the factory should be written about clearly, simply,
without exaggeration or hysteria. The reporters
agreed, but still went about things in their own
way. Today they would ecstatically announce:
"The factory is brilliantly marching forward
to the liquidation of the shortfall," but on
the next day they would sound the alarm:
"Warning signal. The factory isn't fulfilling
the March indicators. Lack of planning is the
decisive factor in the shortfall at the works."
Both statements were equally exaggerated.

Luzgin went to the information room. The
workers had already assembled. They were
nearly all from the hot shops — lean, fire-tanned,
with sharp bronze profiles.

Luzgin prepared his talks with great care.
He had evolved a language that was simple and
polished. He spoke slowly, even stumbling
from time to time, but after each stop he would
begin a passage illuminating the subject from
an unexpected angle. He thought in images
and structured his talks premeditatedly, subor-
dinating himself to them and developing them
to the required expressiveness.

The workers went with a will to Luzgin's
talks.

Luzgin kept a stern eye on the make-up

of his audience. He was delighted above all by the presence of the oldsters. There was a conviction predominant among the factory workers that the old men couldn't be swayed, that they were as stubborn as oxen. Luzgin secretly rejoiced—he was getting more and more of the older men every day.

This time, he talked about events of the Chinese Eastern Road. He sprinkled it with extracts from letters written by Red Armymen, talked about the Far East, where he had spent two years in the Red Army, mentioned, among other thing, the famous explorer of the Ussuriisky Region, Vladimir Arseniev, recommended his book as reading and quoted Gorky's opinion of it.

Luzgin's talks acquired the flesh of life, people, characteristic details and even landscapes. Luzgin noted that this method, by depriving the subject of its abstraction, uplifted the mood of the workers. His method was right. He was hitting the nail on the head.

4

Evening was approaching with all splendour of which the Moscow summer is capable. By five o'clock, the day had acquired the turbid colour of badly strained wine. Hofman was lying on the divan and looking at the masses of the black gardens ready at any moment to tumble into the bright water. He could see Sparrow Hills from the window.

He was tired. He had had to argue a great deal, draw weighty conclusions at short notice and prove what, in his opinion, needed no proof.

The dispute had taken place on the Construction Committee premises. Hofman had been summoned by a notice in which was stated: "Report of Comrade Ivanitsky on the disadvantageousness of building rest centres of the The Fifth Day type", and, at the end, "Your attendance is obligatory."

Hofman was afraid of public speeches. He did not know how to talk. His small stature, in his own eyes, diminished his authority. He was harassed by respectable engineers in fine English suits who casually uttered what seemed to be incontrovertible truths. He was being persecuted by certain research graduates from the Construction Institute who attributed almost world-wide but negative importance to the building of The Fifth Day. They garnished their discourse with a great many "isms", and Hofman was amazed: one "ism" after another meshed with the precision of cogged transmission gears. With his whole being, Hofman knew that they were wrong, but he was unable to prove it.

Nothing was left of The Fifth Day at the conference by the time they had finished with it. The research graduates said that Hofman had made many mistakes and had shown a needless functionalism in his design. They said that the house had been built like a machine: solely of working parts, American style—in other words, tightly and rationally to the point of tedium. One of them called The Fifth Day a silo tower. Hofman flared up and delivered a pile of asperities. He was profoundly convinced that the research students were crediting him with precisely what he was opposing.

The engineers listened respectfully to the research graduates, but absent-mindedly. In their opinion, it was far more important that The Fifth Day had been expensive and had consumed a lot of building materials. The engineers regarded the construction of such houses as an extravagance. They were supported by the representative of the Workers' and Peasants' Inspectorate.

"You see, my dear comrade," said engineer Rozenblit through his nose, squeezing a creaky yellow briefcase between his knees, "you see, there's one thing I can't understand. In winter your holidaymakers will be sleeping with the louvres open. Is that not so? In other words, the house will be converted into a sieve for the night. Besides which it is essential, I presume, for the air temperature not to fall lower than the set norm. In other words"—Rozenblit stood the briefcase on the table as a barrier between himself and Hofman—"in other words, there must always be warm but fresh air in the room. Consequently, there must be heating. Given latticed walls, that is as if"—Rozenblit stood up and put the briefcase under his arm, about to leave—"as if we started heating Sokolnichesky Grove."

"First," replied Hofman, "in light frosts,

the heating can be turned off for the night—the patients use sleeping bags. In severe frosts, heating is necessary, but the louvres will be closed periodically, and in the open position they will be adjusted in such a way as not to allow the temperature to fall below the necessary limit."

Rozenblit laughed briefly and went out. In the next room, he said loudly to someone:

"I have a mass of business today, and I don't want to listen to idle gossip."

Now, lying on the divan, Hofman remembered Rozenblit, flushed, and muttered:

"Idiot! Pompous ass!"

The only one to support Hofman was a man in boots and a stiff new jacket, writing something down.

"If there are not enough materials," he said, "this doesn't mean that we have to build junk. We can build an ideal house too. I have lived and rested in that house as never before, even in the Crimea. It is a remarkable house. This must be firmly stated."

"What organisation are you from?" asked the chairman.

"I am the workers' correspondent from *The Workers' Moscow,* and I shall be covering the meeting."

The resolution was vague—to consider the building of rest centres like The Fifth Day an open question.

"You open and we shall close," said the workers' correspondent, collected up his sheets of paper and went out.

His enigmatic remark drew tense smiles from the engineers.

The day of the session with the Construction Committee was Hofman's last in Moscow. He was leaving on the next day; more precisely, he was flying on leave. He was going to Kharkov by air, and from there he intended to proceed home to the little port of Skadovsk on the coast of the Karkenitsky Gulf.

His things were packed and he had nothing to do. Hofman decided to go home to the Usachevka on foot. He walked past the cramped, Asiatic Zaryadye and went down to the river. Gulls were skimming over water that was blue with petrol fumes. Thick black smoke was pouring from the black throats of the Moscow Power Station chimneys. At Kamenny Most, old men were fishing in the dirty green water. On it floated a pink Kremlin. The reflection was like something out of a fairy-tale, but the old men were spitting coolly into it and approvingly inhaling the foetid cold seeping out from under the arches of the bridge.

Hofman turned down the Prechistenka. In this part of Moscow, the sunlight was free of dust. The doormen were watering the roads. The grey asphalt was turned into shining black puddles that smelt of rain.

"Heat wave!" Hofman recalled that flying can be unpleasant in hot weather; there are many air-pockets.

Little boys were chasing pigeons over the

deserted Usachevka. At home, Hofman lay down and recalled the session for a while; then red and violet patches began gliding past under his closed eyelids and he fell asleep.

He was woken by someone banging at the door. Lelya and Mett had come to say goodbye. Lelya was laughing outside. A delicate stippling of clouds gleamed like gold fish-scales over the city.

Mett smiled with his eyes. He was unable to laugh. Lelya in an unusual dress—short, thin and shiny—was alternately laughing and then thoughtful, staring fixedly to her front. Hofman scrutinised her. Her pupils were dilated unnaturally, and sparks were glittering in the whites— the reflection of an evening full of heat and light. Just as the glittering of the waves shimmers along the white side of a steamship.

It was stuffy indoors. They went down to the river.

"Friends," said Hofman, "if we could go to the sea together. How wonderful that would be! "

The chance combination of several trivial facts frequently inspired Hofman to indulge in flight of fantasy. All it needed was an idle summer's day and a short but sound sleep to start the state of mind which Hofman was now undergoing. He called it "dry drunkenness".

He vaguely imagined the noise of acacias in the dark, the splashing of the sea, sands, steppes from which the dry wind was blowing.

"How wonderful that would be! " he repeated regretfully.

"Everybody's got holidays at different times. It's a stupid arrangement."

Mett began working something out.

"Two hundred and one days in a year," he said precisely, "we sit in dirty rooms. We haven't learned to work in a civilised manner yet. By the end of the day, the air is turning green with smoke."

"Ghastly! " said Lelya.

Hofman could not bear these complaints. The spell of "dry drunkenness" gave way to exasperation.

"How silly," he said. "You're an intelligent person, Mett, but your mind's gone a bit mouldy somewhere. You've decided that scepticism will save you from reality. You live in it like infusoria in a nutritive medium. Deep down inside, you know perfectly well that this is the wrong attitude to the environment. But you're lazy and sensual, and so you swim with the stream."

"Very interesting," said Mett venomously. "Pray continue."

"You're taking the line of least resistance and you're guided by your own feelings, not by reason. Of course, that's easy."

"You harp about that to me every day, " replied Mett calmly.

"Force yourself to think. Imagine the following position; we are surrounded not by enemies, but by friends. No bayonets are levelled against us. Imagine the victory of Soviet system, if not all over the world, then at least in Europe. You are the first to sign contracts with the publishing houses and rush off to Turkey, Greece and Italy. You will write magnificent books, and your life will acquire an unbelievable plenitude. It will take ten years off your life. Then, I hope, you will understand the meaning of the term "cultural revolution". You will be one of its champions. Its values will live within you, like the sum total of your thoughts and moods. Do not think that this will be a sweet and idyllic time. People will die and struggle then too, on expeditions, in laboratories—wherever living human thought exists."

"Vague, but rather attractive," said Mett.

"What is a five-year plan?" asked Hofman. "The greatest possible exertion to bring the future nearer, not with the dreamy tempos of biological life, but with the tempos that are needed by us, living people, who do not expect to last for two hundred years. The five-year plan is a heroic impatience forced into a framework of figures. This is its meaning and its unusualness, young man."

Mett said nothing.

"Would you agree now to leave the USSR for good?" asked Hofman.

Mett stopped smiling.

"Never," he snapped.

"Then why are you playing the fool?"

Lelya burst out laughing.

They went down to the river at Okruzhnaya Doroga Bridge. The colour of the transparent twilight reflected in it was green. Hofman took a boat.

Mauve mercury dripped from the lifted oars. Each drop was suffused with a stream of lights shining from the Park of Culture and Rest. The water went to sleep under the dense, heavy lime-trees.

Hofman took Lelya and Mett almost as far as Boloto. There, they said goodbye. Rowing into the middle, Hofman watched Lelya walking slowly along the embankment. Mett stopped to light a cigarette and fell behind.

"O, my friends! " said Hofman, turned the boat round and, in a series of short pulls, rowed toward · the noisy   darkness of Neskuchny Gardens.

5

Luzgin's father passed away in July. The old man died suddenly of a heart attack.

On the next day, Luzgin sent the body to the   crematorium and   himself   went by bus. There   was   no one   there except Luzgin. A very polite man walked carefully about in overalls, and the   organ sobbed   in   the   bass register.

Luzgin had a sense of relief. With the old man's death, the past had receded; it could now be erased from memory for ever.

Luzgin walked from the Donskoi Monastery to Kaluzhskaya Street. It ran through a belt of gardens and hospitals as far as Sparrow Hills. It was four o'clock. The drought had reached

the stage at which colours are burned away.
The foliage of the trees, the houses and even
the sky had been bleached grey. The buildings
of the Oil Institute gone white, as if covered
with salt.

Luzgin knew that Lelya worked as a typist in
the Oil Institute. He went into the courtyard,
which looked like a parade-ground, and opened
the door. The cool, bright silence of concrete
halls and passages acted on him like a sudden
shower.

He was shown the room. He went in—the
colourful Zamoskvorechye was wilting outside
the window. Lelya was typing to dictation.
She jumped to her feet, pushed up a chair for
Luzgin and asked him to wait a moment while
she finished the page.

Embarrassed by Luzgin's presence, an inconspicuous man in a grey Moscow store suit was
dictating a report on the rejuvenation of sectors
in the Grozny oil fields.

Lelya typed in bursts, her lips compressed.
The typewriter rattled in time to her confused
thought:

"What's he come for?.. Wasn't expecting it...
How nice that he's come, all the same... I'm
ashamed... I've been complaining to him about
my job, and it's good here as never before—
bright and clean, Myatlikov is dictating an interesting report... Does he know that Hofman's
flown to Kharkov... He didn't come for nothing... They don't come that far for nothing...
Why am I jittery?.. Why, why, why?.."

Lelya did not have time mentally to answer that question. Myatlikov said, "That's all," and, discreetly waiting until Lelya had removed out the typed sheet, took the report and, taking his leave, went out hurriedly. He was afraid of delaying Lelya or inconveniencing her for one unnecessary moment. Lelya never ceased to marvel at the kindness and consideration of the scientists in matters far removed from oil, cracking plants and light or heavy grades. She thought about it a great deal, but could not find any explanation. She could only assume that, in the scientific books among the incomprehensible formulae and integrals, microscopic bacteria of respect for man had been born and had insinuated themselves into the minds of the scientists and were now living modestly in there.

"Well, what is it, what is it?" said Lelya hurriedly, going up to Luzgin. "How did you find me here? You've come at just the right moment. I haven't been myself since morning—I feel beastly, as if I was alone in all Moscow."

Luzgin grasped that Lelya was referring to his arrival as a breakthrough in her life. He had dropped in by chance but, on listening to Lelya, he realised something that he had not noticed himself; the decision to meet her had been latent in him ever since the time of the skiing party to Bear Mountain. This meeting had been approaching like a cloud—in the restless rustling of the leaves, in the sudden gusts of wind, in the uncertainty of his mood; he wanted to shout with excitement and terror.

"I was hereabouts on business," said Luzgin, and blushed. What kind of "business" he did not say. He knew that it was impossible to do so at this moment. Lelya would not even hear any words he might say about death; they wouldn't get through to her. They would be drowned by the storm that was raging within her; they would be crumpled up and thrown away by her sudden confusion.

She needed to hear something entirely different.

"I've come for you," said Luzgin. "Let's go to the river."

"Yes, shall we?" asked Lelya happily, as if she had been waiting for this for a long time. Luzgin noticed the broad, tense glitter in her eyes that had struck Hofman not long ago. "It's going to rain. Aren't you scared?"

"On the contrary. It's nice on the river in the rain. Have you got a coat?"

"Yes," said Lelya with a deep sigh. "I won't be a moment."

While she was putting on her hat, Luzgin looked through the window. There was smoke coming from Dorogomilovo. The steam of the railway engines was rising to the sky in white, ominous columns, and an enormous dark-blue cloud was looming up behind Bryansk station through the dust and rumble of the suburbs.

They ran down to the river across Neskuchny Gardens and dropped into a pavilion by the lake for lunch. The approaching thunderstorm had frightened the people out walking—the park was empty.

Lelya didn't eat anything. She told Luzgin about her day.

She had quarrelled with Danilov that morning.

"I've done a write-up on The Fifth Day," said Danilov, wiping himself with a towel.

"Well?"

Lelya had been irritable since the evening before; July was at the end and she hadn't been out of town once. The summer had been enervating on the roads and in rooms full of stagnant air.

"Nothing special. After my article, they appointed a commission to find out if it's worth the trouble building such houses."

"So I heard. Show me what you wrote!"

Danilov held out the newspaper. Lelya soon found the piece and laughed drily. Danilov had written that The Fifth Day, as a little model of formal searchings, was totally alien to the proletariat, and it was a criminal waste of resources to build houses of that type now, when building materials were needed for industry.

"Addle-brains!" Lelya threw the paper on to the table. "Small fry you've been all your life and small fry you'll die! How they can believe you in the editorial office I just don't know. It's a marvellous building, it's anticipated the future, it's got talent and thought — and now this stinking write-up."

"We don't need such houses," replied Danilov icily.

"Who's this 'we'? Who's this 'we'?" shouted Lelya. "Mummy's darlings? Stockbrokers' sons?" (Danilov's father had been a tradesman.) "How dare you talk like that! You're smearing talented people. It makes me sick to listen to you, sick, you understand? Get out!" Lelya snapped her pencil in two and threw it into the corner. "Get out at once, I don't want to see you again! How can I look Hofman in the face again, and Mett, and everybody else?"

"Hysteric!" Danilov hastily began knotting his tie. "Damfool madwoman! Your Hofman is a fraud and a hack. Everyting points to that, and you can't see a damn thing!"

"Get out, I said!"

Danilov left, slamming the door behind him. Lelya collapsed on to the divan and burst into tears. She arrived late for work. The scientists, noticing her tear-reddened eyes, promptly went into the next room and one of them brought her an orange from the canteen. Lelya looked at him, smiled and the tears rained on to the keyboard of the Underwood. The scientist immediately vanished.

Luzgin listened to Lelya, flushing and coughing from time to time. Then, having made up his mind, he said:

"Yes, he's small cheese. The whole point is that it's intolerable to hear how lack of talent" (Luzgin hesitated, but the word had burst out, so he repeated it) "how lack of talent smears such fresh people as Hofman. He's a crank, of course, is Hofman, but we need such eccentrics. They mustn't be swapped for the most sober people."

The river was deserted. A hot wind was rising in gusts over the blind, leaden water. The gardens were stirring restlessly and the dusty leaves were anxiously conversing. Luzgin rowed fast. He wanted to reach the Noev Gardens before the rain. They could already see the notices on the bank: "Do not anchor here—water mains siphon", when a yellow cloud of dust rose over Khamovniki.

"We won't make it," said Lelya.

An iron ripple travelled from bank to bank, and Luzgin was blinded by mingled dust and leaves. He turned the boat into the bank and saw in the middle of the river a wall of water bearing noisily down on Lelya. The rain descended, and at once they smelt the wild scent of damp grass and river sand.

The boat bumped into the bank. Luzgin jumped out and pulled on it. Lelya jumped out, bracing herself heavily on his shoulder.

"Up the steps," commanded Luzgin, feverishly tugging the oars free of their rowlocks.

Lelya ran up the rotting wooden steps. With the heavy wet oars on his shoulder, Luzgin bounded up after her. On top, there was a boarded-up chalet. From a distance away, Luzgin saw a roofed terrace, sheltered from the rain.

Lelya ran on to the terrace, laughing. Dislodged by the rain, glossy lime-tree leaves stuck to her shoes.

The rain boomed with a hollow sound, covering the river with a dense pall. The lightning flashed liquid fires, the thunder crashed, and the rain lashed down even harder.

Without knowing why, Luzgin was smiling and wiping the heavy splashes from his face. The rain was advancing. It began lashing the terrace and crowded Lelya and Luzgin into a corner, the only spot it could not reach. Overjoyed at the wetness, mosquitos began humming in the clumps of the nettles under the terrace floor.

Lelya and Luzgin were standing close together.

"Lelya," said Luzgin, "you know what's going inside here," and he pointed at his forehead.

"Yes," replied Lelya quietly, "and there's more to come, a lot more... Such alarm, we just can't speak. Can't talk about anything when it comes."

She stressed the word "it" slightly.

"How wrong," she continued, laughing, "and how silly people are when they think that to love means one person, that the whole world revolves round that person. It's not like that at all! It's not just one person, it's everything! Everything, d'you understand! Imagine, there's the storm, wet leaves, you, Hofman's house, friendship, quarrels, well, everything, all this is love, not just one person."

"Yes, that's right," replied Luzgin.

He could hear the even booming of the rain in the acrid clumps of nettle, and the rapid beating of Lelya's heart beside him.

"There are things you never forget," he said. "We know perfectly well that nothing's eternal, but there are things that are unforgettable. They exist outside and independent of what can happen to us afterwards."

They returned to Moscow late. The rain had passed over, but the wind blew boisterously till morning. Moscow was noisy with leaves. The raindrops flew from the branches into the open windows of the trams.

Lelya couldn't sleep that night. Danilov was not at home—furious, he had gone to a friend's dacha. Twice, late at night, she quietly phoned Luzgin, and his soft, hollow voice answered her at once in the earpiece. Lelya cursed herself for a silly fool and wiped away the tears as she listened to him joking and laughing.

The windows were open. The harsh night air came in through them. The majestic chimes of the tower clock sailed over from the Kremlin. Lelya had never noticed those chimes before.

6

Mett received a letter written in a shaky senile hand. It was dated 10 August.

"My son, Viktor Borisovich Hofman, men-

tioned your name several times, referring to you
as his friend. I found your address in his note-
book. I therefore consider it my grievous duty
to inform you that Viktor was drowned on 2
August.

"The children from the local kindergarten,"
announced the handwriting, and the shakiness
increased, "were taken by motorboat for a trip
to an island three kilometres from Skadovsk.
The boat was due to return by six o'clock, but
at three, a hurricane blew up with torrential
rain, the sea was rough, and there could be no
question of bringing the children back. People
began worrying in our little town, since the
children had been sent out in light summer
clothing and could naturally catch cold. Further-
more, they were having to spend the night on
an island where there is no accommodation
except for a draughty shed for fishing-nets.
By evening, the storm had reached force seven.

"A fisherman, Kovalchenko, and Viktor volunteered to put out in a dinghy and deliver warm
clothing for children and food. Tarpaulin was
obtained from the harbour management so that
makeshift tents could be put up on the island.

"My Viktor was used to the sea and so I let
him go without fearing very much for the
consequences.

"According to Kovalchenko, they successfully
crossed the bay, taking their bearings from the
lights of Skadovsk; but as they approached the
island, they ran into heavy seas. Viktor and
Kovalchenko jumped ashore so as to pull up the

boat. Viktor was overturned by a wave; he fell
and, apparently, the wave drove his head with
great force against the keel of the boat, or the
keel pinned him to the bottom—it's hard to
understand, but he disappeared. Only ten minutes later did Kovalchenko find his body in the
breakers. He was unable to restore him to life.

"He was buried in Skadovsk. The whole town
came to the funeral. He was very much loved
here, especially by the fishermen, and they were
proud of him as their countryman; they had
read about his beautiful buildings in the papers.

"I have one son left in Tashkent, but compared
with Viktor he has a long way to go. I shall not
write about how I feel now and how the days
pass—I know it is hard to understand an old
man's grief. If you should have the desire and
occasion to visit Skadovsk, I shall be delighted.
I live modestly, as befitting a retired harbour-
master, but I think you will have no cause for
complaint.

"Yours sincerely
Boris Hofman"

"Here's how d'you do!" thought Mett with
a wry smile.

He went over to the window, apprehensively
opened the letter and read it again. Beads of
sweat broke out on his brow.

"How could it be?" he said hoarsely, put
on his hat and went out on to Ostozhenka
Street. "How could it be?" he repeated bump-
ing into passing pedestrians.

He stopped and stared for a long time at a

pink notice. From a distance, it might have
looked as though Mett was reading it carefully.
But he was not reading, he was listening: a
steel string inside him was tightening, ringing
and quivering. It made his heart ache badly.
Mett was waiting for the string to snap and
with it, his heart.

The string stopped quivering. It tightened
and drew his heart up to his throat. Mett shuddered and cried out faintly—the string had
snapped, but his heart had not burst. It began
beating joyously fast. Swaying slightly, Mett
walked away from the notice.

"I must go to Luzgin," he decided. He remembered that it was Luzgin's day off. Where
could he be? On the river, of course. Then Mett
seemed to see the notice before which he had
been standing, printed in a gigantic white letters
on a fresh blue sky. The letters formed into
the words: "Dynamo River Station. 14 August,
Leningrad-Moscow Boat Race".

Mett turned off for the Crimea Bridge and
the Dynamo Station. Colours, flags, splashing
waters, the radiance of the sky and the babbling
of the swimmers calmed him down a little.
He could see Luzgin in dark-blue trunks on the
diving board. Luzgin shouted, sailed off the
board, bending his back in an arch, and began
swimming "brass", spitting and cleaving the
water with his head.

Mett stepped down on to a raft and hailed
Luzgin.

"Get changed, old man!" shouted Luzgin,

swimming up, but then he frowned, climbed out and, shaking himself, went up to Mett.

"You look a bit low," he said sternly.

"I've just received this letter..." replied Mett, not looking at Luzgin. "Hofman has been drowned, apparently."

"Knock it off!"

"Here's the letter."

Luzgin didn't take it; his hands were wet. "Devil knows," he muttered. "What rubbish."

Mett told him about Hofman's death. Luzgin listened as he got dressed.

"Well," he said, after a pause, "it's bad. But that isn't what matters, of course. One must live. Let's have some black coffee and calm down."

On a light terrace, like the deck of a steamer, girls in swim-suits were laughing, and swimmers with numbers sewn onto their chests were engaged in dispute. Luzgin and Mett sat down at the barrier. Mett was silent and looked down at the boat-jetty. A little boy was running naked along it, his wet feet joyously slapping the wet boards. With the perception that comes with a sudden change of circumstances, Mett was scrutinising sunburned hands and the tablecloth tinged with blue from the sky, and listening to the ecstatic screams of children.

"When's the race?" asked Mett.

"Not for a while yet. It's only ten o'clock."

Mett was surprised. He thought it was much later.

"I'm going to Lelya's now." Luzgin was

embarrassed. "She's resting in The Fifth Day. I'll have to break it to her."

Mett nodded.

"Yes," he continued, "a great diviner is dead. Oh well, you're right, we go on living."

They parted. Mett stayed to watch the race and Luzgin went to Bryansk Station.

It would have been inconvenient to call at The Fifth Day; Luzgin and Lelya had arranged to meet on a path in the forest, near the boundary post.

It had been a long hot summer. There was a reek of burning over the clearings and dried-out marshes. The roads smelt of dust and tar. The birches were already turning yellow in the woods. Luzgin took a short cut and went straight across the clearing.

He saw Lelya in the forest among the yellow birches. She walked to meet him. Shadows flitted across her face and lightly rustling dress. She was approaching quickly. The oppressive heat faded away. Lelya brought freshness with her, a vague joy, the breath of autumn, space, the alarm of their new-found love. She seemed to be coming from those lands where the clouds melted.

Luzgin stopped, struck.

"Here we are," Lelya quickly went up to him and lightly pressed his hand.

"Lelya," said Luzgin hurriedly, "Hofman..."

"Yes, I know." Lelya calmly looked him in the eyes. "He's dead. I had a postcard from his father. Oh, well. I haven't been able to get rid of some silly thoughts since he died, I don't know why. He died a good death. He taught me not to be afraid of life."

As he listened to her, Luzgin was watching the clouds. It seemed to him that behind the darkness of the smoke he could see the enormous country from which Lelya had just arrived—a country that was transparent with air and sunshine. Our wild and dreamy ancestors must have imagined the golden age as looking like that.

Moscow, 1931

VALOUR*

The little boy was drawing with crayons. He was very worried and was thinking hard about something. Then he raised his head to look at me, and the tears suddenly began flowing from his eyes. They trickled down his cheeks and fell on to his crayon-smeared fingers, and he could hardly breathe because of them.

"Dad," he said in a whisper, "why haven't they thought of medicines to stop people dying?"

The pilot Shebalin had lost his way in the fog.

The marine met stations had hung out signals to say that powerful masses of tropic air were moving towards Europe.

It was winter. There was no snow, but the crackling of dry leaves reminded the inhabitants of the seaside town about the brittle crack of ice. That sound was characteristic of winter alone.

*English translation © Raduga Publishers 1986

Those experts on sea fogs and smoky murk, the Englishman Taylor and the German Georgi, gave a precise definition of that fog: "Warm tropic air, if carried by winter to Europe, turns first into a pale-blue haze that covers continents for hundreds of miles, and then the murk becomes drizzling rain. Such a fog is very stable."

Pilot Shebalin knew this. Below were Karadag's abysses and jagged summits covered with the lichen and rust of millenia. The fog was enshrouding the summit. It was rushing into the granite wall of the mountain and soaring skywards like a mighty white river. Shebalin was doggedly taking the thrusting machine in wide circles round this column of mist, the only landmark.

The sea boomed callously and hollowly below. A red sun, the sun of early winter, hung suspended in the darkness and cast a shimmering, twilight bronze radiance on the wet wings of the aircraft.

In the cabin, a little boy lay in a fever. His mother was sitting by him and each time Shebalin looked over shoulder he saw the deep, almost masculine wrinkles near her lips. The boy was dying.

Shebalin had flown into the steppe for the little boy and had to deliver him to the hospital in a seaside town. There, three hours back, when the boy was being carried into the cabin, the sky had been dry and cloudless and a cobweb had shone on a thistle. There had been nothing suggestive of fog.

Shebalin knew that even if he succeeded in landing in two or three hours, it would still be too late. There was no chance of saving the boy. There were no gaps in the fog.

The machine was triumphantly tearing the damp, stifling fog to shreds. The little boy tossed and turned in delirium.

Suddenly, Shebalin saw below the shadow of an enormous and swift-flying bird. An aircraft! Shebalin climbed steeply.

"Condensation!" the flight engineer shouted in his face. "They took off just the same!"

Shebalin nodded. The oncoming plane flashed a silver wing. Shebalin recognised Stavridi's aircraft.

Stavridi was flying through the fog and scattering wide bands of electrified dust behind him. The dust was attracting the particles of fog and turning them into heavy rain. The first droplets were already slanting across the windscreen.

Deep chasms were appearing in the fog; already the wet ribs of Karadag were glittering under the mica sun, and Shebalin saw rainwashed ground below him. It was shimmering and dazzling to the eyes.

Shebalin confidently came in to land.

The boy was driven to hospital from the airfield. Shebalin slowly climbed down from the cabin. He was not surprised to find the airfield full of pilots, nor was he surprised at Stavridi's take-off. He knew that dispersing fog was a complicated and expensive business, but that didn't surprise him either—the life of a little boy was more precious. "Who is he?" wondered Shebalin. He had not even asked about it when he received orders to take off.

In the evening, the stop-press editions of the papers announced that Shebalin had brought to the town a seven-year-old boy who was suffering from concussion. The doctors admitted that his condition was almost hopeless, but granted that a successful outcome was possible only under conditions of absolute quiet and rest.

An hour after the papers appeared on the streets, a decree of the Town Council was posted up everywhere in the streets suggesting that all citizens should keep quiet. Squads of militiamen stopped traffic in the vicinity of the hospital.

But these measures were unnecessary. The city needed no orders to hold its breath. And all the more prominent were the voices of the sea, the wind and the dry leaves.

Cars crept furtively round the outskirts. Drivers used to stepping on the accelerator and blasting their horns, sat silent in the darkness of their cabs like conspirators.

The fury of the drivers descended on a battered taxi nicknamed the "water-boiler". This vehicle would suddenly start banging away with a deafening noise. The drivers shook their fists after it and shouted in a whistling whisper:

"Get lost, you blasted kettle! "

The newspaper boys stopped shouting. Loud-speakers were switched off. Pioneers formed detachments to maintain the silence, but they hardly had anything to do.

There were no breaches of the silence, if you discount a trivial incident with the harbour lamplighter. He was a cheerful old fellow.

He would walk along roaring a song, because the seaside town was used to singing and laughing. He used to make up his own verses.

> *The lamp is burning, and even the stars*
> *Aren't needed at all in the heavens above.*
> *There's gladness, yes, gladness within our hearts*
> *Because in the dark we don't have to rove.*

The Pioneers stopped the old man. The quiet conversation did not last long. After it, the tipsy lamplighter sat on the road, took off his shoes, coughing, and tiptoed all the way to his lonely house on the outskirts. He shook his fingers at the side-streets and shushed the passers-by. At home, he let the cat out of the attic so that it wouldn't miaow, took an old watch out of his pocket—a fat turnip—listened to its loud ticking, put the watch on the table, covered it with a cushion and shook his finger at it.

The second incident occurred in the harbour and became a talking point for a long time all along the coast.

It must be said that worthy cargo steamers

had been plying the seas since olden times. Creaking, waddling heavily on the waves, they sailed past the smart motor-vessels, eyeing them malignantly. With a hissing of foam and a churning of screws, they sailed through the nights on the marine horizons like blinding planets.

One steamer, the *Toiler of the Seas,* was carrying a load of roof iron to the town where the boy lay ill in hospital.

Ten miles from the coast, the steamer received a radio signal from the harbour-master. He warned that in view of exceptional circumstances, the unloading of iron in the port was forbidden for an indefinite period.

Two miles from port, the steamer received a second radio signal. It instructed the steamer not under any circumstances to blow her whistle— the shriek of the siren on the *Toiler of the Seas* was notorious.

The crew of the *Toiler of the Seas,* who, like all mariners, was inclined to scoff, excelled themselves in guessing at the possible reasons. But in spite of their mocking mood, there was still a trace of alarm—the elusive link between the two orders spoke of significant events taking place in the seaside town.

As the *Toiler of the Seas* entered the harbour, a motor-launch came out to meet it. The harbour-master climbed up on deck and proceeded to the captain's cabin.

When the harbour-master came out again, the sailors heard part of a baffling sentence:

"Our hospital is right by the sea..."

The captain of the *Toiler of the Seas* went up on to the bridge and tersely ordered that the steamer should proceed to the roadstead and drop anchor. No arguments. They were not going to unload!

The crew murmured. Then the captain assembled them in the foredeck and read them the newspaper bulletins about the little boy.

"You understand," said the captain, "that there mustn't be any noise in the town. It won't do for us to barge in with our cargo just now."

But the waiting on board the *Toiler of the Seas* was not like the usual tedious delay on the roadstead. No one knew the boy, but they thought of him with deep affection.

The wait was full of yarns and reflections, naive and sad. A newspaper from ashore was hurriedly passed from hand to hand. Each was also concealing a sense of pride, in spite of the concealed alarm for the fate of the unknown boy, an alarm that twenty years ago would have seemed to the sailors not only funny, but simply incomprehensible.

Whether it was pride in themselves or in the harbour-master, they couldn't know. But on meeting the harbour-master they snatched off their hats and for a long time watched his dark-blue, glossy tunic as it receded.

The town held its breath. The town was silent. This silence even gave the inhabitants a sensation of solitude and freshness. Just as, after a deep sleep in a room with the windows wide open, morning enters all the pores of the body as deep silence and sunshine. Thought, cleansed of the juices of fatigue and nicotine, launches itself into swift flight and the horizons move, recede and dissolve, revealing new shores, capes and lands, giving new food for excitement and poems.

The town was silent, and all the more distinct were the voices of the sea, the wind and the dry leaves. The pink leaves of the platans rustled particularly loudly. But nothing could compare with the cannonade of the surf.

On the third day of the boy's illness, the town underwent a new trial. A gale warning went up on the mast in the harbour. A storm was coming in from the sea, thundering like hundreds of express trains, a wide-spreading storm of the kind that always breaks when the skies are cloudless. And, like a harbinger of the storm, the sky was already turning dark-blue with an intolerable icy brilliance.

The Town Council issued a second emergency appeal to the population. It stated that measures had been taken to get rid of a noise that is not caused by the will of man, the noise of the elements. Under the supervision of Ernst, the inventor, the assembly of a device was being completed in the hospital which would wholly shut out all external sounds.

The storm was expected at about midnight, and by that time the device, called a "screen of silence", was to be switched on.

The assembly men worked quickly and silently in the hospital. There was not much time left. The wind was already carrying bands of high, transparent cloud over the city. The storm was approaching. The first gusts of wind were sweeping across the town squares and carrying heaps of stiff autumn leaves to the fences.

The boy was expected to undergo a crisis by night-time, and by night-time storm broke. It delivered a devastating blow at the shore with foam, harsh thunderclaps and the shriek of helpless seagulls. The ground shook, the forests swayed on the mountains and began talking in hollow tones, and the smoke from the steamer funnels raced along the dead streets with a prolonged whistle.

A few minutes before the first blast of the storm, Ernst switched on the "screen of silence". He was authorised to go into the ward where the boy was lying, to check the action of the device.

Deafened by the fury of the storm, Ernst slowly climbed the stairs. The silence was so complete that Ernst could clearly hear the air moving in his lungs. Ernst went into the ward, into a silence flooded with the subdued flame of lamps. The only indication of a storm was the trembling of the floors, shaken by the surf nearby.

Ernst noticed none of this. He was looking at the boy. The patient was lying with his lips parted and smiling in his sleep. Ernst could hear his light, regular breathing. He forgot about the "screen of silence" and the storm; he did not notice the doctor and the young woman in white overalls. She was sitting at the boy's bed, and Ernst only afterwards remembered how — and only momentarily—he was struck by the tears in her eyes, tears that were slowly falling on to her knees.

The woman raised her head and Ernst knew that this was the boy's mother. She rose and went up to him.

"He's going to live," she said and suddenly smiled, looking somewhere beyond Ernst, far into the distance. Ernst looked round. There was no one behind him.

"You are a great man!" she said. "I'm so grateful to you!"

"No," he replied, confused. "We live in a great time, and I am as great as every worker in our country. No more. Are you happy?"

"Yes!"

"You see," said Ernst, "to create happiness is a noble task. The whole country is accomplishing it. There is nothing to thank me for."

In half an hour, the town knew about the boy's recovery.

Battling with the storm, the radio hurled these tidings into the night, across the ocean, to the far corners of the land.

The order for silence was cancelled.

The hiss of the dying storm was interrupted by the welcoming sirens of the steamer, the blare of car-horns, the flapping of flags raised over the houses, the jangling of pianos and a new and unsophisticated song from the lamp-lighter.

I've lit up the boulevards, let the land sing a song.
Though I'm old, yet the wine I've been drinking is young.

A holiday was arranged in the town. The storm, as always, gave way to an immeasurable calm. It had receded somewhere beyond the rim of the seas, was splashing on hundreds of miles of beaches, was spilling transparent waters by the rocks and cradling in it the red maple leaves and the low, warm sun.

If you have ever been to the seaside in early winter, you must remember the days with their light breathing, like morning sleep; you must remember the blue air cleansed by the storm when the distant, rusty capes stand in a ridge over the seas, and the seas carefully bring sunny ripples and a fine mist up to their feet.

The sailors from the *Toiler of the Sea* first heard a Beethoven symphony floating over the calm water. The sounds seemed to lift the steamer on a high, smooth wave, and so it was perfectly understandable that the coxswain should have run to the foredeck to make sure that the steamer hadn't slipped its moorings. And there was no cause to laugh at this the way the mechanic laughed.

In the evening, the English steamship, *Song of Ossian,* came into port. The crew were amazed at the sight of the festive town which seemed like a cascade of fire streaming down into the silent sea from the mountains. They politely asked the harbour-master what was happening. His reply was clear and brief.

At this time, Pilot Shebalin came out of his house. Snow had fallen far away in the mountains and the high moon was shining magically over silvery fields of snow.

In the garden near the house, Shebalin met a woman. It was the little boy's mother. She was coming to visit the pilot to thank him for saving her son.

In the light of the lamps and in the darkness of night, her face struck Shebalin with its pallor and joyous beauty. She put her arms round his neck and kissed him, and Shebalin felt a light freshness, as if rime were evaporating on his lips.

They went down into the town, holding hands like children, and saw electric lights twinkling on the mast of an English steamer.

Shebalin stopped. He recognised the Morse alphabet and loudly read out the English signal.

"To the crews of the Soviet ships. We congratulate and envy a thousand times the sailors who have such a marvellous homeland."

The little boy stopped drawing with crayons. The tears dried on his face and only the eyelashes were still damp. He laughed and asked:

"Whose was he, that little boy? Was he public property?"

"Of course he was public property," I replied, taken completely aback by the question.

Yalta, December, 1934

THE GROVES
OF MIKHAILOVSKOYE

A poet whose name I forget once said: "Poetry is all around us even in the wild grass. All you have to do is bend down and pick it up."

It was early morning, and a fine rain was falling as the cart entered a forest of ancient pines. There was a flash of white in the grass by the roadside.

Jumping off the cart I bent down and saw a small board overgrown with bindweed. Something was written on it in black paint. Pulling aside the wet strands of bindweed I read the almost forgotten words: "Many a time did I linger under your canopy, groves of Mikhailovskoye."

"What't this?" I asked the driver.

"Mikhailovskoye," he answered with a smile. "This is where Pushkin country begins. You'll find signs like that all over the place."

After that I would come across these boards in the most unexpected places—the unmown meadows by the River Sorot, the sandy slopes along the road from Mikhailovskoye to Trigorskoye, the banks of Lake Malenets and Lake Petrovskoye. Pushkin's simple lines echoed all around from the grass, heather and wild strawberries, to be heard only by the leaves, the birds and the sky, that pale, timid Pskov sky. "Farewell Trigorskoye, where joy was mine so oft." "I see the azure plains of two lakes."

One day I lost my way in a nut grove. The faint track disappeared among the bushes. A barefooted girl perhaps came once a week with a basket of bilberries here and nobody else. But here too I found a white board in the undergrowth with a quotation from Pushkin's letter to Osipova: "Couldn't I buy Savkino? I would build myself a hut, move my books there and come to spend a month or two among my dear old friends."

At first I could not fathom out why this inscription belonged here, but the path soon led me to the little village of Savkino. Waves of ripe oats reached right up to the roofs of the low wooden houses. There was not a soul to be seen in the village; only a black dog with grey eyes barked at me from behind a wattle fence and sturdy pines murmured quietly on the hills around.

I had been nearly everywhere in my country and seen many wonderful places that left you speechless with emotion, but not one of them made such an immediate lyrical impact as Mikhailovskoye. It was quiet and deserted.

Clouds drifted overhead and their shadows moved across the green hills, the lakes, and the paths of the ancient park. The silence was broken only by the humming of bees.

The bees were gathering honey in the avenue of tall lime trees where Pushkin met Anna Kern. The limes were already losing their blossom. A lively little old woman was often to be found sitting here with a book on a bench. Pinned to the collar of her blouse was an old turquoise brooch. The old woman was reading Fedin's *Cities and Years*. She was Anna Kern's granddaughter, Aglaya Pyzhevskaya, a former provincial actress.

She remembered her grandmother well and readily talked about her. She hadn't liked the old girl. And indeed who could be expected to like this ancient senile old woman who used to quarrel with her granddaughters about the best helping at dinner. The granddaughters were stronger than she was and always took the best helping away from her. Then she would weep at the horrid girls' behaviour.

I met Kern's granddaughter for the first time on the sandy slope where the three famous pines once stood. Now they are no longer. Two of them were struck by lightning before the Revolution and the third was cut down one night by a thieving miller from the small village of Zimari.

The custodians on the Pushkin estate decided to plant three new young pines on the same spot, but it was difficult to establish where the old trees had stood, since all trace of them had disappeared, even the stumps. So they summoned the old locals to calculate the exact spot.

The old men spent the whole day arguing. Their decision had to be unanimous, but three old boys from Deriglazovo refused to agree with the rest. When the three had finally been talked round, the old men began to pace out distances on the slope and make calculations. It wasn't until evening that they finally said:

"Here! This is the spot all right! Go ahead and plant them."

When I met Anna Kern's granddaughter near the three recently planted young pines, she was mending a fence that had been broken by a cow.

The old woman told me, laughing at herself, that she had made herself a niche in Pushkin country and found it hard to leave for Leningrad, although it was high time for her to do so. She was in charge of a small library on Kamenny Island in Leningrad and she lived alone, having no children or relatives.

"No, no," she said, "don't try to dissuade me. I shall definitely come here to die. These places have such a hold on me that I don't want to live anywhere else. Each day I think up some new excuse for postponing my departure. Now I'm going round the villages writing down everything the old men say about Pushkin." "But they're awful liars," she added sadly. "Yesterday one of them was describing how Pushkin was called to a meeting of state powers and asked whether they should fight Napoleon or not. Then Pushkin ups and says: 'What's all this about fightin' then, noble state powers, when your peasants are wearin' nothin' but the same pair of bags day in day out. You ain't strong enough! ' "

Anna Kern's granddaughter was indefatigable. I used to come across her in Mikhailovskoye, Trigorskoye, the graveyard at Voronichi and on the outskirts of Trigorskoye where I lived in a cool empty wooden house. Rain or shine, dawn or dusk she wandered everywhere on foot.

She told me about her earlier life, about famous provincial producers and tragedians who had taken to drink (her stories left one with the impression that the only people with talent in the old days were tragedians) and finally about her love affairs.

"All you can see now is a fussy old woman," she said. "But I used to be gay, independent and beautiful. I could leave some interesting memoirs behind me, but somehow I never get round to writing them. When I finish writing down the old men's tales I'll start preparing for the summer festival."

A summer festival is held each year in Mikhailovskoye on Pushkin's birthday. Hundreds of carts decorated with ribbons and little Valdai bells drive up to the meadow on the other side of the Sorot opposite Pushkin's park.

In the meadows they light fires and dance the *khorovod*. They sing old songs and new ditties:

> *Oh, how beautiful they are,*
> *All our lakes and pine trees.*
> *We are doing all we can*
> *To preserve Mikhailovskoye.*

All the local peasants take pride in their fellow countryman Pushkin and tend the estate as carefully as their own gardens and fields.

I was living in Voronichi with Nikolai, the keeper of Trigorsky Park. The lady of the house did nothing but clatter about with the dishes and nag her husband: a fine husband he was, stuck day and night in that there park, nipping back home for an hour or two, and even then sending his poor old father-in-law or the young boys to the park to keep an eye on things while he was away.

One day Nikolai had just popped home for a cup of tea. Before he even had time to take off his cap the lady of the house rushed in, dishevelled, from the yard.

"Go back to the park, you old skiver! " she shouted. "I was just rinsing my washing in the river when I saw some whipper-snapper from Leningrad nip straight into the park. Goodness only knows what he's getting up to! "

"What could he be getting up to?" I asked.

Nikolai was already at the door.

"Anything under the sun," he said on his way out. "Give him half a chance and he'll go breaking a branch off or something."

But everything was alright in the end. The "whipper-snapper" turned out to be the known artist Natan Altman, and Nikolai calmed down.

The Pushkin estate contains three enormous parks—Mikhailovsky, Trigorsky and Petrovsky—all as different from each other as their owners were.

Trigorsky Park is drenched in sunlight. For some reason it gives this impression even on cloudy days. The light lies in golden pools on the bright grass, the foliage of the limes, the sloping banks of the Sorot and Eugene Onegin's bench. These patches of sunlight give an appearance of mystery and unreality to the heart of the park enveloped in a summer haze. The park seems to have been made for family celebrations, friendly chats and dancing by candlelight under the black canopy of leaves with laughing young girls and playful declarations of love. It is full of the spirit of Pushkin and Yazykov.

Mikhailovsky Park is the haven of the recluse. Made for solitude and reflection, it is not a place for jollity. It is tall, silent, and somewhat gloomy with its old fir trees and runs imperceptibly into ancient deserted forests as majestic as the park itself. Only on the edge of the park through the twilight that always reigns under the canopies of the ancient trees, do you suddenly glimpse an open glade covered with shining buttercups and a quiet pond with swarms of leaping little frogs.

The park's main attraction lies in the high bank of the River Sorot and the small house where Arina Rodionovna, Pushkin's old nurse, lived. This is the only house dating back to Pushkin's time that is still standing. It is so tiny that you feel afraid to walk up the steps to the rickety porch. From the bank over the Sorot you can see two blue lakes, a forest-covered hill and the simple, age-old Russian sky with its slumbering clouds.

Petrovsky Park is where Pushkin's grandfather, the gloomy, self-willed Hannibal, used to live. There is a good view of this park from Mikhailovskoye on the other side of Lake Kuchane (also called Lake Petrovskoye). It is black, damp and overgrown with burdock. Entering it is like walking into a cellar. Hobbled horses graze among the burdock. The flowers are choked by nettles and in the evening the park groans with the croaking of frogs. Squawking jackdaws nest in the dark treetops.

On my way back from Petrovskoye to Mikhailovskoye I once happened to get lost among the forest dells. Little streams were gurgling among the roots and at the bottom of the dell there was a flash of small lakes. The sun was setting. The motionless air was reddish and hot.

From one of the forest glades I suddenly caught sight of a storm rising above Mikhailovskoye on the evening sky in steep banks of coloured cloud, like a huge medieval town surrounded by white turrets. Then came a hollow boom of thunder and the wind swished over the glade dying down in the undergrowth.

It was difficult to imagine Pushkin's horse carrying its silent rider lightly along these simple paths marked by the tread of bast sandals, over the anthills and twisted roots.

I can still see the forests, lakes, parks and sky. These are almost the only things that have remained here since Pushkin's time. The countryside has been completely untouched and is very carefully preserved. When electricity was to be installed in Mikhailovskoye it was decided to lay it underground to avoid putting up poles which would have ruined the essential charm of these parts.

In Voronichi where I was living there was a tumble-down wooden church which everyone called the "old church". It stood morosely, overgrown up to the roof with yellow lichen, barely visible through the elder thicket surrounding it. It was in this church that Pushkin ordered a memorial service to be held for Byron.

Now the church porch was covered with resinous pine shavings. A school was being built alongside it.

Only once during all the time I spent in Voronichi did the hunchbacked priest in a torn straw hat hobble up to the church. He carefully propped his fishing rods up against a lime tree and opened the heavy lock on the church doors. That day a very old man had died in Voronichi and they had brought his body to the church for a funeral service. After the service the priest picked up his rods again and plodded off to the Sorot to fish for chub and roach.

The carpenters building the school watched him go and one of them said:

"The clergy's come down a bit in the world! When Alexander Sergeyevich was alive Voronichi had a priest who was as important as a brigadier-general. And a nasty piece of work he was, too. No wonder Alexander Sergeyevich nicknamed him 'Bully'. But this one's a sorry sort of bloke in his tatty old straw hat."

"What's happened to their power now?" muttered another. "Where's all their silks and velvet gone?"

The carpenters wiped their sweaty brows, the blows of their axes rang out again, and another shower of fresh, pungent shavings flew onto the ground.

Several times in Trigorsky Park I came across a tall man wandering along the deserted paths. He would stop by a clump of bushes and spend a long time examining the leaves. Sometimes he would pick a blade of grass and study it through a small magnifying glass.

One day I got caught in a heavy shower near the pond not far from the Osipovs' house. It suddenly began to pour down and I took shelter under a lime tree. The tall man walked up slowly to where I was standing and we fell into conversation. It turned out that he was a geography teacher from Cherepovets.

"You must be a botanist as well as a geographer," I said to him. "I've seen you examining the plants."

The tall man gave a smile.

"No. I just like trying to find something new in my surroundings. This is my third summer

here, but I don't know a fraction of all there is
to know about these parts."

He spoke quietly and diffidently. With this
the conversation ended.

Our second meeting was on the banks of Lake
Malenets, at the bottom of a wooded hill. The
pines were murmuring dreamily and beneath
their tops the semi-darkness of the forest swayed
with the wind. The tall man was lying in the
grass examining a blue jay's feather through his
magnifying glass. I sat down beside him and he
gave me a slightly ironical, halting explanation
of why he was so attached to Mikhailovskoye.

"My father was a book-keeper in a hospital
in Vologda," he said. "He was a pretty wretched
person — always drinking and showing off. Even
when we were desperately hard up he wore a
carefully ironed and starched shirt front and
boasted about his background. He was a Russianised Lithuanian from a family called
Yagellon. He used to beat me mercilessly when
he was drunk. There were six of us children. We
all lived in one filthy, untidy room, quarrelling
and being beaten all the time. I had an awful
childhood. When father got drunk he used to
begin to recite Pushkin's poetry and burst into
tears. The tears fell onto his starched shirt front
and he would crumple and tear it, and shout
that Pushkin was the only ray of sunshine in the
lives of miserable beggars like us. He couldn't
remember any of his poems all the way through.
He would begin reciting them, but never once
got to the end. This always made me angry,

even though I was only eight and could hardly make out printed letters. So I decided to read Pushkin's poems to the end and went to the town library. I stood at the door for ages until the librarian called me over and asked me what I wanted.

" 'Pushkin,' I said rudely.

" 'Do you mean the fairy stories?' she asked.

" 'No. Not the fairy stories. Pushkin,' I repeated stubbornly.

"She handed me a thick volume. I sat down in a corner by the window, opened the book and burst out crying. I was crying because I had only just realised, that I couldn't read the book, that I couldn't read at all and that there was a whole magical world concealed behind these lines, which had made my drunken father weep. The only two lines of Pushkin which I had learned by heart from him were *I see a distant land, the magic shores of southern climes,* but this was enough for me to be able to picture a different life from ours. Just imagine a man who has been in solitary confinement for years and years. At last he is helped to escape and given the keys to the prison gates. But as he walks up to the gates with freedom, people, forests and lakes on the other side, he suddenly realises that he doesn't know how to open the lock with this key. There is a vast world vibrating only a few inches away behind the iron gates, but to unlock them you must know a stupid little secret which this runaway doesn't possess. He hears the alarm sounding behind him and knows that they will soon grab him and that everything will be just the same as it was until he dies: the dirty window under the ceiling of his cell, the smell of rats and the despair. That is what I went through with the volume of Pushkin in my hands. The librarian saw I was crying, came up to me and said, picking up the book:

" 'What's the matter, my lad? Why are you crying? Didn't you notice you'd got the book upside down?'

"She laughed and I went away. Since then I have been in love with Pushkin. This is my third year running in Mikhailovskoye."

The tall man fell silent. We went on lying on the grass for a long time. You could just hear the faint sound of a shepherd's horn in the meadows on the other side of the curving Sorot.

A few kilometres from Mikhailovskoye is the Svyatogorsky Monastery standing on an elevated piece of ground with Pushkin's grave by the monastery wall. The village round the monastery is called Pushkin Hills.

The village is packed with hay. Night and day the hay carts creak over the large cobblestones, bringing dry hay into Pushkin Hills. There is a smell of bast matting, smoked fish and calico from the shops and stalls.

The one and only teahouse rings with the constant clinking of glasses and teapots. The steam reaches up to the ceiling and in this steam sit farm workers and shrivelled old men from the time of Ivan the Terrible, unhurriedly drinking their tea and eating hunks of grey bread. Where these old men come from with their parchment skin, piercing gaze and hollow, croaking voices no one knows. But there are lots of them and there must have been even more in Pushkin's day when he wrote *Boris Godunov* here.

To get to Pushkin's grave you have to walk through the empty monastery courtyards and go up a flight of weathered stone steps which lead to the top of the hill and the wind-eroded walls of the main church.

At the base of the wall over a steep slope you can see Pushkin's grave in the shade of lime trees, the earth sprinkled with yellowed lime blossom.

The brief inscription "Alexander Sergeyevich Pushkin", the solitude, the creaking of the carts on the hillside below and the clouds brooding in the low sky—this is all you will find. This spot marks the end of the brilliant, turbulent life of a great man. Here is the grave known to all mankind, the "sweet bourn" of which Pushkin spoke during his life. There is a smell of weeds, bark and settled summer days.

And here on this simple grave from which you can hear the hoarse crowing of cocks in the distance it becomes particularly obvious that Pushkin was the first poet of the Russian people.

He is buried in the backwoods of Russia, in

the coarse sandy earth where only flax and nettles grow. From his grave you can see the dark forests of Mikhailovskoye and the distant storms which roll in a stately dance over the bright river Sorot, over Savkino, Trigorskoye and the simple vast fields bringing his beloved, refreshed earth peace and prosperity.

1936

CANES VENATICI

All autumn the wind had been blowing from the ocean. The air quivered and it was very difficult to observe the stars at night.

The astronomer Merot was sick and old. He had not the strength to slide open the observatory's small dome on his own and asked the gardener to help him. Together the two of them pulled the thin cable. The panels of the dome slid apart with a slight creak and the cold starry sky appeared in the inky darkness.

Merot would sit down on the small staircase to have a rest and shake his head sadly: "Wind again, of course! The different densities of air sweeping over the earth are breaking up the light rays again."

Dry oak leaves drifted into the observatory and the trees outside were rustling. The gardener said that if the wind was blowing the leaves off the oak trees it wouldn't die down for a long time.

Merot liked talking to the gardener. There were only eight of them living in the observatory and it was thirty kilometres of difficult, stony road to the nearest small town. His fellow astronomers were a taciturn lot. They had already said all they had to say to each other and now conversations were rare. They evaded questions and pretended to be immersed in their calculations.

The astronomers' simple dinner was cooked for them by an old woman called Teresa, also silent and brusque. Their meals, always taken at the same time and in the same company, became more and more oppressive each month. And with each passing year they grew increasingly accustomed to solitude. So intense was the silence that even the books Merot happened to read from time to time seemed to be full of noises. He did not actually hear any sounds when he was reading, of course, but he imagined them and the more commotion and loud conversations there were in a book, the more irritated he became.

"What a noisy book! " he would say frowning. "The characters shout, argue and cry their heads off... I can't be bothered to try and follow all this racket."

Several years in the observatory had given him an extremely acute sense of hearing. He now heard many sounds which he had never noticed before. They were monotonous ones, like the wind whistling through the cables that supported the pole on which they hoisted the flag on public holidays. Then another sound could he heard—the flag flapping cheerfully in the wind. It brought back memories of childhood holidays, when the sound of the flags in their small town had been so loud that Merot's grandmother had got a headache.

When he was a child there had been lots of sunshine, much more than now, and the sun had been different—huge and very bright, covering half the sky.

"I think the sun is cooling before our very eyes," Merot would say to the gardener. "It just doesn't shine like it used to, as if someone had put a dusty pane of glass over it."

The gardener always agreed—who was he to argue with an educated man like Merot.

There were other sounds besides the wind. In winter the mistral would carry dry snow through the mountain passes and fling it like sand against the windows of the laboratory. Now and then there was an eagle's cry, and sometimes rain would gurgle in the stone gutters. Very occasionally in summer there was thunder. But its rumbling was down in the valleys, not overhead. The thunderclouds clustered way below the observatory.

That was about all, except for the bleating of lost goats, and the hooting of the car once a week when the driver fetched food, newspapers and mail from the town.

The newspapers were snatched up by the young astronomer Neusted, a lumbering Norwegian, who took them to his room and never gave them back. At first the astronomers grumbled about the rude Norwegian, but then they got used to it and forgot that the newspapers existed. Occasionally they would ask Neusted what was happening down below in the world, from which you could expect nothing but trouble. Neusted invariably told them that the world was going on in its mad way as usual, and everyone was satisfied with this reply.

It was at the end of autumn, when Merot had been spending many nights at the telescope studying the Canes Venatici constellation, that he first heard the new sounds. They were like the distant rumble of mountain avalanches. At first they were so faint that Merot could hardly detect them. He racked his brains trying to guess what they were, but did not even attempt to tell the other astronomers about them. They already thought he was a bit of a crank. But the sounds grew in volume and one night the repercussions were so intense that the stars swam together and split in two in the mirror of the telescope.

The sounds came from the direction of the coast. Merot went out onto the iron balcony of the observatory and stared for a long time at the mountains.

Everything was the same as usual—snow, moonlight and the stars topping the peaks like beacons—but there was no sign of the white spray that normally accompanied snowslides.

"Matvei," Merot called to the gardener. "Did you hear something? It must have been snowslides in the mountains."

"Not enough snow for avalanches," said the gardener. "We'd better listen hard."

They strained their ears in silence. Behind the garden wall was the steady splash of water as if it were falling on glass. That was the stream which was already covered with patches of ice. The silence stretched on. Then a heavy thud rang out from the east, hit the mountains and echoed back westwards dying away.

"That's no snowslide," muttered the gardener.

"What is it, then?"

"It's long-range guns," the gardener replied uncertainly. "It's that there is war down below. But it won't come up here. Too high up. No point in coming up here."

Then Merot remembered Neusted's brusque accounts of the Civil War which was devastating the old towns in the valleys and the peasants' miserable plots. He remembered the driver complaining that the only people left in the town were women and old men and that he was always late bacause he had to load the crates himself. He remembered that Teresa's cooking had got much worse, but nobody had taken any notice.

He must find out everything immediately. Merot closed the observatory and went down to the house.

The astronomers were having supper. The chimney in the dining-room fireplace was giving a hollow, sleepy murmur as it had for many a year.

"Listen, friends," said Merot panting hard. He stopped at the doorway pulling off his warm scarf. "I can hear the sound of firing in the distance."

The astronomers looked up from their plates.

"Neusted," Merot went on in a loud, excited voice. The astronomers looked round not at Merot but somewhere in the corner, as if they couldn't believe that this loud voice belonged to the sick old man. "Neusted, you must tell us exactly what's going on."

Neusted did not answer. He looked at his watch and went up to the wireless. Everyone watched him in amazement.

He bent over the knobs. The electric valves lit up with a red glow and a man's voice began to talk sadly about street fighting in Madrid, air raids, hundreds of children mutilated by shells and the destruction of the Alba Palace where paintings by Velázquez and Ribera were burning.

The astronomers listened in silence. The voice suddenly broke off as abruptly as it had begun.

"What do you think of that?" said Merot in the silence that followed, and realised that his question had been somewhat out of place.

Neusted lazily returned to the table. He sat stretched out as if listening to something, gripping the table with his large hands.

A lean old man in a grey suit, the seismologist Dufour who was noted for his refined speech, was the first to break the silence.

"Ever since we came to the observatory," he said with an ironical smile, "each of us has had the feeling of being in a besieged fortress. We are surrounded by mountains without wood, ore or coal. We are besieged by the wind and snow. The world has no time for us, and we have no time for the world. The people in the valleys are running wild, but there is no reason for them to come up here. Here there is nothing but the stars. They can't be melted down for weapons or used to make poisonous gases. Rational mankind has no use for them. Consequently we have nothing to fear."

"Don't play the fool, Dufour," said Neusted. "The war has been on for five months now."

"Nonsense, nonsense," came the grating voice of Hervé who had been silent up to now. It was impossible to guess his age—he could easily be anything from forty to sixty. "I'd like to know something else. How can anyone be upset about a piece of canvas getting burnt even if it was covered with pretty paint? I mean Velázquez' pictures. I've spent all my life studying the stars and it's taught me not to get worried by trifles. What could be more transient than a piece of canvas? People torment themselves, go into ecstasies and even die over it. It's quite incomprehensible. I just don't understand how anyone can bother with such things when there is human thought and the heavens."

He was interrupted by Dufour, who had gone out and returned with a thin strip of paper.

"There," he said proudly. "More proof of

the accuracy of my seismograph. It has recorded nearly two hundred minor earth tremors in the last few days. Obviously these are shell explosions. I've only just realised it."

The astronomers bent over the strip of paper, on which the pencil had traced a jagged line showing the tremors in the earth's crust.

Neusted ran his finger along the line, his eyes screwed up and a cigarette clenched between his swollen, nicotine-stained teeth. He was angry.

"Each curve represents an explosion," he said. "Your apparatus is excellent at registering murders, Dufour."

Before Dufour had time to retort there was a distinct thud outside. The mountain echo turned it into a roll and cast it down into the rocky precipices. All fell silent again.

Merot kept quiet. He didn't want to take part in this futile conversation. All his life he had believed that studying the sky, like the discovery of all the other secrets of the Universe, bound man closer to the earth. Merot was old and kind and was not storing up all his knowledge for himself alone. He had even started writing a book about the sky for those carefree, boisterous youngsters far away in the deep valleys down below, who would envy him, an old man.

Strange thoughts and memories had been crowding into his mind recently. He recalled his childhood, and old men never like dwelling on this period of their life. He remembered the

Christmas tree. Before it was lit up, it had lived secretly in the next room behind locked doors, and only the faint smell of its needles stirred the child's imagination. Then the door was flung open and he walked in timidly and saw the sparkling tree. He could look at it, touch its needles and golden nuts, glass decorations and crackers, and smell the oranges and figs hanging on its branches. He could study the fir tree, but nevertheless the sensation of mystery and wonder filling the room never left him for a single moment.

He had the same feeling from studying the Universe.

"Everything exists for man," Merot used to say. "If people disappear, I'm afraid that I, an astronomer, won't have any use for the starry heavens."

Merot rarely ventured to express these thoughts because they did not meet with approval. He became irritated by the conversation in the dining room. This was the first time that he had noticed how arid the thoughts and feelings of his colleagues were. Coarse, lazy Neusted was perhaps better than the lot of them.

The Civil War in the valleys, the echoes of the fighting and the unpleasant conversation in the dining room did not appear to interfere with the scientists' life. The astronomers worked at night, slept in the morning and spent the evening in the laboratories. There they would compare photographs of the starry heavens on the lookout for the slightest changes. Any change in the familiar jumble of stars was a discovery which gave rise to interesting speculation.

Life went on as usual, but nevertheless the scientists were troubled by a strange unease which only a sharp eye could detect.

Merot would sit by the telescope muttering something to himself angrily. Neusted was twice seen in the daytime turning the telescope onto the distant mountains. The others pretended not to have noticed, since it is accepted among astronomers that only fools use a telescope for observing the earth.

Dufour occasionally said that the sense of the war being so imminent and yet without danger for him steadied his nerves. Formerly when the snow began to fall and the overcast sky stopped their work, the astronomers became moody. Hervé was the most irritable of the lot. But now, after a heavy fall of snow, he remarked that fortunately it would make the road to the observatory impassable for armed detachments. Dufour smirked maliciously.

Baudin, the librarian, had begun to take the newspapers from Neusted and read them all the way through, frowning as if the reports were causing him gnawing pain.

One night in December Neusted came into the observatory while Merot was working. This was against the rules, as the astronomers were not supposed to disturb each other during observation time. Merot looked round and got up.

Neusted stood still, feet apart and hands thrust into his trouser pockets. Both men were silent.

Merot noticed a faint smell of wine. That really was going too far. The young Norwegian's behaviour was becoming provocative.

"I've come to help you close the dome," said Neusted loudly as if he were addressing someone hard of hearing, "because it will hit us all of a sudden."

"He's drunk," thought Merot. This was the first time he had ever seen anyone drunk in the observatory. "What's he talking about?"

"It'll hit us all of a sudden," Neusted repeated angrily. "Do as I say. Come out and look for yourself."

Neusted closed the dome, took Merot by the elbow and led him out onto the iron balcony. Merot did not demur for he had sensed the alarm and threat behind Neusted's words.

"There," said Neusted nodding towards the mountains. "What a magnificent sight! "

A sheer bank of cloud lit by a dim, eery light was rising above the jagged mountain tops. It stretched right across the horizon, and you could see it growing and swelling, obscuring the stars and emitting a weird glow.

"A hurricane," said Neusted with a short laugh. "It'll be here in ten minutes. Just as soon as the wind breaks through the mountains."

"Why is it so quiet?" Merot asked.

"It's always like that just before a hurricane breaks."

The silence was so tense that the sound of their own voices seemed harsh and unpleasant. They could not even hear the familiar sound of the stream. The mountains were already wreathed in grey smoke.

"Here it comes," Neusted whispered.

Merot strained forward listening intently. Far off in the unbearable silence was the faint sound of an engine.

"There's someone out there," he said pointing at the mountains.

Snowy whirlwinds were already leaping convulsively up to the black sky.

"Where?" asked Neusted.

Merot clutched him by the shoulder.

"There, there! " he cried pointing to the mountain tops where Neusted could now see nothing but the swirling hurricane streaming down into the ravines. "I can hear an aeroplane."

"You..." Neusted started to shout but a sudden blast of wind drove the hoarse cry back down his throat. The earth shuddered and the fierce, unbroken howl of the hurricane drowned everything else. The wind whipped Merot from the rail of the balcony and threw him against the observatory wall. Snow was driving into his eyes and mouth, choking him. Neusted grabbed him by the arm and dragged him down the steps. The Norwegian was already white with snow from head to foot.

They forced their way to the house through the leaden current of wind, clinging to trees

and bushes, staggering and using their hands
to protect their eyes from the flying gravel that
was stinging their faces. Everything around was
shaking and howling at different pitches: the
moaning flagpole, the bare garden whistling
like hundreds of shrill flutes, a clattering loose
tile, the rattling windowpanes and the constant
clanging of the iron roofs.

The lamps were not swaying on their posts.
The force of the wind had held them nearly
parallel to the ground and at any minute they
were likely to be ripped off and swept away.

Neusted dragged Merot into the dining room
and only then did he finish the sentence that
had been interrupted by the wind.

"You're wrong," he said taking off his jacket
and shaking the snow off it. "There wasn't
a plane. And even if there was, it's nothing but
a pile of firewood now."

Merot did not argue.

Soon all the astronomers had gathered in the
dining room. Storms bring people together.
They inspire the imagination. Even the most
boring person manages to find words to convey
the excitement that he feels when the wind
is beating wildly outside.

It was very late before they went off to bed.
Merot couldn't get to sleep. He lay on his narrow bed listening to the wind howling and a
terrible feeling of loneliness came over him.
Surely he wouldn't have to spend the rest of
his days here in the mountains, in this white
room like a hospital ward? Would no one ever

come and stroke his grey hair and say, "Go to sleep. I'll sit and read to you until you drop off"?

He lay curled up and felt as if he were a little boy again. He remembered Hervé saying that astronomers shouldn't have anyone who is close to them. "Neither should old men, I suppose," he thought.

He got up, raised the blind and went back to bed. He wanted to be closer to the hurricane and the lowered blind had seemed like an iron curtain. Now the hurricane was right next to him outside the double glass of the windows. It screeched and sang in the rocks, whipping snow against the glass, and emitting a faint bluish light reflected from the snowflakes. It was as if someone had lit large spirit burners outside.

"Why should I bother about sleep?" he muttered and began to think about the aeroplane which had come flying over the mountains ahead of the storm. Steep cliffs were towering up in front of the pilot and he dared not look round. Only his back, his defenceless back sensed the hurricane driving him on like a hound pursuing a hare.

The shutters rattled in the wind. Merot's anguished thoughts became more confused until he eventually dozed off.

He had a strange dream. He was getting into a dusty grey car to drive to the south of Spain. A tall thin old man with a shaking grey goatee beard got in beside him. There was a strange clanking sound from the old man's shabby

creased suit and Merot suddenly noticed with
alarm that his companion was wearing rusty
old armour beneath his jacket.

"We'll drive there and back," said the old
man, his armour grinding in the small car, "and
you will see everything. But try not to weep."

They raced along the narrow road through
the mountains and each time they came to a
pass vast expanses spread out below like the
sea, some brown and parched by the sun, or
dark with the foliage of lemon trees, other
burnished with ripe corn, or blue with the haze
over the forests. And with each new valley the
old man in armour stood up, flung out his arm
with a mighty ring and hailed it solemnly with
the word:

"Spain."

They raced past towns where there was so
much sun that it overflowed from the tiled roofs
and walls of the houses and crept into the far
corners of the cellars where Merot and the old
man sat drinking wine and eating cheese that
smelt of cloves.

They raced past ancient cathedrals that
seemed to be covered with the grey dust of the
heat, past rivers where patient bulls were lazily
drinking the clear water, past schools with
children singing, past palaces where the paintings
of the great masters were gleaming in the
shadows behind linen drapes, past orchards and
fields where each clod of earth was weighed in
the hand and crumbled by the firm palm of the
peaceful peasants, past parks and factories

humming like bees with the wheels of the hot machines, past the whole country rushing forward to hail them in the wind, laughter, songs, greetings and many other sounds of happy toil.

In a small deserted town they sped past a statue of a tall old man with a grey beard. Merot recognised this bronze figure as his companion and managed to read the inscription on the statue which said: "Miguel Cervantes de Saavedra."

"So you are Cervantes?" he shouted to the old man, who took off his hat and replied vaguely:

"Yes, I once lived in this town."

Then they turned back and began to speed past the same towns, lying in ruins, full of the heavy stench of dead bodies, past the schools where dead children with pitiful open mouths lay by the doors, past women crazed with grief running along the roads with unseeing, staring eyes, past people who had been tied to doorhandles and shot, past orchards gutted by fire, past signs scrawled in soot on the white garden walls: "Death to those who talk of freedom and justice! Death to those who are against us! ", past palaces turned into heaps of charred rubbish.

An infantry detachment stopped the car. The soldiers wore heavy boots like buckets and had red faces with ginger moustaches. The officer in charge was fair-haired with protruding ears and a bony pate.

"Who are you?" he shouted.

The old man in armour got up, his eyes dark with anger and his hands trembling.

"Curs! " he shouted. "Hired assassins covered with a bloody coat! Begone from my country! I am Cervantes, the son and poet of Spain. I am a soldier and an honest man."

The old man stretched out his arms to halt the soldiers.

"Fire! " shouted the officer, his voice shrill with anger. The soldiers fired and Merot heard the bullets hitting the old man's rusty armour. The old man fell face down in the dust and stroked the gravel of the road with his thin, warm arms as he lay dying.

"Spain! " he said fervently and a few precious tears fell onto the baking ground. "Spain, mother, land of my children! "

Another spray of bullets hit his armour, more quietly this time.

Merot woke up. Wasn't that someone at the door? He listened intently. The wind could still be heard, but not like yesterday. The hurricane was dying down. A shutter banged and someone knocked more loudly at the door.

"Who's there?" Merot asked almost in a whisper.

"It's me, sir," came the voice of the gardener.

"What's the matter?"

"There's firing in the ravine on the other side of the stream," said the gardener. "Perhaps you wouldn't mind getting up and we could listen together. I think something terrible has happened."

Merot began to dress hurriedly. Surely the war could not have reached them up here in these useless mountains. He remembered his dream and felt as if someone were slowly squeezing his throat.

"It must be the shutters banging, Matvei," he whispered afraid of waking Hervé who was sleeping next door. He wanted to believe that the gardener was wrong and that there was no firing. Why on earth should anyone be firing in this wilderness?

The gardener made no reply and they went out. The snow had stopped, the wind was dying down and huge banks of dark cloud lingering on the mountains were just visible in the east. The sun was beginning to rise. It filtered through the breaks in the heavy sky, and you could already make out the trees with their caps of snow and the green water of the pool where small fish were swimming.

The gardener took Merot up to the wall behind which the deep ravine lay in mist with the mountain stream rippling below. The bottom of the ravine was not visible—darkness always lingers longest in the gorges reluctant to leave them, like the snow.

"Here," said the gardener pointing over the wall.

Merot peered down but could not see anything.

"My eyesight's poor," he said miserably. "I can't see anything. Perhaps you'd better have a look."

"Looking down there gives you the willies," replied the gardener. "Let's keep quiet for a minute and see if we can hear anything."

They listened hard and Merot detected something like a weak groan or a short hoarse shout. It came like a bolt from the blue. Then two hollow shots rang out in the darkness on the bank of the stream.

Merot shrank back from the wall and then set off quickly for the house, followed by the gardener who was confused and baffled by what was happening. Two short shots rang out again.

Still followed by the gardener, Merot went into the laboratory and opened a niche in the wall.

His hands were shaking. He pressed a button and five bells began to ring furiously in various parts of the house and observatory. This was the alarm signal which was reserved for extreme emergencies or for summoning all the inhabitants urgently.

The bells made a deafening noise.

Lights switched on and doors slammed. In a few minutes the excited astronomers had gathered in the laboratory.

Only Neusted remained calm. He went up to Merot, grabbed him firmly by the shoulder and shook him lightly.

"What's happened?" he asked in a very loud voice. No one paid any attention to his rude behaviour.

"There's an injured person in the ravine

signalling for help," Merot replied.

"What makes you think so?" said Dufour angrily. "Is he shouting?"

"He's shouting and firing at regular intervals."

There was silence.

"Who's coming with me?" asked Neusted unexpectedly. "If he's injured four of us will have to go, otherwise we won't be able to get him out."

"I'll go gladly," said the gardener.

"We need two more."

"What about me then?" said Baudin quietly.

"One more. There must be four of us," Neusted repeated.

Merot kept quiet. He knew he couldn't climb down to the ravine. He even got tired going up the mountains by car, just from feeling the straining of the engine.

"Oh, well," said Hervé. "I'm pretty tough although I look like an old man."

"That's not important," said Neusted. "Let's be going."

By the time they had got ready and left the house it was light though misty. Neusted was the first to climb over the wall and begin the descent. He was carrying a rope. After him came the gardener with Baudin and Hervé bringing up the rear. They sent loose stones rumbling loudly down the steep sides.

Merot and Dufour waited by the wall. The sun had risen and the snow was beginning to melt. Large drops of water were dripping from the trees.

Neusted and his companions were swallowed up by the mist. For a while the only sound that could be heard was the stones clattering down the precipice. Then there was a shout from Neusted.

"Halloo there. Halloo," which was answered by a shot from somewhere nearby.

Neusted shouted:

"Shoot upwards, not at the cliffs, blast you! They might ricochet."

An unfamiliar voice repeated several times:

"Over here, over here! On the other side of the stream! "

All the voices were as audible as if they were in the room next door.

"Ricochet," Merot repeated with surprise. He knew what the word meant but this was the first time in his life that he had actually used it.

"Ricochet—what an unpleasant word."

"I imagine we shall hear worse," said Dufour coldly.

The sound of voices could still be heard through the mist, but they were much more muffled than before.

"Give us a knife to cut the ropes. He's got all tangled up," came Neusted's voice. "All right, the shears will do. But make it snappy."

"What's happening?" shouted Merot, but there was no reply.

Then came a clatter, a faint cry and an angry shout from Baudin:

"For heaven's sake, watch you don't slip! "

"Let him have a rest," came the gardener's

voice from somewhere quite nearby.

"Never mind about that. Carry on," said Baudin.

Merot could now see a black smudge moving slowly up the cliff.

"Hold on, Matvei," said Hervé.

"Don't worry," the gardener replied. "I won't let go. My hands are all sticky with blood."

They reached the fence at last and Merot saw that they were carrying a man in blue tarpaulins covered with blood. His face was obscured by a mass of tangled, clotted hair. Neusted's grey trousers were spotted with patches of blood.

They carried the man quickly up to Hervé's room and lay him on the bed. Baudin, who acted as the observatory doctor as well as librarian, undressed the stranger, bathed his wounds and bandaged him up. Neusted helped him.

The rooms smelt of medicine and there were pools of melted snow on the floor from the men's boots.

The observatory inhabitants gathered in the dining room. They looked at the thick drops of blood trailing across the carpet and waited for Neusted and Baudin to appear. It was a long time before they came.

Merot's hands were shaking.

"We ought to have a fire, Teresa," he said. But the old woman was sitting in a corner muttering something under her breath as though she were praying, and did not hear what he said.

The first to appear was Neusted who walked up to the fireplace and began to warm his hands although there was no fire in the grate. Realising this he gave a forced smile and started to fill his pipe.

"So the war's finally reached us, too," he said. "Congratulations, everybody."

"What's the matter with him?" Merot asked.

"It looks as though he's had it," Neusted replied. "He's broken just about everything that is breakable in a man's body. Parachuting in the mountains is always hopeless. He was flying from France to Madrid."

"Is he a soldier?" Dufour asked.

"No. A poet."

"I'm not exactly in the mood for joking," said Dufour in an icy voice.

"I told you. He's a poet," Neusted flared up. "The hurricane threw the plane into a spin and he managed to bail out. The rest should be obvious."

"The main point is not obvious to anyone," drawled Dufour. "You mentioned something about the war."

Baudin came in, took off his glasses and looked round at everyone with his red, shortsighted eyes.

"We need a doctor," he said distractedly. "I don't know enough to be able to save him."

It was decided immediately to send the car to the town for the doctor. Neusted would go along with the driver. Baudin and Merot would keep watch over the man, helped by Teresa.

For the time being all astronomical observations would be carried out by Dufour and Hervé.

"A true scientist would never have acted so hastily as Merot and Neusted," Dufour said to Hervé after the car had left. "I'm not at all convinced that we should allow this useless fussing to interrupt many years of observation. The man's not going to live in any case."

Hervé did not reply.

"War," he said finally, with a deep sigh. "I know astronomers will never shoot each other, and I'd rather not think about the rest."

"But one should bear in mind that our French observatory is on Spanish soil," said Dufour.

Neusted was driving along. The snow had melted and the wet mountains glistened in the sun. Streams of ice-cold water ran down the cliffs. The sky rose higher and higher, losing its colour. Heat was creeping up from the empty valley.

The driver braked sharply and pointed to the red cliffs, at the foot of which Neusted saw a pile of twisted metal and wood.

"His plane," said the driver.

Neusted got out and cleaned the brown blood stains off his trousers with a handful of snow which he found in the shade of the cliff.

"Let's go," he said to the driver. "Or else the old men up there may fuss him to death."

They whizzed down as if the car had suddenly taken wings, the brakes had gone and they could not stop until they reached the town. It skidded at bends sending great showers of gravel into the ravine.

Neusted was in fine spirits. He sang as the earth grew nearer. He could already smell the smoke from the poor hearths. A small herd of goats was grazing on the bare mountain side, tended by a tall old woman in a black scarf, standing by the roadside, who did not even bother to look round when the car raced past.

The town's narrow streets were deserted. A noisy bunch of thin women gathered round the car as soon as it stopped, all speaking at once. Neusted did not know Spanish at all well, but he managed to gather from what they were saying that the scoundrel of a doctor had made off with his family to Huesca leaving no one but the chemist.

One of the women was holding the hand of a little girl who was wearing the same black head-scarf as all the women and the old woman tending the goats. The girl looked up at Neusted fearfully while the woman kept asking him for something, wiping her eyes with her dirty apron.

"What does she want?" Neusted asked the driver.

"She wants us to take the girl with us. The girl's father has just been killed by the fascists—near Huesca. She says it's not so dangerous in the mountains. They won't go up there."

"Who's 'they'?"

The driver shrugged his shoulders:

"Who do you think?"

"We can't take her with us," said Neusted. "Who would look after her? We've got a badly injured man on our hands as it is."

The driver said nothing.

"Who would look after her?" Neusted repeated.

"I do the driving—the rest is up to you."

"Oh, so that's how it is."

Neusted opened the car door and pulled the girl in. Her mother laughed, smoothing her greying black hair, and shouted something to her daughter.

The driver started up the car and it leapt forward up the street to the chemist's. Neusted looked round and saw the women waving their black scarves, like a flock of thin birds silently flapping their wings. The little girl stared hard at the driver's back, her eyes brimming with tears.

"Tell her not to be afraid," Neusted said to the driver. "We'll take her back when it's all over."

The driver nodded.

The chemist was asleep and Neusted asked them to wake him up. A sallow hunchback appeared, greeted them sleepily and stepped onto the platform behind the counter to be higher up.

Neusted did not know what he should buy to treat the injured man, so he explained briefly what had happened and asked for advice. The chemist stared at him in amazement suppressing a yawn.

"I haven't got anything. Honestly, I haven't. All I can give you is a little plaster of Paris, some gauze and six ampules of morphine. You won't be able to manage without a doctor. You've got iodine at the observatory. Mr. Baudin bought enough iodine last year for the whole Republican army, not just one of them."

"What makes you think he's a Republican?"

"Who else would be flying from France at night? Did you find the plane?"

"No," Neusted replied. He didn't feel like chatting.

"You should be worrying about the plane, not the pilot," muttered the chemist and went into the backroom. He searched around, still mumbling something under his breath, and finally came back with a small packet.

Neusted said goodbye and the chemist saw him out onto the stone porch. A grey light hung over the town and the snow on the mountains looked very dreary.

"Where's the fighting now?" Neusted asked.

"Everywhere," answered the chemist with a smirk.

They drove back slowly as the road became steeper and steeper. The little girl sat hunched up, with her round, tearfilled eyes fixed on the driver's back. Not knowing how to comfort her, Neusted whistled and said nothing.

Once more they met the tall old woman with the small herd of goats. She turned round frowning to look at the car.

Above them stretched the faded sky. The mountains were ginger-brown, covered with bare oak bushes, and the valley had become enveloped in a greyish mist.

For the first time Neusted realised how tired he was of life in the observatory, even though it was so close to the sky and the stars. If only he were in Madrid where people were full of vigour and drive, fighting for things that were clear and straightforward. Perhaps all this would not last for long, but so what?

"So what?" he repeated out loud. The girl sat, motionless as ever, and did not look round.

"Poor little thing," he thought looking at her. He would have liked to pat her on the shoulder but didn't dare.

Now that he was down in the valley the inhabitants of the observatory seemed like corpses who were just pretending to be alive and who argued, talked, ate and observed the stars like clockwork toys. That walking clockwork mechanism with the refined ring, Dufour, was particularly irritating. Quiet old Hervé didn't seem a bad chap, but life at the observatory had mummified him.

"There's only Merot, but he's so old that a strong gust of wind might be the end of him," Neusted muttered to himself.

As they turned round a bend and the observatory came into view the driver stopped the car.

"No point in hurrying now," he said. "Look at the flag pole."

Neusted screwed up his eyes and saw that the flag had been lowered to half-mast. He knew all about this tradition. As the son of a sea captain with an interest in astronomy, Neusted was familiar with sea customs and the sight of a flag at half-mast—a sign of mourning—always made him shudder apprehensively. This sea custom had been observed by many European observatories for a long time.

Neusted realised that they were too late.

The observatory gates were closed and nobody came out when they hooted. The driver got out and opened them himself.

Neusted took the little girl's hand and set off to find Teresa.

"What's your name?" he asked her on the way.

"Si," she whispered.

"Cicile?" Neusted queried.

"Si," the little girl repeated, her eyes brimming with tears.

Neusted did not ask her any more questions.

Teresa, her eyes swollen with weeping, accepted the girl as if she had been expecting her all along. She wiped her hands on her apron, squatted down, and began to unwind the torn black kerchief round the girl's head, speaking to her in her gruff, mannish voice. The girl whispered back, but did not cry. Neusted went off bewildered—he just couldn't understand the devilish knack of getting on with children.

He went through to Hervé's room where the dead man was lying. The mirror in the dining room was covered with old sackcloth. In the passage he met Matvei carrying some freshly cut branches of pine and yew with dark leaves. They went into the room together.

The man was lying stretched out on the bed

covered by a sheet. His hair had been combed revealing a deep scar on his forehead.

Matvei scattered the branches over the floor. Two wax candles were flickering on the small table. The shutters had been lowered.

"Teresa lit them," said the gardener in a hushed voice. "Women always know how to look after the dead."

Neusted looked at the stranger's face which bore the imprint of suffering in spite of its youth. His cheeks were cut by two deep furrows like scars, and his mouth looked as if he were calling softly to someone.

"So death has visited us, señor," said Matvei. "Professor Hervé has ordered a grave to be dug by the fence under the old yew tree."

"Where's Merot?" Neusted asked.

"In his room. He's very upset. The man died in his arms."

Neusted took his time before going to see Merot." Hervé came in.

"Well, Neusted," he said with a bitter smile. "Life has invaded our abode at last, even though it took the form of death."

"That's not all," Neusted replied. "I brought a little soul in need of help back from the town."

"Does someone else really need us?" Hervé asked in genuine amazement.

Merot was sitting at his desk with his weak hands pressed against his temples to restrain the tears.

The cold lacquered top of the desk was bare.

He had never written a single line here to anyone dear to him, only calculations and respectful letters to other astronomers. There was no one whom he loved or who loved him. There had been long ago, but Merot had forgotten about them. They had probably died long ago like that young man. "Never forget those who love you. It's better to kill than forget," his mother used to say, and now Merot realised that she was right.

The young man had died while Merot was on duty. He had been groaning all the time and had scarcely said a word, calling to Merot only once.

"Father," he said and Merot shuddered at this forgotten word. "Take the letter and papers from my case... Read them... Send them off... If she comes, tell her... I am thinking of nothing but her, nothing else matters ... nothing else..."

Merot found the letter and the papers. The man fell silent and then became delirious. He sang in his delirium, and it was so terrifying that Merot called Baudin.

The man had died by the time Baudin appeared.

Merot took the letter and papers to his room, but try as he did he could not finish reading them. A host of other thoughts crowded into his brain with every line he read.

They buried the stranger in the evening, standing round silently with bared heads while the gardener and Neusted filled in the grave with wet gravel. On the grave they planted a small stick with a board on which Baudin had written the words:

"Victor Frichard, poet, Frenchman. Crashed whilst flying from France to Madrid. May the name of this stranger in our midst be added to the list of those who have distinguished themselves by their valour.

"The astronomers and staff of the French observatory Sierra del Campo (Pyrenees)."

After the burial the astronomers gathered in the laboratory. Neusted had called them all to be present at what he referred to as his emergency announcement. Everyone was exhausted and silent, for the day had cost them as much as several years of their former smoothly running life.

"Professor Merot," began Neusted, standing up to emphasise the importance of what he was about to say, "has handed me papers and a letter left by the dead man. Before his death he asked that they should be read out and dispatched to their destination. It gives me great pleasure to carry out the wishes of this man, all the more so because the contents of these papers," Neusted placed his heavy hand upon them, "compel me to give up my work at the observatory temporarily and go down to the valley where, as you know, the Civil War has been raging for five months now."

"I always knew you were a philanthropist," Dufour remarked.

"That's a tribute to your perspicacity," replied Neusted calmly. "The man whose life we tried to save and whom we have just buried was a French poet. Astronomers and poets are blood brothers. The beauty of life which surrounds us is to be found not only in the laws governing the firmament but also in the laws of poerty."

"I see," Dufour murmured. "What about reading the letter?"

"If you did see," Neusted continued, "you wouldn't be spending your time now claculating the orbit of planet No. 1,212 which is not more than a kilometre in diameter. I consider such work to be as useless as counting specks of dust on the ground."

"Thank you very much! " Dufour exclaimed with a forced laugh. "And after that you still think of yourself as a scientist, do you?"

"Yes," Neusted replied rudely. "You're Dufour and I'm Neusted and we'll never swop brains. But I haven't finished yet. The poets and writers of France pooled their resources to purchase a few aeroplanes and arms to help the Spanish people's Army. Frichard volunteered to deliver these aeroplanes to Madrid. We know the cause of his death. There are arms in the wrecked aeroplane—rifles, cartridges and machine-guns."

"That's all very well," said Hervé, "but we're not going to use them."

"The letter is addressed to a woman in Briec," continued Neusted as if he had not heard their remarks. "There's little point in mentioning her name. I'll read it to you."

"This letter will be sent to you if I die. Do you remember that last day in Briec when I was leaving, the black cliffs and the smell of the old fishing nets? A piercing wind was blowing from the ocean and your dear little hands were cold. We were alone in the poor town. You and I were quite alone together and you were not only the woman I loved, but my mother, sister and my closest friend.

"In an hour's time I shall be starting for Spain. I carry with me your words that you could not love an unworthy person. It is difficult for some to preserve their dignity in our days when baseness armed with machine-guns and phosgene gas is assaulting all that is good in life and men. Some prefer to flee to far corners and hide in warm burrows on the excuse that we only live once and that each must live his life for himself. But because we only live once, because life is unique and wonderful, I find it easier to look danger openly in the face and win this life for myself or die for it, rather than to write pretty words and suffer from the stench of my own conscience.

"I know that you will understand. I am unable to comfort you. I love this earth because you live on it. I love the air because it touches your face. I love each blade of grass that your eye lights upon, each of your footprints on the wet sand, and the night silence because I can hear the sound of your breathing. And yet I am flying to my death. I am almost certain of it.

"Farewell! Tell the fisherwomen of your

grief, if you have the strength to tell. Nobody can understand it better than these simple women grown old before their time. For none of them have a family which has not known grief."

Neusted finished reading and shuffled his papers on the desk, head bowed. Nobody said a word. Hervé began to cough and pulled out a handkerchief convulsively to blow his nose.

"It's a good thing that you read the letter," said Merot quietly. "But now, if you don't mind, I will go. I can't stay any longer."

Merot left and Dufour sat with a cigarette that had gone out in his mouth.

Merot locked himself in his room, went up to the window and began to cry. A sharp heaviness in his chest hurt him. Merot thought that it would dissolve with the tears which were streaming down his sallow cheeks, but it became sharper until he could not see anything through the window. The stars were swimming about on the glass in blurred blotches.

He was filled with sorrow for the dead man, for the young, bereaved woman, for himself, Hervé and all those who were lost without refuge in this vast, pitiless world.

Late that evening Merot went to see Neusted. The Norwegian was standing by his desk tearing up some papers.

"Neusted, I'm leaving," said Merot. "I want to take the letter to Briec myself. I'll give up my work at the laboratory for a while like you."

"Why not," Neusted replied. "You haven't a son or a daughter. I see why you want to go."

Merot gave him a glance full of gratitude, and Neusted put his arm round the old man's shoulders saying:

"We must never forget each other."

"Of course not," Merot replied.

Back in his room Merot noticed his latest astronomical calculations on the desk and carefully put them away in the drawer.

The faint light of the Canes Venatici was glimmering through the window and as he glanced at it Merot suddenly realised that Briec lay in that direction.

Neither Neusted nor Merot left next morning. A distraught woman from the town rushed into the observatory at dawn. It was the little girl's mother. Her voice hoarse with alarm, she told them that the town had been taken by a small detachment of fascists, that the chemist had told their commander about an injured man hiding in the observatory who had been flying from France to Madrid, and that a platoon was going to set off for the observatory that morning.

"They think he was carrying secret documents and they want to shoot him," said the woman. "That's what the soldiers were saying."

"The only secret document is with me," said Merot, "and I won't hand it over to anyone."

"The woman stared at Merot in amazement. She hadn't understood what the old man was saying.

Another council of war was summoned.

"What are we going to do?" Baudin asked.

"We won't hand him over, even though he's dead," Neusted replied.

"We'll have to defend the stars against them," Dufour said with a wry laugh abandoning his aloof attitude. "Are there many of them?" he asked the woman.

"Thirty."

"Never mind" said Neusted. "Let's get down to some action."

"Of course," Dufour agreed. "Defeating this military detachment won't present any problem for us astronomers. Particularly as it does not include any of our colleagues, so even Hervé can take part in the fighting."

An hour later the driver and Neusted drove back with twenty rifles, cartridges and a machine-gun which they had salvaged from the wreckage of the aeroplane. Some of the rifles were broken, as well as the machine-gun. The driver managed to repair it by midday and wanted to try it out, but Neusted would not allow him to because the firing might put the troops on their guard too soon.

Neusted was fully in command of the situation. By tacit consent he was put in charge of the fortified observatory. Contrary to his expectations nobody questioned the necessity of offering resistance to the detachment marching up from the valley. A strange gaiety took hold of the inhabitants of the observatory, clearly the excitement which people show in moments of great danger.

The plan of defence was simply to take the enemy unawares and catch them in cross-fire. Neusted was convinced that this would be successful.

They set up the machine-gun on a rock not far from the observatory, which was a good point for covering the bend in the road. The driver lay at the machine-gun, with the gardener and Neusted keeping watch nearby, armed with rifles. The gardener had camouflaged the machine-gun and the rock with dead oak branches.

Dufour was keeping watch on the road through the small telescope. Its deserted white bends were clearly visible at a distance of fifteen kilometres. The main entrance to the observatory had been barricaded with heavy boxes of instruments.

Baudin, Hervé and Merot were sitting on a bench near the wall. From their position they could see the same bend in the road as Neusted ensconsed on the rock. Hervé was smoking his first cigarette for many years. The three old men chatted quietly and only the dry glitter in their eyes revealed their excitement.

Their rifles were standing against the wall a little way off. It was a sunny day, with a cool wind blowing from the mountains. A white cockerel hopped onto the fence and crowed, flapping its wings. They could hear Teresa talking loudly to the woman from the town in the kitchen and saying that the old men looked as if they could still stand up for themselves.

None of the astronomers really believed that there would be any fighting. Merot was watching the shadow from the flag pole. First it lay on one rifle, then the next and now it was creeping towards the third.

"Perhaps they've turned back?" said Baudin with a note of alarm in his voice.

"Ho, ho. Be patient, you old Napoleonic guardsman! " said Merot. "You won't be disappointed."

Merot watched the shadow of the flag pole. It was now lying full on the third rifle. Something black crept up beside the shadow.

Merot looked up and saw the flag being hoisted, unfurled and fluttering. This was Dufour's signal to Neusted that the detachment had been sighted on the road.

"Thank goodness, the old boy has picked out the right thing at last," said Baudin.

He was shivering with excitement. Soon Dufour appeared.

"Twenty-five! " he exclaimed animatedly. "Twenty-five royalist cutthroats led by their commander with a fiery shock of red hair."

"How do you know he's the commander?" Merot asked.

"Since when have you doubted the accuracy of our instruments? I saw the stripes on his collar."

"Well, in that case we won't argue with you," said Hervé smiling.

"They'll reach the bend in twenty minutes," said Dufour.

"If I'm not mistaken," Baudin murmured, "that method of firing which Neusted proposed is known as flanking fire?"

"Quite correct," Dufour confirmed. "They will fall into an ambush. But have you thought about what to do if they manage to break into the yard?"

"They won't," Merot said. "Over our dead bodies."

"We must provide for all contingencies," Hervé objected. "We could withdraw to the observation towers. There are three of them and they are all made of granite. Just look—there's a staircase, a small balcony and an iron door. The two narrow windows will do for loopholes."

"Excellent defence points! " Baudin exclaimeed. "Why didn't we think of them like that before?"

"That will be the best solution," said Merot. "At least we shall fall, as they say in military dispatches, at action stations, next to our spectrographs and mirrors."

They all laughed. None believed that there would be any real fighting.

"It's time to get Teresa," Dufour said.

He called Teresa and her appearance silenced their jokes. She was dressed in a short skirt with a dark kerchief wound crosswise over her chest. She examined the rifles and picked the newest one saying:

"When I was a little girl my father taught me to shoot kites. They often used to steal our chickens."

"Well, friends," said Baudin. "Let's get ready."

The old men picked up their rifles. Each of them had already chosen his own firing point by the wall.

Dufour looked at his watch.

"Not long now," he whispered.

They all took up their positions except Merot who had decided not to do so until the last moment because it was difficult for him to stand for long.

"That looks like a cloud of dust," said Baudin meaningfully.

"Look, Teresa."

"The snow's only just thawed," Teresa replied in the same hushed tones. "How could it be dust?"

Merot patted his pocket and the letter to Briec rustled in it. He had told everyone he had the letter and this put his mind at rest.

"Ah," Dufour exclaimed quietly.

Merot hurried up to his firing point. Everyone was watching the road without stirring. The soldiers emerged slowly round the bend. Their rifles were slung over their shoulders and they were walking out of formation.

"Try not to breathe when you pull the trigger," Teresa warned.

"You're a real trooper, Teresa," said Dufour. "But why is Neusted keeping quiet for so long?"

"Our driver used to be in the army. He knows the right moment to open fire."

The road was full of the dark shapes of the soldiers by now. They stopped to let the officer through to the front and at this moment Neusted's machine-gun opened fire with a bursting howl. The yellow oak leaves whirled into the air, and the mountain echo flung the sound of the machine-gun from one cliff to the next. It recoiled from the sheer rockface, plunged down into the depths of the ravines, and soared up again, with a hollow ring which would swell into a deafening crash like steel hammers beating against empty ship's boilers. Gravel and bullets whistled along the road. The soldiers flung themselves behind a stone parapet. The officer shouted something, clutching his head, then fell and lay motionless. Dufour counted ten bodies lying on the road, but then the first bullet cracked against the wall and ricocheted over the garden with a quiet whine knocking some branches off the old pine tree.

"Wake up there, friends," shouted Baudin.

Neusted could not see the soldiers lying behind the parapet, but it was easy to shoot at them from behind the wall. Baudin was the first to fire. Teresa screwed up her eyes. A lock of grey hair kept slipping out from her kerchief and she tucked it back angrily with an impatient gesture. Dufour fired calmly taking aim very carefully. Hervé was aiming for the parapet and his successful shots sent white wisps of dust rising from it. After Merot's first shot his shoulder began to ache from the impact of the butt, but he continued firing scarcely bothering to take aim.

Some of the soldiers had begun firing at the wall and the crack of their bullets became more and more frequent. Frightened by the shooting the white cockerel flew up to the pine tree cackling, fell off and hit the ground with a thud. He had been ripped open by a bullet.

The shooting increased. Merot heard the sound of breaking glass behind him as bullets hit the windows on the first floor. He reflected that it was a good thing the laboratory was on the ground floor because all the instruments would remain intact.

Machine-gun bullets spattered along the top of the wall sending showers of dust into their eyes.

"Everyone aim for the machine-gunner!" Baudin ordered. "They've only got one machine-gun. How on earth did they manage to set it up!"

Merot fired barely conscious of what was happening. It was difficult loading the cartridges into the rifle. He nicked the skin of his palm painfully several times and his finger was bleeding.

He saw the soldiers crawling off slowly down the slope, hiding behind boulders. Judging by the expressions on their faces they were shouting and cursing. He could see the machine-gunner's legs clearly, very thin and bandy, in dirty puttees. Then he saw the man jerk up, fall side-

ways and roll down the steep slope like a green
sack until he got tangled in an oak bush.

The machine-gun was quiet now. There was
only Neusted's gun going. The soldiers jumped
up and ran for their lives crouching low and
leaping from rock to rock, some of them throwing away their rifles.

Merot saw Neusted and the driver move the
gun down quickly to the road, roll it at the run
up to the bend and lie flat. The gun shuddered
and barked again, sending long ribbons of dust
ripping along the road. Neusted waved.

"Congratulations, old men," said Dufour.
"They're retreating."

"So that's the end, is it?" Hervé asked.

The machine-gun stopped firing. A last solitary shot rang out from Teresa. Hervé shook her
by the shoulder. The road was clear except for
a few soldiers who soon disappeared round a
bend.

Merot threw down his rifle and stretched.
The sun was shining overhead and silence lay on
the mountains. He filled his lungs with air and
felt the rich tang of leaves and roots.

The sound of the stream at the bottom of
the ravine could be heard again. The amphithe-
atre of mountains, drenched in sunshine,
sparkled in an ever-changing array of late
autumnal shades. Merot smiled. He knew that he
had a daughter down there in Briec, someone
immensely close to him, and friends, the astronomers, who were old men but courageous ones.
He felt as if he had just won the right to be alive

and possess the whole vibrant world below in the valleys which had once been alien to him.

Teresa smiled at Merot. He embraced her and the two old people kissed one another like brother and sister. They could hear Neusted singing a Norwegian song along the road.

The rest of the fascists were driven out of the town the same day by a detachment of Basques. Merot and Neusted left immediately. They were given a noisy farewell, but no one could conceal their sorrow at this parting.

Silence fell on the observatory once more, and the starry sky shone over it at night as usual listening gravely to the quiet voices of the astronomers, the slow steps of the gardener and the ripple of the old stream at the bottom of the ravine.

1936

THE GOLDEN TENCH *

When they're haymaking in the fields, it's better not to go fishing in the meadow lakes. We
knew this, but we went to the Prorva just the
same.

The trouble started at once, after Devil's
Bridge.

The colourful peasant women were stacking
the hay. We decided to make a detour round
them, but they noticed us.

"Where are you off to, lads?" they shouted,
laughing. "If you cast a line, you won't get
anything!! "

"They're bound for the Prorva, believe me,
girls! " shouted a tall, skinny widow nicknamed
Grusha the Prophetess. "They've got no choice."

The women had been jeering at us all summer.
However much fish we caught, they always said
pityingly:

*English translation © Raduga Publishers 1986

"Caught something for soup, have you? You're lucky to get that. But my Petka brought back ten carp the other day. Whoppers they were, as if fat was dripping off their tails! "

We knew that Petka had only brought back two skinny ones, but we said nothing. We had our own score to settle with that Petka; he had cut off Reuben's English hook and had tracked down the places where we were feeding the fish. By all the laws of fishing, we ought to have beaten up Petka for that, but we forgave him.

When we came to the unmown meadows, the women stopped shouting.

Sweet horse sorrel brushed our chests. The lungwort smelt so strong that the sunlight, drowning the horizons of Ryazan, seemed like liquid honey. We breathed the warm air of the grasses, hornets buzzed around us and crickets chirped.

The leaves of centuries-old willows whispered overhead like tarnished silver. From the Prorva came a scent of water-lilies and pure cold water. We calmed down and cast our lines, but an old gaffer nicknamed "Ten Percent" came rolling up from the meadows.

"So how's the fish?" he asked, peering at the water that was glittering in the sunshine. "Are they biting?"

Everybody knows you're not supposed to talk when you're fishing.

The old man sat down, lit a cheap cigarette and started taking his shoes off. He stared for a long time at his torn bast shoe and sighed noisily.

"Ripped them haymaking. No-o, they won't bite for you, the fish have gone funny. The devil alone knows what kind of bait they need."

The old man was silent. A frog began calling sleepily on the bank.

"My, he's jabbering away some," muttered the old man, and he looked up at the sky.

A dull, rosy haze hung over the meadow. There were glimpses of pale-blue patches in it, and a yellow sun hovered over the hoary willows.

"It's sultry," sighed the old man. "You can bet your boots there's going a real downpour in the evening."

We said nothing.

"And the frogs aren't croaking for their health," he explained, slightly put out by our glum silence. "Frogs, my friend, always get jittery before a storm, they jump all over the place. I spent the night with the ferryman the other day. We boiled some fish soup in a pot by the fire, and a frog—he weighed a kilo if he weighed a gram, hopped straight into the pot and got boiled alive. 'Vasily,' says I, 'you and me have had our fish soup.' And he says, 'To hell with that frog. I was in the German war in France, I was, and they eat frogs there. Help yourself, don't be scared.' So we supped the fish soup."

"Was it all right?" I asked. "Edible?"

"Very tasty," replied the old man, screwing up his eyes, and he thought a moment. "Want me to make you a jacket out of bast, laddie?

I made a whole three-piece out of bast for the All-Union Exhibition—jacket, trousers and waistcoat. There isn't a better bast-shoemaker on the whole collective farm."

It was two hours before the old man went away. Our fish, needless to say, didn't bite.

No one in the world has as many different kinds of enemies as the fisherman. Worst of the lot are small boys. At best they stand for hours behind you and stare hypnotised at the float.

At worst, they start swimming in the vicinity, blowing bubbles and diving like horses. Then all you can do is reel in your lines and find somewhere else.

Apart from small boys, peasant women and garrulous old men, we had more serious enemies; submerged logs, mosquitoes, duckweed, thunderstorms, rainy weather and rising water in the lakes and rivers.

It was a great temptation to fish where there were submerged logs; that was where the big, lazy fish used to lurk. They used to bite slowly and firmly, pulled the float right down, then they would snag the line on a tree-trunk and tear it off together with the float.

The thin whine of the mosquitoes used to make us tremble. For the first half of summer we went about all bloody and bumpy with mosquito bites.

On hot windless days, when the same clouds, as fluffy as cotton wool, hung in the same place in the sky for days and nights on end, a fine weed, like mould, appeared on the creeks and lakes. This was duckweed. The water would be covered with a stickly green film so thick that even your weight wouldn't sink through it.

The fish also stopped biting before a thunderstorm. They were afraid of the thunder, of the lull, the moment of calm when the earth is shaken dully by distant thunder.

In bad weather and when the water was rising, the fish didn't bite either.

But how beautiful were the fresh misty mornings, when the shadows of the trees reached far across the water, and the leisurely, bulging-eyed chub came in shoals right up to the bank! On such mornings, the dragonflies loved to settle on the feathered floats, and with sinking hearts we watched as the float and its dragonfly suddenly, slowly and slantways, dipped into the water; the dragonfly flew away, its paws wet, and a strong and cheerful fish swam down to the bottom on the end of the taut line.

How beautiful were the rudd falling like quicksilver into the dense grasses and hopping about amid the dandelions and clover! Beautiful were the sunsets that filled half the sky over the forest lakes, the thin smoke of the clouds, the cold stems of the lilies, the crackle of the campfire, the quacking of ducks in the distance.

Grandad was right: a thunderstorm blew up by evening. It growled in the forests for some time, then rose to the zenith like a wall of ash, and the first flash of lightning darted into the distant hayricks.

We sat in the tent till nightfall. At midnight, the rain eased off. We lit a big fire and dried ourselves out.

The night bird called sadly in the meadows, and a white star shimmered over the Prorva in the sky just before dawn.

I dozed off. I was awoken by the cry of a quail.

"Queep, queep, queep"—it was calling somewhere close by, in the undergrowth of clumps of briar and buckthorn.

We went down the steep bank to the water, holding on to roots and grass. The water shone like black glass. I could see the tracks left by snails on the sandy bottom.

Reuben cast his line not far from me. After a few minutes I heard him calling me with a low whistle. It was our fishermen's language. A short whistle three times meant "Drop everything and come at once! "

I went cautiously up to Reuben. He silently pointed to his float. A strange fish was biting. The float was bobbing, shifting now to the right, now to the left, trembling, but not sinking.

It stopped slantwise, dipped slightly and again bobbed up.

Reuben froze: only a very big fish nibbles like that.

The float quickly moved to one side, stopped, straightened up and began going down slowly.

"It's sinking," I said. "Pull! "

Reuben heaved. The rod bent into an arc, the line cut into the water with a whistle. The invisible fish was stiffly and slowly pulling the line round in circles... The sunlight fell on the water through clumps of white willow and I saw a bright bronze gleam under the surface. It was a caught fish flexing and backing into the depths. It took us several minutes to land it. It turned out to be an enormous, sluggish tench with swarthy gold scales and black fins. It lay in the damp grass, slowly moving its tail.

Reuben wiped the perspiration from his brow and lit a cigarette.

We did not fish any more, reeled in our lines and went to the village.

Reuben carried the tench. It hung heavily from his shoulder. It was dripping, and its scales glittered dazzlingly like the golden domes of the former monastery. On clear days, you could see those domes thirty kilometres away.

We purposely went across the meadows past the women. When they saw us, they stopped work and stared at the tench, shading their eyes with their hands, as when people look at the intolerably bright sun.

They said nothing. Then a faint whisper of delight travelled along their colourful ranks.

We walked calmly and independently through the lines of women. Only one of them sighed, and picking up her rake, said after us:

"That's a real beauty you've got there. It hurts your eyes to look at it! "

We slowly carried the tench all through the village. The old women poked their heads out of the windows and stared at our backs. The little boys ran after us pestering.

"Where did you catch it? What was your bait?"

Grandad "Ten Percent" slapped the tench on its hard gold gills and laughed.

"Now the women'll hold their tongues! Always giggling and sniggering they were. Now they'll change their tune! "

Since then, we haven't bothered to avoid the women. We've gone straight towards them, and they've shouted after us affectionately:

"Mind you don't catch too many fish! It wouldn't harm you to bring us some too! "

In this wise, justice triumphed in the end.

1936

THE RUBBER DINGHY*

We bought an inflatable dinghy for fishing.
We bought it in Moscow, in the winter, and since then we couldn't get any peace. Reuben was the most restless of all. It seemed to him that he had never known such a long, drawn-out and tedious spring in whole his life, that the snow was deliberately melting very slowly and that summer would be cold and the weather inclement.

Reuben clutched his head in his hands and complained of bad dreams. He dreamed that a big pike was towing him in the rubber dinghy over the lake and the dinghy was plunging into the water and bobbing up again with a deafening bubbling noise; or he dreamed of a piercing robber's whistle—it was the air rushing out of the boat which had been punctured by a submerged branch, and Reuben, to save himself, was vigorously swimming to the shore with a packet of cigarettes between his teeth.

*English translation © Raduga Publishers 1986

The fears only passed off in summer when we brought the dinghy to the village and tried it out in a shallow place near Devil's Bridge.

Dozens of little boys were swimming near the boat, whistling, laughing and diving to see it from underneath. The dinghy rocked calmly, grey and fat, like a tortoise.

A shaggy white dog with black ears, Murzik by name, barked at it from the bank and kicked up the sand with his hind-paws. This meant that Murzik would bark for at least an hour. The cows in the meadow lifted their heads and all, as if by order, stopped champing at the same moment.

Some women were going over Devil's Bridge with their baskets. They saw the rubber boat, shrieked and started upbraiding us.

"Why, you rascals, what are you up to? Upsetting folks like that! "

After the trial, an old man nicknamed "Ten Percent" felt the dinghy with his gnarled hands, kicked it, smelt at it, slapped it on its inflated sides and said respectfully:

"An airblown thing."

After these words, the boat was accepted by the entire population of the village, and the fishermen even envied us.

But our fears were not over. A new enemy for the boat appeared—Murzik.

Murzik was clueless, and he was always having accidents. He would be stung by a hornet and lie squealing on the ground and flattening the grass, or his paw would be crushed, or he would steal honey, smearing his shaggy muzzle with it up to the ears, so that leaves and chicken feathers stuck to his nose and our little boy had to wash Murzik with warm water.

But most of all, Murzik wore us out with his barking and his attempts to chew anything that came his way.

He barked mainly at things he couldn't understand: at Stepan, the black cat, the samovar, the primus stove and the wall-clock.

The cat would sit at the window, washing himself thoroughly and pretending not to hear the pestiferous barking. Only one ear quivered oddly with hatred and contempt for Murzik. Sometimes the cat looked at the puppy with bored, bold eyes, as if to say:

"Beat it or I'll fetch you one! .."

Then Murzik would jump away and, instead of barking, whined with his eyes shut. The cat would turn his back on Murzik and yawn loudly. He wanted to humiliate his foe with his whole appearance, but Murzik would not let up.

Murzik used to chew things in silence and for a long time. He always carried the gnawed and slobbered-on objects up into the attic, where we used to find them.

For instance, he chewed up a book of poems by Vera Inber, Reuben's braces and a remarkable porcupine needle float—I had bought it by chance for three rubles.

Finally Murzik got round to the rubber dinghy.

He spent a long time trying to grip it by the side, but the boat was very tightly inflated and his teeth slid off it. There was nothing to get hold of.

Then Murzik climbed into the boat and found the only thing that could be chewed—the rubber bung. It was used to plug the valve that let the air out.

We were having tea in the garden at the time and had no suspicions of foul play.

Murzik lay down, held the cork between his paws and growled. He was beginning to like it.

He gnawed it for a long time. The rubber wouldn't give way. Only an hour later did he finally chew through it. And then a truly terrible and incredible thing happened.

A dense jet of air rushed out of the valve with a roar like water from a fire-hose, hit Murzik in the muzzle, ruffled his fur and tossed him into the air. Murzik sneezed, squealed and fled into a clump of nettles, but the boat went on whistling; it growled, its sides shook and it became visibly smaller.

The hens cackled all over the neighbouring yards. The black cat raced at a heavy gallop across the garden and shinned up a birch-tree. From there he watched for a long time as the strange boat gurgled away, spitting out the last gouts of air.

After this incident, Murzik was punished. Reuben smacked him and tethered him to the fence.

Murzik tried to apologise. As soon as he saw one of us, he swept up dust near the fence with his tail looking us guiltily in the eyes. But we were adamant: vandalism must be punished.

We were soon past the twenty-kilometres to Lake Glukhoye, but we didn't take Murzik. When we left, he whined and wept at the end of his rope by the fence. Our little boy felt very sorry for Murzik, but hardened his heart.

We spent four days on Lake Glukhoye. On the third night, I was awakened by a warm, rough tongue licking my nose.

I raised my head and, by the light of the campfire, saw Murzik's muzzle, shaggy and wet with tears.

He was whimpering with joy, but didn't forget to apologise; he kept sweeping up the dry pine needles with his tail. A piece of chewed rope dangled round his neck. He was trembling, his fur was filthy and his eyes were red with exhaustion and tears.

I woke all the others up. The little boy laughed, then wept, then laughed again. Murzik crawled up to Reuben and licked his heel, asking for forgiveness for the last time. Then Reuben opened a tin of stewed meat and gave it to Murzik. He gobbled it up in seconds.

Then he lay down next to the little boy, pushed his nose under his armpit, sighed and began whistling through his nose.

The boy covered Murzik with his coat. Murzik breathed heavily in his sleep with fatigue and shock.

I thought how terrible it must have been for a little puppy to run through the forests at night, sniffing out our trail, missing it, baring his teeth, lifting his paw and listening to the sobbing of the owl, the crack of twigs and the incomprehensible noise of the grass; and, finally, to run full pelt, ears flattened back, when he heard the quavering howl of a wolf somewhere on the very edge of the earth.

I could understand Murzik's fear and exhaustion. I once happened to spend the night in a forest without my comrades, and I shall never forget that first night on Lake Bezymyannoye.

It was September. The wind was tearing the damp, fragrant leaves off the birches. I sat by the fire, and it seemed to me that someone was standing behind me and staring fixedly at the back of my head. Then, in the depth of the undergrowth, I heard the crackle of human footsteps over the brushwood.

I stood up and, prey to a sudden and inexplicable terror, drenched the fire, although I knew that there wasn't a soul for tens of kilometres around. I was completely alone in the night forests.

I sat until dawn at the extinct campfire. A bloody moon rose in the mist, in the autumnal dampness over the black waters and its light seemed baleful to me and deathly.

When we returned from Lake Glukhoye, we put Murzik in the rubber dinghy. He sat quietly, his paws apart, looking sideways at the valve and wagging the tip of his tail, but growling softly. He was afraid that the valve might play another nasty trick on him.

After this incident, Murzik became used to

the dinghy and always slept in it.

Once, Stepan the cat climbed into the boat and decided to have a nap in there too. Murzik bravely hurled himself on him. With a terrible hiss, as if someone had splashed water on to a red-hot, greasy grid iron, the cat flew out of the boat and never went near it again, although he sometimes very much wanted to sleep in there. He merely looked at the dinghy and Murzik with envious eyes from a clump of burdock.

The dinghy lasted till the end of summer. It did not burst, and not once was it punctured by a submerged branch. Reuben was exultant. Before leaving for Moscow, we made a present of Murzik to our friend Vanya Malyavin, the grandson of the forester from Lake Urzhenskoye. Murzik was a country dog, and in Moscow he would have found life hard amid the asphalt and noise of the big city.

1936

LUMP SUGAR

One northern summer I arrived at the small town of Voznesenye on Lake Onega.

It was midnight when the boat drew into the harbour and a silver moon was shining low over the lake. There was no need for it here because we were well into the season of white nights with their colourless lustre. There was scarcely any difference between the long days and the short nights. Both day and night, the whole of this low-lying forested landscape seemed to be melting away in the half-light.

The northern summer always provokes a feeling of uneasiness. It is very unstable. At any moment its precarious warmth may suddenly disappear. For this reason you begin to treasure the slightest breath of warm air and the gentle sun which transforms the lakes into sheets of quiet, gleaming water. This northern sun does not shine, but seems rather to glimmer through a thick pane of glass. It is as though winter had not yet disappeared and was only hiding away in the forest or at the bottom of the lake still giving off a tingling scent of snow.

The birch trees in the gardens were losing their blossoms. Fair-haired, barefooted boys were sitting on the landing stage fishing for smelt. Everything seemed to have turned white except for their large black floats. The boys's eyes were fixed on them in frowning concentration and they would ask each other in a whisper for a cigarette.

A militiaman with freckles and a cap stuck on his tousled hair was fishing with the boys.

"Now then. No smoking on the landing stage. No messing about here! " he would shout from time to time, and immediately several lighted cigarettes would flash into the white water, hiss and go out.

I set off for the town to find somewhere to spend the night accompanied by a fat, apathetic man with a crew cut who had tagged on to me. He was bound for the River Kovzha on business and carried a large worn briefcase full of reports and calculations about timber. He talked clumsy officialese like a rather incompetent business man, using such expressions as "curbing travelling expenses", "checking accounts", "organising a bite to eat", and "overfulfilling the timber rating norms".

The sky grew pale from boredom with his very presence.

We walked along the planked footways with the smell of bird cherry wafting from the cold, nocturnal gardens and pale lights gleaming behind the open windows.

A quiet, bright-eyed little girl was sitting on a bench by the garden gate in front of a wooden house singing her rag doll to sleep. I asked her if it would be possible to spend the night there. She nodded silently and then led me up a steep, creaking flight of steps into a clean room. The man with the crew cut persisted in following me.

An old woman in steel-framed glasses was knitting at the table and a thin dusty old man was sitting, eyes closed, leaning back against the wall.

"Grandma, here's a traveller who wants a bed for the night," said the little girl pointing at me with her doll.

The old woman rose and bowed low to me.

"You're welcome, my dear," she said in a sing-song voice. "You're welcome as an honoured guest. But we haven't much room, I'm afraid. We'll have to make up a bed for you on the floor."

"So things here are a bit primitive, citizen," said the man with the crew cut censoriously.

At this the old man opened his eyes—they were almost white like those of a blind man—and replied slowly:

"Some people never learn. Be thankful for small mercies."

"Now you just mind who you're talking to, my man," said the man with the crew cut.

The old man said nothing.

"Don't take offence at what the old man said," the old woman quavered pitifully. "He's got no home of his own, the poor old wanderer. You can't hold him to answer."

The man with the crew cut became animated. His eyes narrowed into a hard expression and he hit the table loudly with his briefcase.

"The old man's certainly an alien element," he said pompously. "You should be more careful who you let into your house. We'll soon find out who he is. Now, then, you there. What's your name and where were you born?"

The old man gave a wry smile. The little girl dropped her doll and her lip began to quiver.

"The world's my home and I'm at home everywhere in it," replied the old man calmly. "And my name is Alexander."

"Occupation?"

"I reap and sow," said the old man in the same calm voice. "When I was a young man I would reap and sow the crops. Now I sow a kind word and reap other wonderful words. The trouble is that I can't read or write, so I have to take everything in by ear and rely on my memory."

The man with the crew cut said nothing for a while, puzzled.

"Any papers?"

"Yes, I have papers. But they're not intended for the likes of you, my lad. Them's valuable papers."

"I see," said the man with the crew cut. "Then we'll find the person they are intended for."

And he went out slamming the door behind him.

"There's a right thick 'un for you," said the

old man after a pause. "Nothin' but fuss and
bother from the likes of him."

The old woman set the samovar going, apol-
ogising contritely in her wavering voice for
not having a lump of sugar in the house because
she had forgotten to buy it. The samovar provided a mournful accompaniment to her lament.
The little girl laid the table with a clean tablecloth of unbleached linen which smelt of rye
bread.

Outside the open window a single star was
shining. It was misty and very large and looked
strange on its own in the vast gloaming sky.

This tea-making in the middle of the night
did not surprise me. I had discovered a long time
ago that northerners stay awake until very late
in the summer. Outside by the gate of the house
next door two young girls were standing with
their arms round each other gazing into the dim
waters of the lake. As always on a white night,
the girls' faces looked pale with emotion, sad
and beautiful.

"That's the two Komsomol lassies from
Leningrad," said the old woman. "Captains'
daughters. Always spend the summer here."

The old man was sitting quietly with his
eyes closed as if he were listening for something.
Suddenly he opened his eyes and sighed.

"He's bringing him! " he said sadly. "Forgive
me for being such a fool and a nuisance,
Grandma."

The steps outside creaked and there was a
sound of heavy footsteps. The man with the

crew cut came in without knocking, followed by a worried, tousle-haired militiaman in a cap—the one who had been fishing on the landing stage. The man with the crew cut nodded in the direction of the old man.

"Now then, Grandad," the militiaman said sternly. "Come on and establish your identity. Let's have your papers."

"I'm a simple enough person," the old man replied. "But it's a long story. Sit down and I'll tell you all about it."

"Mind you're quick, then," said the militiaman. "I haven't got time to sit around. I've got to take you down to the station."

"There's plenty of time for us to get down to the station, my lad. They don't waste any words there. No one to have a good talk to. I've turned sixty and I might pop off any day now in a strange place. So you just listen to what I have to say."

"Come on then," the militiaman agreed. "But don't you go making it all up, mind."

"Why should I? My life is a simple one and there's no getting away from it. All of us Fedosievs were coach drivers and singers from way back. My grandfather Prokhor was a great singer. His mighty voice would ring out and weep all along the highway from Pskov to Novgorod. A person should look after his voice. It's not given to a man for nothing. My grandfather looked after his well until one sad day when he forgot and that was the end of it. Happen you know that our famous coutryman .Alexander

Sergeyevich, the poet Pushkin, lived in Pskov gubernia.''

The militiaman grinned.

'' 'Course I know that.''

"Well, it was because of him that my grandfather ruined his voice. One day they met at the fair in the Svyatogorsk Monastery. My grandfather was singing and Pushkin stood there listening to him. Then the two of them went into a drinking house and sat there all night. Nobody knows what they were a-talking about, but my grandfather returned home as merry as a lord altho' hardly a drop of wine had passed his lips. Later on he told my grandmother: 'I got drunk from his words and laughter, Nastyusha. He spoke so beautifully—much more beautifully than my singing.' There was one song my grandfather knew that Pushkin was real fond of.''

The old man paused for a moment and then suddenly burst into song in a powerful, anguished voice:

> *Over the plains so broad and white*
> *The snow our bitter tears hath buried.*

The girls walked up to the window and listened, their arms round each other. The militiaman sat down cautiously on a bench.

"Aye," the old man sighed. "A fair time after that my grandfather died at a ripe old age and bade his sons and grandsons sing that song after him. But that's not what I meant to tell you about. One winter's night grandfather was woken up by knocking on the window and ordered to harness the horses on urgent state business. He comes out on to the steps and sees the place a-swarming with policemen, walking about and rattling their broadswords. So we're taking off another bunch of convicts, he thinks. But instead of prisoners there's a black coffin lying there bound with rope. Who can that be, he thinks, carried to his grave in fetters? God have mercy on him. Who is it that the Tsar fears even after death? He goes up to the coffin, brushes the snow off the black lid with his sleeve and asks the policeman: 'Who are we taking?' 'Pushkin,' says the policeman. 'He's been killed in St. Petersburg.' Grandfather started back, flung off his cap and bowed low before the coffin. 'Did you know him then?' said the policeman. 'I sang to him.' 'Well, you won't be singing to him any more! ' The night was so bitter cold, that you could hardly breathe. Grandfather tied the bells so that they would not ring, climbed up to the coachman's seat and set off. There was silence all around except for the swishing of the runners and the sound of the broadswords knocking against the coffin. His heart was heavy, his eyes smarted with tears and he burst into song at the top of his voice:

Over the plains so broad and white...

"The policeman hit him on the back with his scabbard, but grandfather went on singing, paying no heed to him. He got home and went to bed in silence—the cold had ruined his voice. From that day onwards he could speak only in a hoarse whisper."

"He really put his heart into his singing, then," murmured the militiaman in a moved voice.

"No use doing anything unless you put your heart into it," said the old man. "And here you are going on at me about who I am and what I do. I sing songs. That's what I do. Just go about singing to people. And when I hear a new song I try to remember it. For example, it's one thing to say something, but if you sing it that's quite a different matter. Then the words go straight to the heart. We must cherish the power to sing. People who don't like singing are not worth a farthing. They don't understand the meaning of life. And don't you go worrying about my papers. I'll show you one."

The old man put a shaking hand inside his shirt and drew out a grey pouch from which he took a piece of paper.

"There. Read this."

"Why should I?" said the militiaman offended. "I don't need to read it now. I can see who you are without that. You just stay where you are and have a good rest, Dad. And as for you, citizen," he said turning to the man with the crew cut, "you'd better go and spend the night at the hostel. That will suit you better. Come along and I'll show you the way."

They left. I took the piece of paper from

the old man and read the following:

"This is to certify that Alexander Fedosiev is a collector of folk songs and stories for which he receives a pension from the government of the Karelian Republic. Local authorities are requested to render him all necessary assistance."

"Dear me," said the old man. "There's nothing worse than a person who has a dried-up soul. They make life wither like grass from the autumn dew."

We sat drinking tea. The girls with their arms round each other went down to the lake, and their simple cotton dresses showed white in the light nocturnal twilight. A pale moon was descending into the water and somewhere in the garden among the birch trees a night bird called.

The bright-eyed little girl went into the street and sat down again by the gate to sing her rag doll to sleep. I could see her through the window. The tousle-haired militiaman in the cap came up to her and pushed a bag of sugar and biscuits into her hands.

"Take these to the old man," he said blushing hard. "Tell him it's a present. I haven't got time myself—got to get back on duty."

He went off quickly and the little girl brought the bag of lump sugar and biscuits to the old man who burst out laughing.

"Ee, but I'd like to go on living for a long time yet," he said wiping his wet eyes. "It's such a pity to die and leave such good people behind. Such a pity. And when I look at the forest, the bright water, the young lads and the wild grass, I just haven't got the heart to die."

"You just go on living, my dear," said the old woman. "Why should you do anything else with a life as easy and simple as yours."

The following afternoon I left Voznesenye for Vytegra. The small *Svir* sailed along a canal, its sides brushing against the willow-herb which grew along the banks in profusion.

The little town gradually disappeared into the sunny haze, the silence and the distance of the summer day, and the low-lying forest enveloped us in a dark circle. Around us lay the pale northern summer, as shy as the bright-eyed local children.

1937

LYONKA FROM LITTLE LAKE

We were following a map compiled in the eighteen seventies from "information obtained from the local inhabitants" as a footnote in the corner explained. We were not overjoyed by this note in spite of its frankness, for we too had obtained information from the local inhabitants and it was almost invariably inaccurate.

They would shout long and heatedly, contradicting each other and referring to a lot of landmarks. Their directions were usually something like this: "As soon as you get to the ditch make a sharp turn across to the forest, then just go on and on across burnt clearings until you reach the badger's hole. From there you make straight for the big hill that you can just see in the distance, and once you've reached the hill it's just a matter of crossing the tussocks to the lake. You can't miss it."

We would follow these instructions to the letter and never find the place we were looking for.

So today we were using a map, but had got lost all the same among the dried-up marshes overgrown with small sparse trees.

The autumn day was rustling with crisp leaves. Then a fine rain began to fall which felt like cold dust on our faces. About three o'clock we found ourselves on a sandy bank covered with dry fern in the middle of the marshes. The light was fading fast, and dusk was gathering under the unfriendly sky, heralding the approach of night—a bleak night in the marshes, with nothing but the cracking of dead branches, the pattering of rain and an unbearable feeling of loneliness.

We shouted and listened hard. The wind moaned back at us through the lifeless thickets bearing the harsh cawing of crows.

Then suddenly we heard a long, faint answering call in the far distance. The calls grew nearer and there was a cracking sound among the aspen trees. A boy with a freckled face emerged from the thicket. He looked about twelve years old and was picking his way carefully over the dead branches barefoot, carrying a pair of old boots. He came up and greeted us shyly.

"I heard this shouting," he said and added with a laugh. "Got a bit scared, because you don't expect to find anyone here at this time of year. You get women picking berries in the summer, but it's not the season for berries any more. Are you lost?"

"Yes," we said.

"You wouldn't last long here," said the boy.

"A woman got lost last summer and they didn't find her until spring. Just a heap of bones."

"What are you doing here?"

"I live here. By Little Lake. I'm looking for a lost calf."

The boy took us to Little Lake. It was almost night by the time we got out of the marshes onto hard ground and reached the overgrown path. The wind had driven the clouds southwards and the stars were blazing over the pine trees, but the familiar constellations looked different through the tangled branches, and it was even difficult to find the Great Bear.

"I made that up about the calf," said the boy after a long silence. "I wasn't looking for a calf at all."

"What were you after in the marshes, then?"

"A falling star. Saw it fall the night before last behind the big hill: woke up and heard Manka the cow mooing and tossing about. Thought there must be a wolf outside, so I went to have a look. I stood in the yard listening and then something blazed across the sky, sailed low over the forest and fell somewhere behind the hill. It was a meteor. Made quite a noise, like an aeroplane."

"What do you want a meteor for?"

"I'll take it to school and we'll examine it. Do you know what stars are made of?"

We began a nocturnal discussion about stars and spectral analysis.

It was almost midnight when we arrived at the forest lake with the starry autumn sky reflected in its black waters. There were several cottages on the bank and the boy knocked at the door of the far one where an oil lamp was still burning in the window.

"Where on earth have you been, you little rascal," said a woman's voice angrily behind the door. "Wearing out your boot leather! "

"I took them off, Ma," said the boy.

There was a rattling of bolts being drawn and we groped our way into a little passage smelling of hay and fresh milk.

We spent the night in the boy's cottage—his name was Lyonka Zuyev—smoking a cigarette with his father, an elderly quiet man with steel-rimmed glasses, and then going to sleep on the straw near the warm stove. A cricket was chirping and sleepy hens were clucking in the passage.

I was woken in the middle of the night by the sound of a powerful woman's voice giving a passionate rendering of the well-known aria from *The Queen of Spades* accompanied by a host of high-pitched violins. Stars were shimmering through the misted windowpanes and the cricket had stopped chirping to listen to the singing.

"That there radio's disturbing you," said Lyonka's mother from her bed above the stove. "Lyonka made it himself. It'll prevent you from sleeping, but I don't know how to stop it. Haven't got the education. I'll wake up the lad."

"No, don't bother. Let him have his sleep."

"But we love listening to Moscow singing,

we really do," she went on in the dark, her voice hushed and wistful. "Somehow it's so strange and sad and gay, all mixed up together. You can go on listening to it until the cock crows even though you were ready to drop after a hard day's work."

She paused for a moment.

"And it's all our Lyonka's doing," she continued, obviously smiling to herself in the dark. "He's a right one for finding out about things. Takes after his father."

"What does his father do, then?" I asked her.

"Semyon? He's been in the Party since nineteen eighteen. Never a thought for himself. Give away his last crust, he would, and live on his books."

The next morning we found out all about Semyon Zuyev. He had started off as a tailor's apprentice in Ryazan. The Lysov firm where he worked was considered to be the best tailors in the town and was patronised by the governor, the military and the legal profession. Semyon had ruined his eyesight sewing silk braid by hand onto lawyers' trousers. It was very painstaking work.

Lysov, a devout old fogy with a face as green as a frog, spent all his time reading religious books or Karamzin's *History of the Russian State*. He spent a thousand rubles on beautifying the town's dusty streets by having steel plates with quotations from Karamzin put up on houses. Each extract had a footnote saying: "See Mr. Karamzin's *History*", volume so-and-so, page so-and-so.

"So I began with Karamzin and finished up reading Lenin," said Semyon. "Lenin's voice penetrated right into the most remote backwaters. You'd read at night and then go out into the street in the morning to be greeted by dust everywhere, geese waddling about among the puddles and scraps of red sealing wax all over the shop where they sold vodka. The bells were ringing in the church and the beggars beating each other with their staffs for the sake of a farthing. In other words, primeval Russia in all its glory. And the stirring words would be ringing in your head like the dawning of a new life."

After the Revolution Semyon went to live by the lake, built himself a cottage and began the hard job of reclaiming land from the dense forest. There were already five families living there now.

In the morning Lyonka took us to the main road. A white sun was shining through the thinning branches and its cold light picked out each leaf as it fell from the aspen and birch into the lake. Occasional gusts of wind would send the leaves showering and rustling down, tickling our faces.

A few days later Lyonka appeared in our village with a piece of "falling star" in the form of a pointed burnt-out fragment covered with soot and rust, which he had discovered in a twisted old tree stump behind the hill.

From then onwards he and I became great

friends. I liked wandering round the forest with him. He knew every path, every nook and cranny. He could name all the plants, bushes, mosses, mushrooms and flowers and tell all the birds and animals by the sound they made.

Lyonka was the first of the many hundreds of people I had met to tell me how and where fish sleep, how dry marshes smoulder under the ground for years, how old pine trees bloom and how tiny spiders, as well as birds, migrate in the autumn. They hang suspended from their cobwebs and get carried along by the wind, dozens of miles southwards. Lyonka had two books by Kaigorodov which he had read until they were falling apart. He had searched through them in vain to find an explanation of the spiders' autumn flight.

"The one thing I don't understand is how such tiny spiders can weave so much cobweb. If you were to wind it all into a ball it would be forty times their size."

Each day Lyonka went ten kilometres to school and he had only stayed away twice in the whole winter. This was when a strong snowstorm had covered their house in snow right up to the eaves, but Lyonka didn't like talking about it. He was ashamed of having missed school.

In the winter he would leave the house when it was still dark. The spiky stars were shivering in the bitter cold, the pine trees creaked, and the snow crunched underfoot. Lyonka was terrified that he might be heard by the wolves, who used to come right up to the lake in winter and live in the haystacks.

The worst time of all was late autumn, November, when the paths were covered with a slushy mixture of snow and rain, and gusts of wind from the lowering sky lashed your face and froze you to the marrow.

In the summer Lyonka and his mother would plough the field, dig up the vegetable garden, sow, and mow the hay. Semyon could not do that sort of work any more. He suffered more and more from a weak heart that made his face sallow and puffy, and was racked by fits of dry coughing.

"I'm more dead than alive," he would say spreading out his hand on his thin chest. "That dog's life ruined my system. The Revolution must have come too late for me. Never mind, Lyonka will finish the job off for me."

So Lyonka and I became friends and I used to send him lots of books from Moscow. I got into the habit of coming to the lake every autumn.

I would always arrive unexpectedly, walking through the quiet autumn forest, deserted except for the birds, and recognising the familiar tree stumps, the twists and turns of the overgrown path and the bright forest clearings. I knew every pine tree on the edge of the forest and it was Lyonka who had taught me to love them.

I usually arrived in late twilight when the pale stars were heralding a cold night and the smell of smoke seemed to be the most delicious odour in the world. It conjured up the nearness of the lake, the warm house, lively conversations, Lyonka's mother complaining in her singsong voice, and beds of dry hay. It reminded me of the chirping cricket and the endless nights when I would wake up to a torrent of strings playing Beethoven or Verdi, drowning the tremulous howls of hungry wolves.

Each time Lyonka would leap out of the house to greet me. He was too shy to show how pleased he was and just gave me a firm handshake. Then we talked for a long time about the books he had read, the harvest, winter in the Arctic, an eclipse of the sun and loach fishing. We were never at a loss for interesting topics of conversation. Semyon used to tell us tales about his young days and the students who had brought revolutionary leaflets to Ryazan.

We became really close friends. Wherever I was, I knew that I would return to the lake in late autumn and see Lyonka and Semyon, and that my contact with these people would make me increasingly certain that life was getting better all the time. There seem to be more and more days when you are suddenly aware of the rushing sound of the wind in the forest, the cold springs gurgling in the moss, and you realise the tremendous value of books, quiet meditation and friendship with a country lad who has been dreaming for three years of coming to Moscow and seeing the metro, the Kremlin and a live elephant at the zoo.

This year Lyonka saw me off as usual. The

funny little local train, which the inhabitants call "The Old Gelding", was puffing along through the forest. Each clearing revealed gold and crimson copses. In one of the clearings Lyonka was standing right by the railway track, waving his father's old cap. The kettle-like steam engine gave an angry whistle at him, but he just laughed and shouted:

"We'll be waiting for you. I'll write you a letter about everything. Don't forget to send me Brem! "

It was a long time before the ruddy-faced lad running after the train through the wet, pungent autumn copses, disappeared from view. He ran waving his satchel of books and smiling his shy, open smile to me, the forest, the sun and the whole world.

1937

THE OLD BOAT*

The train stopped. A wasp was buzzing trapped in the window-curtain.

"What station is this?" asked a drowsy voice from the sleeping compartment.

"We've stopped on the line," answered the conductor. He hurried along the carriage, wiping his hands on a piece of tow.

Natasha put her head out of the window. From a high embankment to the horizon stretched forest. Over it hung a dense cloud, covering half the sky. Flocks of white birds were floating in front of it like a dandelion clocks.

Thunder boomed at the ends of the earth and rolled cumbersomely over the forest. It rumbled for so long that it seemed to be travelling all the way round the vast land, dying down when absorbed by a grove but, when it broke out into the fire-lanes and glades, growling even more grimly than before.

*English translation © Raduga Publishers 1986

"What a storm! " said someone behind Natasha.

She looked round. Her travelling companion, a young theatre director, was standing in the compartment doorway.

"What a storm! How well done! " he repeated peering at the thundery sky as if it was a stage-set! "D'you know what those birds are?"

"They are doves," said the elderly forester in a horn-rimmed spectacles, and he smiled at Natasha. "Fancy you not knowing. And you a tenth-former! "

"I'm city born and bred," replied Natasha, embarrassed.

The train jolted and began crawling backwards. Suddenly, darkness fell.

The wind snatched at the curtains and overturned a tumbler of flowers on the table. The yellow water spilled noisily on to the floor.

Lightning lashed across the window, and at once there was a dry terrifying crack in the forest, as if a tall pine had been snapped in two.

"What's happened?" asked a shrivelled, lilac-pyjama'd little woman in a tearful voice. Her twittering beauty had vanished with the first clap of thunder.

The passengers were hurriedly raising the windows and looking at the cloud. The lightning flashes revealed ominous caves within it, the funnels of whirlwinds, turbid tresses of rain. Enormous continents of black soot and white cinders were tumbling down to earth. In the terrifying blackness, the same silver birch kept blazing up in the glare of the lightning. It was incomprehensible why that intermittent light was picking this particular birch out of the darkness, when thousands of other trees around it were sighing in the wind.

"Just what's happened, conductor?" cried the woman in the lilac pyjamas. "Why are we going back?"

"The track's flooded ahead," replied the conductor morosely. "You see what a storm it is! They're taking us to Sinezerki. We'll stay there till the line's been repaired."

"Disgraceful! " said the little woman; she screwed up her eyes in fright and slammed the compartment door.

The dead forest shuddered at the turbid glare and suddenly came to life; the branches, like ragged black sleeves, were shaking in the wind, all reaching out in the same direction, towards the last gap under the low canopy of clouds. The trees seemed to be clutching at the clear departing sky and calling for help.

Torrential rain drummed hard on the carriage roof.

"Swift is the lightning's flight, and it smites with a blow that is heavy," said the forester unexpectedly.

The director smiled with his eyes alone.

"Where's that from?"

"Lucretius."

By all appearances, the forester was happy and embarrassed. He was happy because he was going for his holidays to the Crimea, which he hadn't seen since childhood. He still had memories of sheer cliffs, steep capes overgrown with brambles, and lapping waters that floated up to their feet from somewhere terribly far away.

He was embarrassed by his fellow-passengers. He was embarrassed by their politeness to him, by the pyjamas, by the conversations about seaside resorts. They talked to one another without ever speaking to him. When they casually discussed hotels, porters and Lincolns, he felt that they were people from another world and he, a forester, who had put on a new grey suit for the journey, was of no interest to them whatever. They were sharp, his fellow-passengers, and they seemed to know that his suit was the only one he owned and had been made by a second-rate tailor from Kostroma. He took care of it and envied the stage-director. Lounging on the seat, his pale hands thrust into the pockets of his thin trousers, the director smoked Elite cigarettes and was not in the least bothered that his unbuttoned jacket was getting creased, or that the cigarette ash was falling on to his dazzling, loosely knotted necktie.

The only fellow-passenger who did not embarrass the forester was Natasha, a slim, modest girl. The wind coming through the window ruffled her hair occasionally and several times a day it blew dust into her eyes.

Once, the forester helped her take a speck of dust out of her eye, but was embarrassed again when Natasha offered for the purpose a diaphanous, lightly scented handkerchief.

"Forester," he thought to himself, "damned yokel! "

"What a marvellous name, *Sinezerki*! " murmured the director. *"Sinezerki! Sinezerki!* Blue lakes! Must remember that."

"There's a lot of lakes here, in the forests," said the forester.

"You know the vicinity?"

"Yes, a bit... I worked here about fifteen years back, planting trees."

"Ah, how interesting," drawled the director, but the forester could see from his face that it was of no interest to anybody. "We're really out of luck. Why couldn't the storm have burst tomorrow instead of today?"

"Yes, very annoying," agreed the forester.

He was thinking that for a long time now he had been intending to go to Sinezerki, to the old places, but he would never get round it. And now the train would stand in Sinezerki for an hour or two until the track had been repaired and he would see nothing except familiar deserted station, where the hens wandered about the platform on their own business.

"Yes, it's a pity! " sighed the forester.

Natasha also was upset. She had never been to the Crimea before, and to her it was dark-blue, misty, and fragrant with carnations. She wanted to see the sea as soon as possible. She had heard that it revealed itself suddenly and was like a lofty cloud in the sky.

Sinezerki was deserted. A paraffin lamp burned in the duty station-master's window, and it was hard to understand whether it was already evening' or whether it was dark because of the rain.

The rain died down. There was an odour of wet woodshavings from the forest.

Grandpa Vasily turned over the damp hay in the wagon and glanced from time to time at the train. "What are folks toing-and-froing all the time like that for?"

His nag pushed its head up to its ears in a bag of oats, champed hurriedly, listened to Grandpa muttering, and waited for the familiar call: "Come on, you devil! You've had enough feed on the state! " After that shout, there was nothing left to do but heave a ponderous sigh and glumly tow the cart over the sandy road back to the lake.

But Grandpa Vasily suddenly threw down the reins and hastened to the train. He went up to the illumined window of a first-class carriage and tapped the window-pane with the handle of his whip.

"Pyotr Matvev! " he shouted in a weak, faltering voice. "Pyort Matvev! "

The forester was standing in the corridor and talking to Natasha. He stared at the old man and opened the window.

"Don't you know me?" asked Grandpa, and he laughed shrilly. "I recognised you all the way from the wagon back there. Fancy us meeting again like this! "

"Vasily! " exclaimed the forester and he

quickly went to the carriage door, jumped down on to the sand and embraced the old man. "Still alive?"

"Still alive," replied Grandpa, wiping his face with his sleeve. "Still alive and kicking. Death hanging about in the offing, but he hasn't got round to calling on me yet. You forgot us, Pyotr Matvev, honest you forgot us. And without you, I'll tell you straight, life's not been worth living."

"Why? What's wrong?"

"You mean you don't know?" asked the Grandpa mistrustfully. "Haven't you been reading the papers, Pyotr Matvev?"

"What is it, then? Tell me, don't look over your shoulder."

"There's nobody for me to look over my shoulder at. Our district papers printed it goodness knows how many times," said Grandpa with a sigh. "They printed it and they printed it, and when it came to, they were wasting their time. It's plain to see, you can't get things done just by writing. You won't save the forest."

"What are you blethering about?" asked the forester. "Stop beating around the bush and talk straight."

Grandpa took off his hat and hurled it down on the oilblackened sand.

"Pyotr Matvev, Pyotr Matvev! Your young forest was supposed to live for a long time! "

"Has it burned down?" asked the forester in a fright.

"Why burned down? God preserve us, we haven't had any fires. But the caterpillars have been chewing it up ever since spring, yes, chewing it up as if on orders, and they've gobbled up half of it already, the swine! The new forester'll never cope. They don't give him any elbow-room, you know, so he sits and writes papers and he sends them here, there and everywhere, but it makes no difference if you go to him, all you get is words: 'No reply from the district centre.' So we sit here and twiddle our fingers. 'No, no reply! ' And the forest! " said Grandpa, and he snivelled loudly. "What a forest you and I planted, Pyotr Matvev! Choice pines, like beautiful sisters! By God, believe it or not, but when I go into it, I take off my hat and I stand like I was in a trance, it's such a lovely forest! "

Grandpa picked up his hat, inspected it and crammed it down over his tangled white locks.

"What are we to do?" said the forester, and he looked round. Natasha was standing on the carriage steps and, her brow wrinkled, was listening to Grandpa's complaints.

"When a father leaves his children uncared for," said Grandpa mournfully, "his conscience gnaws him; yes, and he can be sentenced by a People's Court. But a tree? A tree can't talk. Who's a tree got to complain to? Only a fool of a forest warden like me."

"So what's to be done, Vasily?" asked the forester in confusion.

"Pollen clouds," muttered Grandpa, who had

not heard the forester. "The pollen ripened this spring, the wind started blowing, and carried it over the lake like golden smoke. I've never seen such dust before in all my life."

He was silent for a moment.

"Pyort Matvev," he said imploringly and he plucked the forester by the sleeve. "Do an old man a favour—let's go to the lake and have a look. You just tell me how to save it, the forest, I mean, and then God be with you, I'll manage somehow on my own."

"You're crazy! " said the forester. "The train's leaving in two or three hours. What d'you think you're up to?"

"It won't leave," said Grandpa confidently. "It's got nowhere to go. Two kilometres of track washed away. It'll start off tomorrow at noon, but not before."

The forester looked round again at Natasha. Still wrinkling her brow, she was watching Grandpa.

"Let's go to the duty station-master," said Grandpa firmly, "and if he has a scrap of conscience, he'll back me up."

"What am I going to do with you?" said the forester angrily. "You've got me all confused with your gibberish."

"Off you go, Pyotr Matveyevich," said Natasha unexpectedly. "You'll make it in time! "

"You think I will?" asked the forester, and he laughed, conscious of a sudden freshness in his heart. "You think I'll be in time?"

"Can I go with you?" asked Natasha.

"Ah, dear miss, beautiful comrade," said Grandpa, bowing low to Natasha. "How could we not take you for your true words? Let's go. While we're marching round the forest, you can stay by the lake. Our lake has silver water, there isn't one like it in all the Soviet Union..."

"Let's go to the duty station-master," said the forester. "You've really got me muddled, Grandpa."

The duty station-master said that the track was unlikely to be repaired before midday.

The forester, Grandpa and Natasha left for the lake. Their departure caused among the passengers the disapproving bewilderment usual in such cases and vague exclamations such as: "Really! Well, I never! " "I wouldn't have expected it! "

The little nag pulled the cart at his own speed, wiggling his ears—you can't see a sick forest at night anyway, and you can't have any brain-waves.

The wheels squeaked over the dark, grassy roads. In the forest, a silence reigned that seemed to Natasha as deep as night water. Only in the damp copses did strange birds cry out very occasionally.

By midnight the clouds had gone, and over the pine tops the sky began to glitter with cold lights. But Natasha did not recognise the stars; the constellations were tangled up in the tree branches and had lost their familiar outlines.

The forest land, mysterious and vast as the ocean, was spread all round them in the gloom of the   night, in the scent of damp, rotting foliage, and in the endless glitter of the sky. Natasha talked in a whisper, and even Grandpa and the forester spoke in undertones.

"This is our preserve," murmured Grandpa with a sigh. "These forests run to the end of the world. There's nothing better on this earth."

"Sleep, sleep! " cried a newly awakened bird somewhere overhead. "Sleep, sleep! "

"I'm sleeping anyway," thought Natasha and she laughed with sudden joy. She even felt cold with happiness and wanted the night to last forever, the wagon to rattle slowly over the roots forever, and forest to become even more dreamy and wild.

"Seems like we're here," said Grandpa.

It was lighter. Natasha looked round and couldn't understand it. The starry sky was lying by the road and plashing softly as it ran up to an unseen shore.

"The lake," said the forester. "Look at all the stars in it, same as in autumn! "

A dog began barking gruffly. The wagon stopped near a watch hut, under some black willows. Hens flapped their wings on a perch. Grandpa went into the hut, lit a tin paraffin lamp and showed the way for Natasha and the forester.

Natasha went into the hut. There was a strong, acrid smell of stove ashes, dry mint and the warmth of an old wooden building.

Natasha drank some milk and promptly fell asleep on the broad bench that was glossy with age. Grandpa put a new peasant's coat under her head.

She woke up very early. A white sun hung over the forest. There was no one in the hut, only a black dog sitting under the table, eyeing Natasha with astonishment from time to time and fleaing itself.

"I had to go and be late! " thought Natasha, flustered. She jumped up and straightened her hair.

The wall clock had stopped, a long time ago, most likely. A bottle of water had been suspended under it instead of a weight; it was covered in cobwebs.

Natasha went out into the cool passage. The dog followed her and, fawning, thumped its tail against the buckets and horsecollars lying on the floor.

There was no one about. Natasha opened the door leading to the porch and sighed. The bright round lake lay right there, on the very threshold, in a scarcely visible mist. Tall trees were reflected in the surface. The water at the white sandy beach was so pure that it seemed very light and weightless. Small silver fishes were asleep in it, hardly moving their tails.

An old boat, grey with age, had been pulled up on to the beach. Natasha bathed in the lake, got dressed and went to the boat. There was still a bench inside it. Natasha sat down. It had been warmed by the sun.

Tall flowers and grasses had grown up through the cracks in the boat. At Natasha's feet, a graceful willow-herb was in blossom. In the bows, where the boat was braced with a rusty iron rod, a marigold was in flower, and some spotted orchis had pushed through the sand on the bottom of the boat. There was a strong, sweet fragrance of tar and pine-shavings. The black dog lay down near the boat and yawned. Mole crickets were calling deep underground.

"What about the train?" wondered Natasha, and to her surprise, the thought did not cause her the slightest alarm.

She stayed there for about an hour. She could hear the cranes quietly holding converse about semething of their own in the glades beyond the lake; then a dusk quacked wildly and everything was quiet again.

The first to come was Grandpa. He greeted Natasha warmly, sat down on the sand by the boat and said:

"Don't you fret about the train. I'll just have a smoke, then I'll harness up Malchik and take you to the station. I'll wave you goodbye; and off you'll go to live by the warm, waters in the town of your dreams and find your happiness there."

"But where's Pyotr Matveyevich?"

Grandpa grinned.

"He'll be here in a moment. Nothing else matters to him now! "

"What is it?" said Natasha in fright.

"He'll tell you all about it," replied Grandpa, knocking out his cracked pipe against the side of the boat. "Listen. Know how old this boat is? Same age as me. See, it's overgrown with all kinds of flowers and grasses. It's what we call *dryoma.*" Grandpa pointed at the spotted orchis. "Just look at it with all its flowers. It dozes in the daytime and at night it opens up and smells of honey right until morning. To tell the truth, it's a poor boat, it's served its time. The forester came here one of these days and laughed at it. 'Vasily,' says he, 'why don't you cook your spuds with it, you've got good firewood going to waste there.' And I think to myself, 'No, it's too soon to cook spuds with it; must wait for that business.' "

"Are you sorry to part with it?" asked Natasha.

"Of course I'm sorry. Just think; gone completely rotten, but it's useful in life."

"How's that?" asked Natasha. "I don't understand."

"What is there to understand?" said Grandpa crossly. "This boat's dead rotten, but there's a flower coming up in every gap. I look at it, and I think, 'Perhaps something useful for life'll come out of me, an old man.' See, I'm getting old. Don't you be afraid of white hair. The main thing is that your heart should be all right. Have I spoken rightly or not?"

"Rightly," said Natasha, and she laughed.

"That's it! You take my word for it! "

The forester arrived. Grandpa stood up, coughing, and went to harness up Malchik. The forester looked grim and worried. He asked Natasha how she had slept and whether she had drunk any milk in the morning, but that was all he said to her.

"Won't we be late?" asked Natasha.

"I don't think so," replied the forester. He flushed and added, without looking at Natasha: "The fact is, I'm not going."

Natasha was silent in amazement.

"No, I'm not going," said the forester angrily. "The situation here is... Well, in a word, nothing'll come of it without me. The forest'll be ruined. I planted it myself, you know, and I feel sorry..."

"I do understand," said Natasha.

"I'll be better off here, I must admit, than in the Crimea. Pity, though—waste of a holiday voucher. Oh well, to blazes with it! But I have a big favour to ask of you: give my suitcase to Grandpa. He'll bring it back for me."

"Oh, all right, then," said Natasha, and she sighed. "I even feel envious."

"Gee-up, you devil! " shouted Grandpa hoarsely by the watch hut, "You've overeaten on state feed."

"Well, then, goodbye," said Natasha, and she timidly shook the forester's hand.

The train travelled round a smooth bend, and Natasha recognised the spot where the thunderstorm had caught them the day before. The carriage sped with a rattle over a clean little river, and Natasha managed to read on a board near the bridge a dusty inscription:

"River Moshka".

A broad rainbow arched over the forests:

over there, somewhere beyond the lake, it was raining slightly.

To Natasha the rainbow looked like the entrance to protected, mysterious realms where Pyotr Matveyevich and Grandpa were the lords and masters, and the cranes cried out at dawn.

Bright water glittered somewhere far among the trees. Was it the lake? Natasha put her head out of the window and gazed for a long time at the gleam of water amid the foliage and at the rainbow, and her heart winced. If only she could have stayed there till autumn!

The engine shrieked in farewell, and the woods began to throw the brief call from one to another, bore it away into the impenetrable thickets and unexpectedly sent it back as a ringing, many-voiced echo.

1939

THE INHABITANTS
OF THE OLD HOUSE[*]

The trouble began at the end of summer when Funtik, the bow-legged Dachshund, appeared in the old village house. Funtik had been brought from Moscow.

Stepan, the black tom cat, was sitting on the porch as always and washing himself in a leisurely manner. He would lick his splayed-out paw, then, frowning, wipe the licked paw behind his ear with all his strength. Suddenly, Stepan sensed that someone was staring intently at him. He looked round and froze with his paw still behind his ear. His eyes turned white with fury. A little red dog was standing beside him. One ear was turned out. Trembling with curiosity, the dog extended its damp nose towards Stepan—it wanted to sniff this enigmatic creature.

"So that's it! "

Stepan chose his moment and hit Funtik on his out-turned ear.

War was declared, and from that moment on

*English translation © Raduga Publishers 1986

life lost all its savour for Stepan. There was no
time now even to think of lazily rubbing your
muzzle against the cracked door-posts or lying
near the well in the sunshine. You had to go
about with apprehension, on tiptoe, look round
as often as possible, and always select in advance
a tree or fence in order to escape Funtik in time.

Like all cats, Stepan was a creature of
ingrained habits. He loved going round the
garden, overgrown with celandine, the house.

The cock flapped his wings triumphantly,
raised a thick cloud of dust, pecked at the wet
crust and threw it aside in disgust—the bread
probably smelt of dog.

Funtik stayed under the house for several
hours, only emerged towards evening and,
steering well clear of the cock, made his way
indoors. His muzzle was covered with dusty
cobwebs and shrivelled spiders.

Far worse than the cock was a skinny black
hen. She wore a shawl of coloured down and
she looked like a gypsy fortune-teller. They
made a mistake when they bought that hen.
Not for nothing did the old women in the village
say that hens turn black with malice.

This hen could fly like a raven, fought, and
could stand for several hours on the roof clucking without cease. It was impossible to dislodge
her from the roof, even with a brick. When we
came back from the meadows or the forest, we
would see her from afar, standing on the
stove chimney and looking as if cut out of tin.

We thought of the medieval inns—we had

read about them in the novels of Walter Scott.
On the roofs of these inns stood tin cocks or
hens on a perch instead of a sign.

As in the medieval tavern, we were met at
home by dark timbered walls caulked with yellow moss, blazing logs in the stove and the fragrance of caraway seeds. For some reason, the
old house was permeated with the scent of caraway and rotting wood.

We read Walter Scott's novels on dull days
when the warm rain was making a peaceful
noise on the roofs and in the garden. The
blobs of the tiny raindrops shook the wet
leaves on the trees, and water flowed in a thin
transparent stream from the drainpipe under
which a small green frog sat in a puddle. The
water would be pouring straight on to its head,
but the frog never moved and merely blinked.

When there was no rain, the frog sat in the puddle under the washstand. Once a minute, cold
water dripped on to its head from the water di-
spenser. We knew from the same novels by Walter Scott that the most terrible torture in the Middle Ages was just this slow dripping of icy water
on to the head, and we were amazed at the frog.

Sometimes, in the evenings, the frog came
into the house. It hopped over the threshold
and could sit for hours watching the flame of
the paraffin lamp.

It was hard to understand what the frog
found so attractive about that flame. We guessed
that the frog had come to watch the bright light
as children gather round the tea-table to hear

a fairy-tale before bedtime. The flame would flare up, then die down because of the greenflies being consumed in the lampshade. It must have looked to the frog like a huge diamond; if you stared at it long enough, you might see in each facet whole countries with golden waterfalls and rainbow-coloured stars.

The frog was so carried away by this fairy-tale that it had to be tickled with a stick before it would wake up and go back to its place under the rotting porch—dandelions had somehow managed to flower on its steps.

When it was raining, the ceiling leaked here and there. We used to put copper bowls on the floor. At night, the water dripped into them with a particularly resonant and rhythmic noise, and this noise coincided with the loud ticking of the clock.

The clock was very cheerful, decorated with luxuriant rose-blossoms and trefoils. Each time Funtik walked past it, he would growl slightly, probably so that the clock would know that there was a dog in the house, so let it watch out and not allow itself any liberties; no gaining three hours in every twenty-four or stopping without any cause whatever.

There were many old objects in the house. They had once been needed and necessary to the residents, but now they were gathering dust and drying up in the attic, and the mice were busy amongst them.

Very occasionally we used to arrange excavations in the attic and, among the broken window-frames and curtains of shaggy cobwebs, we would find a box of oil-paints covered with petrified, multicoloured drops, or a broken mother-of-pearl fan, or a copper coffee-mill dating back to the defence of Sebastopol, or an enormous book of ancient historical engravings or, finally, a packet of transfers.

We transferred them. From under the wet paper film appeared vivid, sticky views of Vesuvius, Italian donkeys decorated with garlands of roses, girls in straw hats with pale-blue satin ribbons playing quoits, and frigates wreathed in puffy little balls of gunsmoke.

We once found a black wooden casket in the attic. The lid bore an inscription in copper lettering: "Edinburgh. Scotland. Made by Master Galveston".

The casket was taken down into the room, the dust was carefully wiped off it and the lid opened... Inside were copper rollers with fine steel pins. Near each roller was a bronze lever on which sat a copper dragonfly, a butterfly or a beetle.

It was a music box. We wound it up, but it wouldn't play. In vain we pressed on the backs of the beetles, flies and dragonflies—the music-box was broken.

At evening tea, we discussed the mysterious Master Galveston. We all decided that he must have been a cheerful, elderly Scot in a tartan jacket and a leather apron. At work, shaping the copper rollers in a vice, perhaps he whistled a song about the postillion whose horn rings out in the misty dales, and about the girl gathering firewood in the mountains. Like all good craftsmen, he used to talk to the things he was making, and he foretold them their destiny. He could never, of course, have guessed that this black casket would turn up from beyond the pale Scottish skies into the wild forests beyond the Oka, into the village where only the cocks crow as in Scotland, but nothing else is in the least reminiscent of that faraway country in the north.

Since that time, Master Galveston became, as it were, one of the invisible inhabitants of the old village house. Sometimes it even seemed to us that we could hear his hoarse cough when he accidentally inhaled the pipe smoke. And whenever we were knocking something together—a table in the summerhouse or a new birdhouse—and were arguing about how to hold the plane or fit two boards together, we often referred to Master Galveston, as if he was standing beside us, and, his grey eyes screwed up, was looking on in amusement at our fuss. And we all sang Galveston's last favourite song:

Farewell, bright star above the well-loved mountains,
Farewell forever, warm home of my fathers...

We put the casket on the table with a geranium blossom and finally forgot about it.

But late one autumn a glassy, shimmering sound was heard in the old, echoing house, as if someone were hitting bells with tiny hammers, and from these wonderful chimes there flowed a melody:

Home to our mountains
You shall return...

The music-box had suddenly woken up after many years sleep and had started playing. At first we were frightened, and even Funtik listened, warily lifting up first one ear, then the other. Some spring in the music-box had evidently clicked into action.

The music-box played for a long time, now stopping, now filling the house again with its mysterious chimes, and even the clock was silent in amazement.

The music-box played all its tunes and fell silent; but however hard we tried, we could not get it going again.

Now, in late autumn, when I am living in Moscow, the music-box stands there alone in the empty, unheated rooms and, perhaps, in the impenetrable and quiet nights it wakes up again and plays, but there is no one to hear it except the timorous mice.

Afterwards, we whistled the tune about the beloved mountains many times over, until it was once whistled back to us by an elderly starling who lived in the bird-house near the side-gate. Until then he had sung strange wheezy songs, but we listened with delight. We guessed that he must have learned these songs during the African winter, listening to the black children as they played their games. For some reason we were glad that next winter, somewhere terribly far away, in the dense forests on the banks of the Niger, the starling would sing under the African sky a song about the old, abandoned mountains of Europe.

Every morning we scatted breadcrumbs and seed on the wooden table in the garden. Dozens of perky tomtits used to fly down and peck up the crumbs. These birds had fluffy white cheeks, and they all pecked at once, as if dozens of little white hammers were hastily hitting the table.

The tits quarrelled and twittered, and that twittering, like the rapid drumming of nails on a glass tumbler, merged into a cheerful melody. It seemed that a live, chirruping music-box was playing on the old table in the garden.

Among the inhabitants of the old house, apart from Funtik, Stepan the cat, the cock, the clock, the music-box, Master Galveston and the starling, there were also a tame wild duck, a hedgehog that suffered from insomnia, a small bell inscribed "A Gift from Valdai", and a barometer which always pointed to "Severe Drought". I shall tell about them some other time, as it's already late.

If, however, after this little story you dream of the merry nocturnal playing of a music-box, the tinkle of raindrops falling into copper bowl, Funtik growling his displeasure with the clock, and the coughing of dear old Galveston, I shall know that I didn't tell you my story in vain.

1940

NASTYA THE LACEMAKER[*]

A thunderstorm was booming hollowly in the mountains of Alatau. Frightened by the noise, a big green cicada jumped through the hospital window and settled on the lace curtain. The wounded Lieutenant Rudnev sat up in bed and looked for a long time at the cicada and the curtain. The piercing blue lightning flashes kept picking out the complex pattern of gorgeous roses and tiny crested cockerels.

Morning came. The thunderous yellow sky was still smoking in the window. Two rainbows arched over the mountain summits. The wet blossoms of the wild peonies glowed on the window-sill like incandescent coals. It was close. Steam was rising over the wet crags; a brook in the abyss snarled and rolled its pebbles over and over.

"That's Asia for you!" sighed Rudnev. "But that lace curtain is ours, from the north. And it was made by a beautiful woman called Nastya."

*English translation © Raduga Publishers 1986

"What makes you think that?"

Rudnev smiled.

"I can remember," he said, "something that happened in my battery near Leningrad."

He told me the story.

In the summer of 1940, the Leningrad artist Balashov left to go hunting and work in our desolate North.

At the first village that took his fancy, Balashov got off the old river steamboat and settled in the village schoolmaster's house.

A girl named Nastya lived in the village with her father, a forest warden. She was famous in those parts for her lace and for her beauty. Nastya was quiet and grey-eyed, like all the girls in the North.

Once, out hunting, Nastya's father wounded Balashov in the chest with a careless shot. Depressed by this accident, the old man sent Nastya to look after the victim.

Nastya cared for Balashov, and her first girlish love came out of pity for the wounded man. But her love was so shy that Balashov didn't notice anything.

Balashov had a wife in Leningrad, but he never told anyone about her, not even Nastya. All the village people were convinced that he was on his own.

As soon as the wound healed, Balashov left for Leningrad. But first he called uninvited to thank Nastya for looking after him and to give her some presents.

Nastya accepted them.

It was Balashov's first visit to the North. He did not know the local customs. These are very stable and long-lasting in the North, and they do not surrender quickly to the pressure of the new times. Balashov did not know that a man who called uninvited at a girl's home and brought her a present was regarded as her betrothed if the gift was accepted. That is how they declare their love without words in the North.

Nastya shyly asked Balashov when he was coming back from Leningrad to see her in the village. Balashov unsuspectingly replied that he would be back very soon.

Balashov left. Nastya waited for him. A radiant summer passed. So did a wet and bitter autumn, but Balashov did not return. Nastya's impatient and joyful hopes turned to alarm, despair and shame. They were already whispering round the village that her betrothed had deceived her. But Nastya didn't believe it. She was convinced that some misfortune had overtaken Balashov.

Spring brought more distress. It came late and lasted a long time. The rivers were in spate and would not stay within their banks. Only at the beginning of June did the first steamer sail past the village without stopping.

Nastya decided to run away secretly from her father to Leningrad and look for Balashov there. She left the village at night. In two days she reached the railway and learned at the station that war had broken out that morning. A peasant girl who had never seen a train before, she managed to travel across that enormous country as far as Leningrad and find Balashov's flat.

The door was opened to Nastya by Balashov's wife, a thin woman in pyjamas with a cigarette between her teeth. She looked in bewilderment at Nastya and said that Balashov was not at home. He was at the front outside Leningrad.

Nastya had learned the truth. Balashov was married. That meant he had deceived her and made a mockery of her love. It was terrible for Nastya to talk to Balashov's wife. She felt terrible in the city flat amid the dusty silk divans, scattered powder, and the insistent telephone calls.

Nastya fled. She walked in despair round the magnificent city, now converted into an armed camp. She did not notice the anti-aircraft guns on the squares, or the monuments piled round with sandbags, or the cool centuries-old gardens, or the majestic buildings.

She went down to the Neva. The river was bearing its black waters along as high as the granite banks. Here, in these waters, she might find the only possible deliverance from her unbearable pain and from her love.

Nastya took off her old headscarf, a present from her mother, and hung it on the balusrtade. Then she straightened her heavy braids and put her foot on the volute of a baluster. Someone seized her by the arm. Nastya looked round. A thin man with floor-brushes under his arm was standing behind her. His working clothes were stained with yellow paint.

The floor-polisher simply shook his head and said:

"What are you up to at a time like this, you fool?"

This man, the floor-polisher Trofimov, took Nastya to his home and handed her over to his wife, a lift-attendant, noisy and decisive, who despised men.

The Trofimovs gave shelter to Nastya. She lay ill for a long time in their cubby-hole. Nastya first heard from the wife that Balashov had not wronged her in any way, that no one could be expected to know their northern customs and that only such a goose as she, Nastya, could have been silly enough to fall in love with the first passing stranger.

The wife upbraided Nastya, but Nastya was delighted. She was delighted that she had not been deceived, and she still hoped to see Balashov.

When Nastya recovered, the wife fixed her up on a course for nurses. The doctors, Nastya's instructors, were impressed by her skill at tying bandages and the dexterity of her thin, strong fingers. "But I'm a lacemaker," she replied, as if trying to justify herself.

The blockaded Leningrad winter passed with its iron nights and its bombardment. Nastya finished the course and waited to be posted to the front, thinking in the nights about Balashov and about her old father—to the end of his days he would probably never understand why she had secretly left home. He would not curse her, he would forgive everything, but as for understanding, that he would never do.

In spring, Nastya was finally sent to the front outside Leningrad. Everywhere, in the wrecked palace parks, amid the ruins, fire-gutted dugouts, on the batteries, in the woods and in the fields, she tried to find Balashov and inquired about him.

Nastya met the floor-polisher, and the garrulous fellow told the men in his unit about the northern girl trying to find the man she loved at the front. The rumour about her began to grow and spread like a legend. It went from unit to unit, from battery to battery. It was carried about by motor-cyclists, lorry-drivers, ambulance men and signallers.

The soldiers envied the unknown man whom the girl was trying to find, and they remembered their own dear ones. To each man they were part of peace-time life, and each cherished memories of them in his heart. Telling one another about the girl from the North, the soldiers changed the details of the story according to their powers of imagination.

Each swore that Nastya was a girl from his own part of the country. The Ukrainians thought of her as their own, the Siberians likewise, the people of Ryazan, and even the Kazakhs from the faraway Asiatic steppes said that the girl had probably come to the front from Kazakhstan.

The rumours about Nastya reached the shore

battery in which Balashov was serving. The artist, like the soldiers, was moved by the story of the unknown girl looking for the man she adored and was impressed by the power of her love. He often thought about her and began envying the man who meant so much to her. How could he have known that he was jealous of himself?

Balashov's personal life had not gone well. Nothing had come of his marriage. And now others were having all the luck! All his life he had dreamed of a great love, but it was too late to think of such a thing now. His hair was greying at the temples...

It so happened that Nastya finally found the battery in which Balashov was serving, but him she did not find—he had been killed two days before and buried in a pine-forest on the shore of the gulf.

Rudnev was silent.

"What happened next?"

"Next?" asked Rudnev. "What happened next was that the soldiers fought like men possessed, and we made mincemeat of the German defence line."

"And Nastya?"

"Fancy asking about Nastya! She's looking after the wounded. She's the best nurse on our sector of the front."

1942

SNOW

Old Potapov died a month after Tatyana Petrovna moved into his house. Tatyana Petrovna remained alone there with her daughter Varya and the child's old nurse.

The little three-roomed house stood on a hill at the town limits, overlooking the northern river. Beyond the house and the now naked garden gleamed a white birch grove. Jackdaws cawed there from morning to night, soaring in swarms over the bare treetops and calling down gloomy weather on the town.

After Moscow it had taken Tatyana Petrovna some time to grow accustomed to the deserted little town with its tiny houses and creaking garden gates, to the evenings when it was so still that you could hear the flame spluttering in the paraffin lamp.

"What a fool I was!" Tatyana Petrovna had thought. "Why did I leave Moscow, why did I give up the theatre and my friends! I could have sent Varya out to her nurse's place in Pushki-no—there weren't any air raids there—and remained behind in Moscow myself. Goodness me, what a fool I was! "

But now it was too late to return to Moscow. Tatyana Petrovna decided to give performances in the army hospitals—there were several in the town—and stopped worrying. She even began to grow fond of the town, especially when winter came and smothered it in snow. The days were mild and grey. The river did not freeze for a long time; mists kept rising from its green waters.

Tatyana Petrovna had grown used both to the little town and to the stranger's house. She had grown used to the piano that was out of tune, and to the yellow photographs of cumbersome armoured battleships of the coastal fleet pinned up on the wall. Old Potapov had once been a ship's mechanic. On the faded green baize of his desk stood a model of the cruiser *Gromoboi,* on which he had served. Varya was not allowed to touch anything.

Tatyana Petrovna knew that Potapov had a son, a naval officer now serving in the Black Sea Fleet. There was a picture of him on the desk, next to the model of the cruiser. Sometimes Tatyana Petrovna would pick it up and frown, thoughtfully gazing at it. She felt she had seen that face somewhere long, long ago, before her unsuccessful marriage. But where? And when?

The sailor gazed back at her with calm, slightly mocking eyes, as though he were chiding her: "Well, how about it? Can't you remember where we met?"

"No, I can't," Tatyana Petrovna would reply very quietly.

"Mummy, who are you talking to?" Varya would call from the next room.

"To the piano," Tatyana Petrovna answered laughing.

In the middle of the winter letters addressed to Potapov began to stream in, all written in the same hand. Tatyana Petrovna stacked them up on the desk. One night she suddenly awoke. The snow was emitting a faint glow outside the window. The grey tomcat Arkhip, Potapov's legacy, was dozing on the couch.

Tatyana Petrovna slipped on her dressing gown, went into Potapov's study and stood there at the window. A bird swept some snow off a bough as it flew out of a tree. The snow floated down in a fine white dust and filmed the window.

Tatyana Petrovna lit the candle on the desk and sank into an armchair. She gazed at the flame for a long time—it was burning without even the slightest flicker. Then she carefully picked up one of the letters, opened it, and, glancing round, began to read.

"Dear old Dad," Tatyana Petrovna read. "I've been in hospital a month now. My wound is not a very serious one, and it's healing well.

But for goodness sake don't you start worrying and smoking cigarette after cigarette. Please!

"I often think of you," Tatyana Petrovna read on, "and of our house and our little town. It all seems far, far away, at the other end of the world. I close my eyes and see myself opening the gate and walking into the garden. It is winter and there is snow on the ground, but the path has been cleared to the arbour overlooking the river. The lilac bushes are all covered with hoarfrost. Inside the house the stoves are crackling. There is a smell of birchwood smoke. The piano has been tuned at long last and you've put the yellow convoluted candles—the ones I brought from Leningrad—in the candlesticks. The same music lies on the piano: the overture to *The Queen of Spades,* and *For the Shores of My Distant Country*. Does the doorbell work? I didn't get a chance to fix it before I left. Will I really see it all again? Will I really wash myself in water from our well out of the blue jug when I get back? Remember? Ah, if you only knew how I have grown to love all this from afar! Don't be surprised when I tell you in all seriousness that I used to recall it all during the most difficult moments of battle. I knew that I was defending not only my country but also that little corner of it, dearest to my heart— you, our garden, our mischievous little village boys, the birch groves beyond the river, and even our tomcat Arkhip. Please don't laugh and don't shake your head.

"I may be able to come home for a short

leave after my discharge from hospital. But
I don't know yet. Better not to count on it."

Tatyana Petrovna sat at the desk for a long
time, staring fixedly out of the window at the
dawn spreading over the dark blueness outside.
She was reflecting that any day now a strange
man, evidently a calm, courageous person, might
arrive from the front, and that it would be difficult for him to bear the sight of strangers living in the house and to find everything quite
different from what he had been looking forward to.

In the morning Tatyana Petrovna told Varya
to take a wooden shovel and clear the path to
the arbour overlooking the river. The arbour
was a ramshackle affair. Its wooden posts had
turned grey and were overgrown with lichen.
Tatyana Petrovna mended the doorbell herself.
It bore the amusing inscription: "I hang at the
door, so ring some more! " She rang the bell. It
gave a highpitched tinkle. Arkhip twitched his
ears with displeasure, and, taking this as a
personal affront, stalked out of the entrance hall.
To his mind the merry tinkle was obviously
nothing short of outrageous.

Later in the day Tatyana Petrovna, flushed
and vivacious, her eyes sparkling with excitement, brought an old piano tuner in from town,
a Russianised Czech who tuned pianos when he
wasn't repairing primus and oil stoves, dolls
and accordions. When he had finished, the

Czech said that it was an old piano but a very good one. Tatyana Petrovna was aware of that herself.

After he had gone she looked carefully into all the drawers of the desk until she found a package of thick yellow candles. She put two of them in the candlesticks on the piano. In the evening she lit the candles and sat down at the piano, and the house became filled with sound.

When she finished playing and blew out the candles, the same sweet smell that one associates with Christmas trees spread through the rooms.

Varya could not contain herself any longer.

"Why do you touch other people's things?" she said. "You won't let me, but you touch them yourself! You've touched the bell, and the candles, and the piano. And you put somebody else's music on the piano."

"Because I'm a grown-up," said Tatyana Petrovna.

Varya pouted and glanced at her with disbelief. Just then Tatyana Petrovna did not look at all like a grawn-up. She was all pink and radiant and looked more like the girl with the golden hair who lost her glass slipper in the palace. Tatyana Petrovna herself had told Varya about the girl.

While he was still in the train Lieutenant Potapov had calculated that he could not spend more than twenty-four hours at home. His leave was very short, and the journey took up almost all of it.

The train arrived in the afternoon. At the station the lieutenant learned from the stationmaster, an old acquaintance, that his father had died a month before and that a young Moscow singer and her daughter were living in his house.

"Evacuees," the stationmaster explained.

Potapov said nothing. He gazed through the window at the passengers in padded jackets and felt boots scurrying up and down the platform with teapots. His heart sank and he grew dizzy.

"Aye," said the stationmaster. "He was a good soul. Didn't live to see his boy come home."

"When can I get a train back?" Potapov inquired.

"At five in the morning." The stationmaster paused and then added, "You can spend the night with me. My old woman will give you some supper. There's no need for you to go home."

"Thanks," said Potapov. He went out.

The stationmaster shook his head as he gazed after him.

Potapov walked through the town to the river lying under a soft grey sky. A light snow was slanting down between sky and earth. Jackdaws hopped about the dung in the road. Twilight was deepening. A wind blew from the woods on the opposite bank whipping tears into his eyes.

"Well!" said Potapov. "I'm too late. And now I don't belong here any more—the town, and the river, and the forest, and the house."

He turned and gazed at the distant hillside above the river. There they stood—the frost-covered garden and the house. Smoke was curling up from the chimney. The wind carried the smoke to the birch grove.

Potapov walked slowly in the direction of the house. He decided not to go in but only to walk past it, and perhaps enter the garden and stand for a moment in the old arbour. He could not bear the thought that strangers who cared nothing for him and for his father were living in his father's house. It would be better not to see anything, not to torment himself—to leave and to forget the past.

"Well," thought Potapov, "you grow older as time passes and learn to see things with harder eyes."

He reached the house at dusk. He opened the gate carefully, but it creaked just the same. The white garden seemed to give a start. Snow fell rustling from a bough. Potapov turned round. The path leading to the arbour was cleared of snow. He went over to the arbour and put his hand on the rickety rail. In the distance, beyond the forest, the sky was tinged pink—the moon must have been rising behind the clouds. He took off his cap and passed his hand through his hair. It was very quiet. Only below, at the foot of the hill, women were clattering their empty pails as they went to the ice hole for water.

Potapov leaned his elbows on the rail.

"I just can't accept it," he murmured.

He felt a light touch on his shoulder and turned to face a pale, grave young woman with a thick kerchief on her head. She looked at him with her dark, attentive eyes. Snow was melting on her cheeks and eyelashes—it must have slipped from a branch onto her face.

"Put on your cap," she said softly. "Or else you will catch cold. And come into the house. You mustn't stand here."

Potapov said nothing. The woman took his hand and led him along the cleared path. Near the porch he stopped. He felt a sudden lump in his throat and could not breathe. The woman said in the same soft voice:

"It's all right. And please don't take any notice of me. It'll soon pass."

She stamped her feet to shake the snow off her boots, causing the little bell to tinkle and resound through the entrance hall. Potapov took a deep breath.

He entered the house, muttering something in his confusion, and took his coat off in the hall; a smell of birchwood smoke assailed his nostrils. He saw Arkhip sitting on the couch and yawning. Near the couch stood a little girl with pigtails, gazing with delighted eyes at Potapov; she was not looking at his face, though, but at the gold stripes on his sleeve.

"Come along," said Tatyana Petrovna. She ushered Potapov into the kitchen.

There was the blue jug filled with cold water

and the familiar linen towel embroidered with green oak leaves.

Tatyana Petrovna went out. The little girl brought Potapov a cake of soap and watched him while he washed. Potapov still felt embarrassed.

"What does your mummy do?" he asked the girl, reddening.

He had asked the question just for the sake of saying something.

"She thinks she's a grown-up," the girl said, in a mysterious whisper. "But she isn't at all. She's even more of a girl than I am."

"Why?" asked Potapov.

The girl did not reply. She laughed and ran out of the kitchen.

All evening Potapov could not shake off the strange sensation that he was living in a gossamer, but very sound, dream. Everything in the house was just as he had hoped to find it. The same music lay on the piano. The same yellow candles spluttered as they illuminated his father's small study. Even the letters he had written from the hospital lay on the desk—under the same old compass, where his father had always placed his letters.

After tea Tatyana Petrovna took Potapov to his father's grave, beyond the grove. A hazy moon had risen high in the heavens. The birches gleamed in its light, casting soft shadows on the snow.

Then, late in the evening, Tatyana Petrovna sat down at the piano. Running her fingers lightly over the keys, she turned to Potapov and said:

"I have a feeling that I've seen you somewhere before."

"So have I," answered Potapov.

He looked at her. The candlelight slanted down, lighting up half her face. Potapov rose, paced the room and came to a stop.

"No, my memory fails me," he said in a husky voice.

Tatyana Petrovna turned and shot an alarmed glance at Potapov, but she did not say anything in reply.

Potapov's bed was made up on the couch in the study. He could not fall asleep. Each minute in this house was precious, and he was loath to lose a single one.

He lay listening to Arkhip's stealthy tread, to the ticking of the clock, to Tatyana Petrovna whispering something to the nurse in the next room. Then the voices died away and the nurse went out, but the strip of light under the door remained. Potapov heard the rustle of pages—Tatyana Petrovna was evidently reading. He guessed that she was sitting up so that she could wake him in time for the train. He wanted to tell her that he was not sleeping either, but he did not dare to call out to her.

At four o'clock Tatyana Petrovna quietly opened the door and called him. He stirred.

"Time to get up," she said. "I do hate to wake you up so early! "

Tatyana Petrovna saw Potapov to the station

through the sleeping town. They said good-bye after the second bell. Tatyana Petrovna held both hands out to him.

"Write to me," she said. "We are almost relatives now, aren't we?"

Potapov said nothing. He only nodded.

Several days later Tatyana Petrovna received a letter from Potapov, written on the journey back:

"I hadn't forgotten, of course, where we met, but I didn't feel like talking about it back there at home. Remember the Crimea in the autumn of 1927? And the old plane trees in the park in Livadia? A darkening sky, a pale sea. I was walking along the path to Oreanda. On the way I came upon a girl seated on a bench by the path. She must have been about sixteen. She saw me, got up and walked towards me. As we came to a level I glanced at her. She passed by quickly and lightly, holding an open book in her hand. I stopped and gazed after her for a long time. That girl was you. I could not have been mistaken. I gazed after you and suddenly felt that a woman who could either ruin my whole life or make me ecstatically happy had walked past me. I felt that I could have loved that woman to distraction. I knew then and there that I must find you at all costs. That is what I thought, standing there, but I did not move from the spot. Why—I do not know. Ever since then I have loved the Crimea and that path where

I saw you for only a fleeting moment and lost
you forever. But life has been kind to me.
I met you again. And if everything ends well
and you should want my life, it is yours, of
course. Oh yes, I found my opened letter on
father's desk. I understood all and can only
thank you from afar."

Tatyana Petrovna put away the letter and
stared misty-eyed at the snow-covered garden
outside the window.

"Oh dear!" she murmured. "I've never been
to the Crimea in my life, never! But can that
make any difference now? And is it worth
disillusioning him? Or myself!"

She laughed and then covered her eyes with
her hand. Through the window a dim sunset
glowed faintly; somehow its lights could not
fade away.

1943

GLASS BEADS

Dawn in a peasant cottage is much the same wherever you may be—in the parts where I come from near Kostroma, in the Ukraine, or in the little Gutsul village in the foothills of the Carpathians. There is a sourish smell of bread and the sound of an old man sighing, sleepy hens clucking in the yard and the rapid ticking of the clock on the wall.

The darkness outside begins to turn blue and you can see from the misted panes that there is a spring frost and dew on the grass outside and it will be a clear day. You gradually begin to make out the black crucifix over the door, the sheepskin jerkin on the stool, covered by a faded felt hat, and then you remember that you are not near Kostroma. You are on the exreme western border of the Soviet Union in Gutsul country. And those remote blue clouds through the window are not clouds at all. They are the Carpathians. Far off in the mountains, beyond the forest and mist, there is a protracted sound of cannon fire. Another day of battle is beginning.

You go into the yard to wash. The cold water clears your head and everything that happened yesterday comes back to you vividly.

There are so many daisies in the clearing in front of the house that the soldiers are reluctant to trample on them and go round the edge instead. A solitary briar bush is flowering in the clearing. Its scent is more powerful in the morning coolness than in the heat of day. The sun is still behind the mountains but the tree tops on the western slopes are already glowing russet in its early rays.

This cottage is the home of Old Ignat and his granddaughter Ganya. Ignat is old and sick. He used to be a woodcutter but has been unable to wield his heavy axe for a year now. "Thank God I still had the strength to cross myself when I saw the Russian guns," he says. Even walking as far as the church is difficult for him, so Ganya helps him along. He kneels in front of the altar which is decorated with blue paper flowers. His grey shaggy hair quivering, he whispers thanks for his daily bread, for the liberation of his country from the cursed Swabians, and for the joy of living to see another spring in his native land.

What a magnificent land it is, swathed in light mists which seem to rise above its gentle hills from the breathing of the early spring grass, flowers and leaves, the ploughed earth and the green shoots.

Small rainbows shimmer over the splashing water wheels, spraying the dark willows on the bank.

One line of hills follows the next and they ripple in waves of greenness and light from one end of the horizon to the other. The sky is so pure and solid that you cannot help wanting to use its old name, the firmament. The sun is shot with yellow. With every breath you inhale a bracing infusion of pine bark and the vestiges of snow still left on the mountain tops.

It was only yesterday that we occupied the village. It was empty except for old women, children and doddery old men. The rest of the inhabitants were still hiding in the woods from the Germans, who had now retrenched not far away on the other side of the gorge overlooking the only mountain road. We needed a guide to take us to the cliff called Cheshske Lono above the Germans' position. This was the only point from which we could dislodge the Germans and clear the road.

Instead of a guide they brought a ten-year-old girl to our lieutenant. She was wearing new leather moccasins, a long maroon skirt edged in white, a sleeveless yellow jacket with lots of pearl buttons and a silk head scarf. The little thing stood there with downcast eyes in her Sunday best twisting the hem of her blue apron.

"Surely you can find someone older?" said the lieutenant, taken aback.

The old men standing nearby exchanged glances, took off their felt hats, scratched their heads and explained that this girl was the granddaughter of Old Ignat, a famous hunter and woodcutter in these parts, and that unfortunately no one knew the way to Cheshske Lono better than she did. Ignat himself knew it, of course, but he was very weak now and hadn't been into the mountains for a year or so.

The lieutenant shook his head doubtfully.

"Will you get us there? You do know the way?"

"Yes," said the girl blushing.

"So not even a bird will notice us?"

"No," she said, blushing even deeper.

"Aren't you afraid?" the lieutenant asked sternly.

His men were standing around frowning. What sort of guide was this? It didn't sound like a serious conversation.

The girl did not reply. Instead she looked up at the lieutenant with her big grey eyes, smiled and looked down again. The lieutenant involuntarily smiled too, and then the soldiers. No one had expected to see such a shy, happy smile under these dark eyelashes.

There was a silence broken only by the envious cry of "Ee, Ganka" from a shock-headed lad with shifty eyes who was looking round the wattle fence. The girl scowled, the soldiers looked round and the boy disappeared. The old men shook their heads. Yes, the lad really had something to be jealous about, I'll say he did.

The little girl led the soldiers up to Cheshske

Lono and the road was cleared of Germans. She came back in the evening with a soldier called Maleyev who had been wounded. He was a fine, brave lad and the only criticism you could make of him was that he tended to be somewhat talkative.

That evening he was sitting on a stone near Ignat's house, drinking milk and chatting with the old men, resting his bandaged right arm. They listened to him with respect and affection, but probably understood very little of what he said. Maleyev was from Ryazan and it was difficult for the old Gutsuls to make head or tail of his conversation.

"Our high-ups will reward her for this. Indubitably. For being a canny, brave lassy. We know how to reward bravery. So don't you have no doubts on that score, citizens."

The old men nodded and smiled.

"But leavin' aside the high-ups," he went on, "our lads are right grateful to that lassy. Can't praise her enough. And she ought to have something from the lads for what she's done. The trouble is what! A soldier doesn't carry anything round with him except emergency rations and cartridges, as you well know. But she ought to have a doll or something like that."

While he was expounding on these aspects of a soldier's life, Maleyev kept giving sly winks and glances at the embarrassed girl and jingling something in his pocket, but no one understood his subtle hints. He was jingling a string of glass beads which the lieutenant had given to him and asked him to present to Ganya next morning. If possible it should be a surprise. He wasn't just to pull them out and thrust them into her hands with a "Here you are, take these!" The whole thing must be handled with more delicacy.

Maleyev understood what he was being asked to do and agreed enthusiastically although he thought it a difficult, ticklish job.

The old men went their separate ways into the night. The stars blazed on over the Carpathians and the rushing of the waterfalls grew louder. A smell of dampness and wild plants wafted from the evening forest.

Old Ignat, Maleyev and Ganya sat on for a long time outside. Maleyev stopped talking for a while and Ganya asked him timidly:

"Are your rivers near Moscow like ours, or are they right different?"

"They're different," Maleyev said. "Yours are nice and so are ours. Our rivers are wide and clear with lots of flowers and grasses. They flow into the Crimean seas a long way away. White boats with red silk flags sail along them and there are hundreds of shining, twinkling towns on their banks."

"And is the forest different?"

"Yes, that's different too. Our forests are full of mushrooms. Stretch for thousands of miles, they do. The mushrooms are all different kinds. There's a clever old bird in our forests called the woodpecker. He goes round tapping the trees with his beak and when he finds one that's dead or rotten he leaves a mark on it that means: 'Chop this one down. It's no good.' "

Maleyev stopped talking, but when Ganya did not ask him any more questions he went on again.

"Why don't you ask me anything about the people, then? What our people are like?"

"I know what they're like already," answered Ganya smiling.

"So you do!" said Maleyev. "It's real fun talking to you."

In the morning Maleyev woke up very early and went outside. Looking round, he took the beads out of his pocket and hung them on the fence by the house, then hid behind a corner and began to wait. Ganya had gone to fetch water from the river and should pass the fence on her way back. Maleyev was sure that she would notice the beads. He had spent a long time breathing on them and rubbing them on his greatcoat, and now they were sparkling in the sunshine like a handful of diamonds.

She appeared walking along the path. Maleyev's eyes were glued to her.

Suddenly she noticed the beads, stopped short, smiled and put her buckets down on the ground. Then she began to walk slowly towards the fence with one thin hand stretched out hesitantly for the beads. She was walking carefully as if she were afraid of frightening a bird.

Suddenly she screamed, grabbed hold of the ends of the scarf tied round her head and began to sob. Maleyev dived out of his hiding place in surpise and saw the shock-headed boy rushing along by the fence with the shining beads clutched in his hand.

"Thievin' rascal!" thought Maleyev and thundered:

"Drop it, I say. Or you'll be sorry."

The boy looked round, flung the beads into the grass and made off faster than ever.

Then everything happened just as the lieutenant hadn't wanted it to. Maleyev picked up the beads, walked over to the tearful Ganya and thrust them into her hand, mumbling gruffly:

"Here. These are for you."

So it was all done very crudely and there was no surprise. But Ganya gave him such a look with her beaming, wet eyes that he stepped back in confusion and could only mutter:

"The high-ups do things their own way. But this is from the lads."

Old Ignat was standing in the doorway grinning. When they came up to him he took the beads from Ganya and shook them so that they tinkled and flashed in the sun. Then he hung them round her neck and said:

"This necklace is more beautiful than gold. Ee, my little darlin', your pretty eyes will live to see happiness with folk like these."

Ganya put her buckets on the ground and looked shyly down at the beads with shining eyes. The water in the buckets splashed reflecting the sun onto the beads and they sparkled on the little girl's brown skin in a myriad of twinkling lights.

1944

THE TELEGRAM*

The weather that October was uncommonly cold and inclement. The wooden roofs turned black.

The tangled grasses in the garden were flattened, and only one little sunflower kept trying to bloom, but simply couldn't manage it so as to scatter its seeds.

Shedding a persistent rain, the scraggy clouds trailed over the meadows from the far side of the river and clung to the leaf-stripped willows.

It was no longer possible to use the roads, and the herdsmen gave up driving their cattle into the meadows.

The shepherd's horn was silent until next spring. Katerina Petrovna found it even harder to get up in the morning and see the same thing every time: rooms with a stagnant, bitter smell of unlit stoves, a dusty *Vestnik Evropy***,

*English translation © Raduga Publishers 1986
** *Herald of Europe*—a periodical.—*Tr.*

yellowing cups on the table, a samovar that had not been cleaned for ages and pictures on the wall. Perhaps it was too dark in the rooms, or dark water had already appeared in Katerina Petrovna's eyes or, perhaps, the pictures had been dulled by time, but it was impossible to distinguish anything on them. Katerina Petrovna only knew from memory that this one was a portrait of her father and that little one in the gilt frame was a present from Kramskoi, a sketch for his "Unknown Woman".

Katerina Petrovna was ending her days in an old house built by her father, a well-known artist.

In his old age, he returned from Petersburg to his native village, lived in peace and busied himself in his garden. He could not paint any more; his hand was shaky, his vision had weakened, and his eyes often ached.

The house was, as Katerina Petrovna said, a "monument". It was under the protection of the regional museum. But Katerina Petrovna did not know what would happen to the building when she, its last occupant, died.

And in the village of Zaborye, there was no one with whom she could chat about pictures, life in Petersburg, or the summer when she and her father were living in Paris and saw Victor Hugo's funeral.

It was no use talking about such things to Manyushka, the daughter of her neighbour, a local shoemaker, a girl who used to come every day to fetch water from the well, sweep the floors and light the samovar.

Katerina Petrovna gave Manyushka for her services a pair of wrinkled gloves, ostrich feathers, and a black hat covered with bugle-beads.

"What do I want with that," asked Manyushka huskily, wrinkling her nose. "Am I an old clothes merchant or something?"

"You sell it, my dear," whispered Katerina Petrovna. She had weakened much in the last year and could not talk loudly. "You sell it."

"I'll give it to the rag-and-bone collectors," decided Manyushka, she picked up all the things and left.

Very occasionally the thin, red-haired Tikhon used to look in. He was the watchman at the fireman's shed and he could remember when Katerina Petrovna's father arrived from Petersburg, built the house and began running an estate.

Tikhon was a little boy then, but he would keep his respect for the old artist all his days. He would look at his pictures and sigh loudly:

"Very lifelike! "

Tikhon often fussed about for no particular reason, mainly out of pity; but even so, he helped with the household chores, cut down the dead trees in the garden, sawed them and chopped them up for firewood. Each time, as he left, he would stop in the doorway and ask:

"I haven't heard anything, Katerina Petrovna, any letters from Nastya at all?"

Katerina Petrovna would say nothing, sitting

on the divan, bent, tiny—forever sorting through some papers in a russet leather handbag. Tikhon would sniff and shift his feet for a long time on the threshold.

"Well," he would say without getting a reply, "I expect I'll be going now, Katerina Petrovna."

"Go, Tikhon," Katerina Petrovna would whisper, "go, and God be with you!"

He would leave, carefully closing the door, and Katerina Petrovna would begin weeping softly. The wind whistled outside the window in the bare branches, blowing off the last few leaves. The paraffin night-light trembled on the table. It seemed to be the only living thing in the abandoned house—without that feeble glow, Katerina Petrovna would never have survived till morning.

The nights were as long and burdensome as sleeplessness. The dawns took longer and longer to come, they kept being late, seeping reluctantly through the unwashed windows where, between the panes, lay last year's cotton wool and leaves that had once been yellow but were now black and rotten.

Nastya, Katerina Petrovna's only daughter and all she had left of her family, lived far away in Leningrad. She had not been home for three years.

Katerina Petrovna knew that Nastya no longer had any time for her, an old woman. The young people had their own affairs, their incomprehensible concerns, their own happiness. It was better not to interfere. And so Katerina Petrovna wrote very seldom to Nastya, but thought about her all her days, sitting on the edge of the crushed divan so quietly that a mouse, deceived by the silence, would run out from behind the stove, sit erect on its hind legs and, its nose twitching, sniff at the stale air.

There were no letters from Nastya either, but once every two or three months, Vasily, the cheerful young postman, would bring Katerina Petrovna a remittance for two hundred rubles. He carefully held Katerina Petrovna's arm when she signed so that she wouldn't put her name in the wrong place.

Vasily would go away, and Katerina Petrovna would sit there distraught, holding the money in her hands. Then she would put on her spectacles and read the few words on the postal remittance form. The message was always the same: Nastya was so busy that she hadn't time to come or even write a proper letter.

Katerina Petrovna carefully counted over the banknotes. In her old age, she had forgotten that these notes were not at all the same as the ones that Nastya had handled, and it seemed to her that the money smelt of Nastya's perfume.

Once, in the night, at the end of October, someone banged for a long time at the little back garden gate that had been boarded up for many years.

Katerina Petrovna became flustered and spent a long time wrapping her head in a warm shawl, put on an old coat and went outside the house for the first time that year. She walked slowly, feeling her way. The cold air gave her a headache. Forgotten stars looked penetratingly down at her. Fallen leaves got in her way.

Near the gate, Katerina Petrovna asked quietly:

"Who's knocking?"

No one answered behind the wall.

"I must have dreamed it," said Katerina Petrovna, and she turned back.

Gasping for breath, she stopped by an old tree, took hold of a cold, wet branch and recognised it as a sycamore. She had planted it a long time ago, when she was just a giggly girl, and now it was standing there, stripped of its leaves, shivering, chilled; it had nowhere to shelter from that windy, inhospitable night.

Katerina Petrovna felt sorry for the sycamore, touched its rough trunk, went back to the house and wrote a letter to Nastya that night.

"My darling," wrote Katerina Petrovna, "I shan't live through winter. Come for at least one day. Let me look at you and hold your hand. I'm old and weak, it's horror for me to sit or lie down, let alone walk—death has forgotten the way to me. The garden is withering up—it's not the same any more—and I can't see it. This is a bad autumn. It's so hard; all life, it seems, was never so long as this one autumn."

Manyushka, sniffing, took the letter to the post. She was a long time putting it in the letter box, and she peeped inside. What was in there? But she couldn't see anything, just a tin void.

Nastya worked as secretary at the Artists' Union. There was a lot of work to do. The organisation of exhibitions and competitions, all went through her hands.

She received the letter from Katerina Petrovna when she was at work. She put it in her handbag unread; she decided to look at it afterwards. Katerina Petrovna's letters always made Nastya sigh with relief; if her mother was writing, that meant she was alive. But they were also a source of profound unease, as if each letter was a silent reproach.

After work, Nastya had to call at a studio of a young sculptor named Timofeyev to see how he was getting on and to make a report to the board of the Union. Timofeyev had been complaining of the cold in his studio and, in general, that he was being obstructed and not allowed to show his talent.

On one of the landings, Nastya took out her pocket mirror, powdered her face and smiled—she now liked the look of herself. The artists called her Solveig because of her fair hair and big, cold eyes.

The door was answered by Timofeyev himself—small, decisive, malignant. He was wearing a coat. He had swathed an enormous muffler round his neck, and Nastya noticed ladies' felt boots on his feet.

"Don't take your coat off," snapped Timofeyev, "or you'll freeze. Come this way!"

He led Nastya along a dark corridor, climbed several steps and opened a narrow door into the studio.

There was a smell of stove fumes inside. A paraffin stove was burning near a barrel of wet clay. Sculptures draped with wet clothes stood on stands. The snow slanted across the wide window, shrouding the Neva in mist and melting in its dark waters. The wind whistled in the frames and stirred the old papers lying on the floor.

"My God, how cold it is!" said Nastya, and it seemed to her that the studio was made even colder by the white marble bas-reliefs hung randomly all over the walls.

"Admire it!" said Timofeyev, moving up a clay-stained armchair for Nastya. "It's a wonder I haven't conked out in this hole. And Pershin has warm air blowing from the heaters, like from the Sahara."

"You don't like Pershin?" asked Nastya cautiously.

"An upstart!" said Timofeyev angrily. "A commercial hack. His subjects don't have shoulders, they have coat-hangers. His kolkhoz woman is a stone idol with her apron tucked up. His worker looks like Neanderthal Man. He moulds with a wooden spade. And he's crafty, my dear, as crafty as a Jesuit."

"Show me your Gogol," requested Nastya to change the subject.

"Not there," said the sculptor glumly, "no, not there. Over there in the corner. That's it!"

He took the wet cloths off one of the figures and studied it critically from all sides, squatted

down near the paraffin stove to warm his hands
and said:

"There he is—Nikolai Vasilievich!"

Nastya started. Mockingly, as if he knew her
through and through, a beaky-nosed, round-
shouldered man was staring at her. Nastya could
see the sclerotic vein throbbing on his temple.

"And you haven't opened the letter in your
handbag," Gogol's keen eyes seemed to be saying. "Oh, you flibbertigibbet!"

"Well?" asked Timofeyev. "Not bad, eh?"

"Remarkable!" answered Nastya with an effort. "It's really superlative."

Timofeyev laughed bitterly.

"Superlative," he repeated. "They all say
superlative. And Pershin, and Matyash, and all
the experts from all kinds of committees. But
when my fate as a sculptor is being decided that
same Pershin only hums and hahs vaguely and
that's that. If Pershin hums and hahs, that means
it's curtains!.. I can't sleep at night!" shouted
Timofeyev and he began running about the studio, his boots clumping. "I've got rheumatism
in my hands from wet clay. I've read every word
about Gogol for three years. I see his characters
in my dreams!"

Timofeyev picked up a stack of books off the
table, shook them in the air and, with an effort,
threw them down again. Plaster dust flew off
the table.

"That's all about Gogol!" he said, and suddenly calmed down. "What? I haven't scared
you, have I? Sorry, my dear, but by God, I

feel like fighting someone! "

"Well, we'll fight together," said Nastya, and she stood up.

Timofeyev firmly pressed her hand and she went out, determined to rescue this talented man from obscurity at all costs.

Nastya returned to the Artists' Union, went to the chairman and talked to him for a long time, passionately arguing that an exhibition of Timofeyev's works should be organised at once. The chairman tapped his pencil on his desk, spent a long time weighing something up in his mind and finally agreed.

Nastya returned home, to her old room on the Moika, with its moulded gilt ceiling, and only then did she read Katerina Petrovna's letter.

"How can I go there now! " she said, standing up. "What hope have I got of getting away from here?"

She thought of the overcrowded trains, the change to the narrow-gauge line, the jolting ride in the wagon, the withered garden, her mother's inescapable tears, the unrelieved boredom of days in the country, and she put the letter in her desk drawer.

For two weeks Nastya was busy arranging Timofeyev's exhibition.

Several times she quarrelled and made peace with the intractable sculptor. Timofeyev was sending his work to the exhibition as if he were condemning them to extinction.

"You won't get a damn thing out of it anyway, my dear," he said to Nastya maliciously, as if she was arranging her own exhibition and not his. "I'm simply wasting my time, honestly!"

At first, Nastya despaired too and took offence, until she grasped that all these whims came from wounded pride, that they were an affectation and that, deep in his heart, Timofeyev was very pleased about his forthcoming exhibition.

The exhibition opened in the evening. Timofeyev was in a bad mood and said that sculptures shouldn't be viewed by electric light.

"Dead light!" he grumbled. "A deadly bore. Even paraffin would be better!"

"What lighting d'you need? You're impossible!" flared up Nastya.

"I need candles! Candles!" shouted Timofeyev in a martyred voice. "How can you put Gogol on show by electric light? It's absurd!"

Sculptors and artists attended the opening. Any outsider who heard the sculptors talking would not always have been able to guess whether Timofeyev's work was being praised or abused. But Timofeyev grasped that the exhibition was a success.

A white-haired, excitable artist went up to Nastya and patted her on the arm.

"Thank you! I've heard you dragged Timofeyev into the light of day. You did marvellously. We've got a lot of people burbling about attention to the artist, care and sensitivity, but when it comes to action, you're up against a brick wall. Thanks again!"

The discussion began. They talked a lot,

paid compliments, became excited, and the thought let drop by the old artist about attention to the man, to the young and undeservedly neglected sculptor was repeated in every speech.

Timofeyev sat looking glum studying the parquet floor; but he still kept glancing furtively at the speakers, not knowing whether to believe them or whether it was still too early.

The Union messenger appeared in the doorway, the good-natured and dim-witted Dasha. She signalled to Nastya, who went up to her. Smirking, Dasha handed her the telegram.

Nastya returned to her place, discreetly opened the telegram, read it and could not make sense of it:

"Katya's dying. Tikhon."

"What Katya!" wondered Nastya desperately. "What Tikhon? This must be for someone else."

She looked at the address. No, the telegram was for her. Only then did she notice the fine printed letters on the paper tape. "Zaborye."

Nastya crumpled up the telegram and frowned. Pershin was speaking.

"In our days," he was saying, trying to hold his spectacles in place, "care for the man is becoming the beautiful reality which helps us to grow and work. I am happy to note a manifestation of this concern in our milieu, the milieu of sculptors and artists. I refer to the exhibition of comrade Timofeyev's work. For this exhibition, we are wholly indebted to—and I am sure the management will not take offence at this—to one of the rank-and-file members of the Union, our dear Anastasia Semyonovna."

Pershin bowed to Nastya and all applauded. They applauded for a long time. Nastya was embarrassed almost to tears.

Someone touched her arm from behind. It was the old and excitable artist.

"What is it?" he whispered, and he glanced pointedly at the crumpled telegram in Nastya's hand. "Nothing unpleasant, is it?"

"No," replied Nastya. "It's just... From a friend..."

"Ah!" muttered the old man, and he resumed listening to Pershin.

All eyes were on Pershin, but Nastya felt someone else's heavy and penetrating stare on her all the time, and she was afraid to look up. "Who could it be?" she wondered. "Has someone guessed? How silly. My nerves are getting the better of me again."

She raised her eyes with an effort and turned away at once. Gogol was looking at her with a smile on his face. It seemed to Nastya that Gogol said quietly through his clenched teeth: "Oh, how could you!"

Nastya quickly stood up and went out, hastily put on her things and ran out into the street.

It was sleeting heavily. A grey rime had grown on St. Isaac's Cathedral. The bleak sky was sinking lower and lower over the city, over Nastya herself and over the Neva.

"My darling," said Nastya to herself, thinking of the letter. "My darling!"

Nastya sat down on a bench in the gardens

near the Admiralty and wept bitterly. The snow thawed on her face and mingled with her tears.

Nastya shivered with cold and suddenly realised that no one had loved her as much as that frail, forsaken old woman out there in dismal Zaborye.

"It's too late! I shan't see Mum again," she thought, and remembered that it was the first time in a year that she had used that dear childhood word, "Mum".

She jumped up, quickly walked against the snow lashing her face.

"What is this, Mum? What is it?" she thought, not seeing anything. Mum! How could it happen this way? I haven't got anyone in the world. There'll never be anyone dearer to me. If only I can be in time, if only she can see me, if only she can forgive me."

Nastya came to Nevsky Prospekt, to the city railway station.

She was too late. There were no tickets left.

She stood near the booking office, her lips trembling. She could not speak, feeling that if she uttered a single word, she would sob her heart out.

The elderly, bespectacled booking-clerk looked through the window.

"What's the matter, citizen?" she asked irritably.

"Nothing," replied Nastya. "My mother..."

Nastya turned round and quickly made for the exit.

"Where are you going?" called the booking-clerk. "You should have said so first! Wait a moment!"

Nastya left that evening. All day it seemed to her that the "Red Arrow" was hardly moving, whereas the train was rushing through the night forests, enveloping them in steam and hailing them with a prolonged warning shriek.

...Tikhon arrived at the post-office, whispered something to Vasily the postman, took a telegram form from him, turned it over and for a long time, wiping his moustache with his sleeve, wrote in a crabbed script on the form. Then he carefully folded it up, pushed it into his hat and made his way back to Katerina Petrovna.

Katerina Petrovna had not left her bed for ten days. She was not in pain, but a morbid weakness was oppressing her chest, her head and her legs; she had difficulty in breathing.

Manyushka had not left Katerina Petrovna's bedside for six days and nights. She slept in her clothes on the crumpled divan. Sometimes Manyushka imagined that Katerina Petrovna was not breathing any more. Then she would whimper in fright and call:

"Ma'am, are you alive?"

Katerina Petrovna's hand would stir under the blanket and Manyushka would calm down.

A November darkness filled the rooms every morning, but it was warm. Manyushka would light the fire. When the cheerful glow illumined the timbered walls, Katerina Petrovna would sigh cautiously; a fire made the room comfortable and cosy, as it had been a long time ago when Nastya had still been there. Katerina Petrovna would close her eyes; a single small tear would trickle down the yellow temple to mingle with her white hair.

Tikhon came in. He coughed, blew his nose and was evidently agitated.

"What is it, Tikhon?" asked Katerina Petrovna.

"It's turned a bit colder, Katerina Petrovna!" said Tikhon briskly and he looked uneasily at his hat. "It'll snow soon. It's for the best. It'll be easier for her to travel."

"Who?" Katerina Petrovna opened her eyes and began convulsively smoothing the blanket with a withered hand.

"Who else but Nastasya Semyonovna," replied Tikhon, smiling wryly, and he took the telegram out of his pocket. "Who else would it be?"

Katerina Petrovna wanted to sit up but she couldn't and sank back on to the pillow again.

"Here!" said Tikhon. He opened the telegram carefully and offered it to Katerina Petrovna.

She did not take it, but looked imploringly at Tikhon.

"Read it," said Manyushka hoarsely. "Ma'am can't read any more. Her eyes are too bad."

Tikhon looked fearfully over his shoulder, straightened his collar, smoothed his sparse red hair and in a hollow, uncertain voice, read: "Hold out, am on the way. Your everloving daughter, Nastya."

"Don't Tikhon!" said Katerina Petrovna quietly. "Don't, my dear. God be with you. Thank you for the kind word and the affection!"

Katerina Petrovna turned to the wall with an effort and then seemed to fall asleep.

Tikhon sat with bowed head in the cold passage on a bench, smoking, spitting and sighing, until Manyushka came out and beckoned him into Katerina Petrovna's room.

Tikhon went in on tiptoe and wiped his face with the back of his hand. Katerina Petrovna lay there, small and pale, as if she had peacefully fallen asleep.

"She didn't wait," muttered Tikhon. "Poor old thing! And you watch it, you fool," he said angrily to Manyushka, "pay for good with good, don't be mean. Sit here, and I'll go to the village Soviet and report."

He went out, and Manyushka sat on the tuffet with her knees tucked up, trembling and never taking her eyes off Katerina Petrovna.

They buried Katerina Petrovna next day. A frost had set in. A fine snow was falling. The day was white, and the sky was dry and bright, but grey, as if someone had spread out a washed and frozen linen sheet overhead. The vistas beyond the river were blue-grey. From them came the sharp and cheerful tang of snow and willow-bark caught by the first frost.

Old women and children had gathered for the funeral. The coffin was taken to the cemetery by Tikhon, Vasily and the two Malyavin brothers—little old men who looked as if they were overgrown with flax. Manyushka and her brother Volodya carried the coffin lid, looking straight and unblinkingly to their front.

The cemetery with its tall lichen-yellowed pussy willows, was behind the village, over the river.

They met the schoolmistress on the way. She had recently arrived from the regional town and no one in Zaborye knew her yet.

"Teacher's coming, teacher's coming!" whispered the little boys.

She was young, shy, grey-eyed and still a mere girl. She saw the funeral, stopped timidly and looked apprehensively at the little old woman in the coffin. Stinging snowflakes were settling on the old woman's face and not melting. Back in the regional town, the teacher had left her mother—just as tiny, eternally worried about her daughter and just as white-haired.

The teacher stood there for a moment and then slowly began walking after the coffin. The old ladies looked round at her, whispering that she was such a quiet girl, look you, and she would have a hard time with the children at first, they were a very independent and mischievous lot in Zaborye.

The schoolmistress finally made up her mind and asked one of the old ladies, the peasant Matryona.

"I take it, the old lady was alone, was she?"

"Eh, my dear," chanted Matryona at once, "you might say she was all alone. And was so genuine, so kind. She'd sit alone on her little divan all the time, and nobody to talk to. Such a pity! She had a daughter in Leningrad, only she's gone up in the world, by the look of it. But this one died without anybody, without her family, without her relatives."

They put the coffin down in the cemetery near the fresh-dug grave. The old ladies bowed to the coffin, their dark hands touching the ground. The schoolmistress went up to it, bent over and kissed Katerina Petrovna's withered yellow hand. Then she stood up quickly, turned away and went to the ruined wall.

On the other side of the wall, under the light snow, lay her beloved, slightly sad native soil.

The schoolmistress watched and listened for a long time as the old men talked among themselves behind her, the soil thudded on the coffin-lid and, far away, cocks in their yards crowed with different voices, foretelling clear days, light frosts and winter silence.

Nastya arrived in Zaborye two days after the funeral. She found a fresh grave-mound at the cemetery—the earth on it was frozen into lumps—and Katerina Petrovna's cold, dark room from which life seemed to have departed long, long ago.

Nastya wept all night in that room until a

murky and heavy dawn glimmered dark-blue in the windows.

Nastya left Zaborye furtively to avoid being noticed by anyone or asked about anything. It seemed to her that no one but Katerina Petrovna could assuage the intolerable burden of her guilt.

1946

A NIGHT IN OCTOBER

Personally, I find it far easier to write in the country than in town. In the country everything helps you to concentrate: even the sputtering of the small paraffin lamp and the moaning of the wind in the garden — and then, in between these sounds, there is that complete hush when the earth seems to have come to a standstill and hangs soundlessly in space.

And so, late in the autumn of 1945, I left town to work in a village near Ryazan. There was a country house there, with a garden that was completely overgrown. Its mistress was an old lady named Vasilisa Ionovna, a retired Ryazan librarian. I had been there previously, and upon each new visit had found the garden wilder and the house and its mistress more aged.

I left Moscow on the last boat of the season. Rust-coloured banks drifted past outside the windows of my cabin, and grey little waves sent out by the paddle wheels lapped up against

them. In the saloon a small red bulb burned all
night long. I felt as though I was alone on that
boat, for the passengers seldom left their warm
cabins. Only a lame army captain with a weather-beaten face wandered around on deck and
gazed smilingly at the banks. They were ready
for winter: the leaves had long since been shed,
the grass lay flat, the potherbs had turned black,
and little white wisps of smoke curled over
the cottages of the villages—the stoves were already being heated everywhere. The river, too,
was ready for winter. Almost all the quays had
been shifted to the back-waters. The buoys
had been removed, and it was only thanks to
the grey moonlight sheathing the earth that
our boat was able to proceed at night.

I struck up a conversation with the sapper
captain to our mutual delight and satisfaction.
It appeared that Captain Zuyev was also getting
off at Novoselki and that he, like myself,
intended to cross over to the other bank of
the Oka and walk to the village of Zaborye over
the meadows. Our boat was due to arrive at
Novoselki that evening.

"I'm not stopping at Zaborye, though,"
the captain told me. "I'll push on a bit farther
to the forestry office out there; but we can go
together as far as Zaborye. I've fought at the
front and have seen a thing or two in my life,
but I don't quite fancy plodding through those
deserted places at night by myself. Before the
war I was a forester, and now that I've been
demobbed I'm going back to the old job. It's a

wonderful job—looking after those forests!
I'm a graduate silviculturist. Come and visit
me. I'll show you some spots that will take your
breath away. At the front I dreamt about them
almost every night."

He laughed, and his face grew visibly younger.

When the boat reached Novoselki late in the
evening, there was nobody on the quay except
the watchman with his lantern. Zuyev and I
were the only passengers to go ashore. No soon-
er had we stepped off the damp gangplank
than the boat got under way, enveloping us in a
cloud of steam. The watchman with the lantern
departed at once, leaving us to our own resources.

"Let's not hurry," said Zuyev. "We might as
well sit down on a log, have a smoke and work
out what to do next."

Judging by his voice, the way he drew in the
smell of the river water, glanced about him and
laughed when the boat gave a short whistle
as it rounded a bend, and the night echo picked
up the sound and rolled it on and on until it
drifted away into the forests beyond the Oka—
judging by all this, I could see that Zuyev was
in no special hurry for the simple reason that
he was experiencing an extraordinary and unexpected joy at finding himself in this familiar
place to which he had almost lost hope of returning.

We had our smoke and then made our way up
the steep bank to the lodge of the beacon-keeper
Sofron. I tapped on the window. Sofron came

out so quickly that I doubted whether he had been asleep. He recognised me and we shook hands.

"The water's been rising today," he said. "All of two metres during the last twenty-four hours. Looks like it's raining higher up. Did you hear anything about it?"

"No."

Sofron yawned.

"Autumn, nothing to be done about it. Well, shall we cross?"

At night the Oka seemed to be very broad, much broader than by day. The current was strong along the entire width of the river. Fish were splashing about here and there, and in the faint moonlight we could see how the rings formed by the splashes were swiftly carried along by the current and stretched out of shape.

At length we reached the opposite bank. The meadows gave off the smell of withered grass and the sweetish scent of willow leaves. We walked along a barely visible path and soon came to a country road. It was very quiet. The moon was sailing earthward; its light was already on the wane.

We next had to negotiate a meadow island about six kilometres wide, cross an old bridge spanning a second, very still and overgrown, bed of the Oka, and there, beyond a stretch of sand, lay Zaborye.

"I recognise it all," said the captain excitedly, "every little landmark. It seems I haven't forgotten a thing. See that cluster of trees? Those are the willows on the Prorva. Am I right? I told you so! Look at the mist over Lake Sel-yanskoye! And not a bird to be heard. I've come too late, of course—the birds have all flown off. And the air! Just smell that air! It's infused with the smell of the grasses. I've never breathed such air anywhere else. Can you hear the cocks crowing? That's in Trebutino. Lusty devils, they are! You can hear them four kilo-metres away! "

The farther we went, however, the less we spoke, and soon we stopped talking altogether. An opaqueness lay over the creeks, the black haystacks and the clumps of bushes. The si-lence of the night had communicated itself to us.

On our right spread a reed-choked lake whose surface gave off a dull gleam. Zuyev found it hard to walk because of his bad leg. We sat down to rest on a willow that had been blown down by the wind. I knew that willow well—it had been lying there for several years now and was all covered with low-growing dog rose.

"Life's pretty good, when you think about it! " sighed Zuyev. "I've been intensely aware of it ever since the war ended. You can laugh if you like, but now I could spend the rest of my life growing pine trees. Absolutely. Am I talking nonsense?"

"On the contrary," I said. "Not at all. Have you a family?"

"No, I'm an old bachelor."

We continued on our way. The moon disappeared behind the steep bank of the Oka. Dawn was still a long way off. In the east the darkness was as in the other parts of the sky. We found walking more and more difficult.

"There's one thing I can't understand," said Zuyev, "and that is why they've stopped bringing the horses out for night grazing. They used to keep them out at night all the way up to the first snowfall. And now there isn't a single horse in the meadows."

I had noticed this also but had not attached any significance to it. The meadow all around was so desolate that there seemed to be no other living creatures on it but ourselves.

Presently I made out a broad strip of water ahead of us. It hadn't been there before. I peered into the darkness and my heart sank—was the old bed of the Oka flooded as badly as that?

"We'll soon see the bridge," Zuyev said gaily. "And beyond that lies Zaborye. We've practically arrived."

On the bank of the old channel the road led right into the black water. The water lay there at our feet lapping against the low bank. There were dull splashes here and there as lumps of the bank collapsed into the water.

"Where's the bridge?" Zuyev asked anxiously.

There was no bridge. It had either been washed away or flooded by water. Zuyev switched on his torch. We saw muddy waves and the swaying tops of bushes.

"We-e-ll! " said the puzzled Zuyev. "We're cut off. By water. Now I understand why the meadows are so deserted. It looks like we're the only ones here. This wants some thinking over."

He fell silent.

"Shall we try shouting?"

But it was no use shouting. Zaborye was still quite a distance away. And in any case, nobody would have heard us. Besides, I knew that there was not a single boat in Zaborye to take us off the island. The ferry had been set up about two kilometres downstream, by the Pustynsky forest.

"I suppose we'll have to go down to the ferry," I said. "Of course —"

"Of course what?'"

"Oh, nothing. I know the way."

I had been about to say: "Of course, if the ferry is still there." But I had thought better of it. If the meadows were already deserted and they were being flooded by the autumn waters, then it stood to reason that the ferry had been removed. And Vasily the ferryman, that stern and sensible old fellow, would not be sitting in his little hut for nothing.

"Oh well! " agreed Zuyev. "Come along, then. Look how dark the night's become, curse it! "

He switched the torch on again and let out an oath—the water had already covered the tops of the bushes.

"This is getting serious! " Zuyev muttered. "We'd better hurry."

We set out for the ferry. A wind blew up out of the darkness; it came slowly, with a hum, sweeping snow-flakes before it. The splashes made by the collapsing bank grew more frequent. We plodded along, stumbling against hillocks and clumps of old grass. There were two small gullies which had always been dry. Now we waded across them up to our knees in water.

"The gullies are filling up," said Zuyev. "I hope we don't get caught in this. I just can't understand why the water is rising so fast! "

Not even during the heaviest autumn rains had the water risen so rapidly or flooded the island.

"I can't see any trees here," Zuyev remarked suddenly. "Nothing but bushes."

There was a cart-track leading to the crossing. We found it thanks to the mud and the smell of manure. The bank on the other side of the old channel was steep and covered with pines now moaning in the wind.

The night kept growing darker and colder. The water was hissing. Zuyev switched his torch on again. The river was now on a level with the bank, and narrow tongues of water were already darting out over the meadow.

"Fer-r-ry! " Zuyev shouted. He listened. "Fer-r-ry! "

Nobody responded. The pines moaned.

We shouted for a long time, until we became hoarse, but nobody answered. The snow gave way to rain. Scattered drops began to thud heavily on the ground.

Again we shouted. The pines continued to moan indifferently.

"The ferryman's gone! " Zuyev said crossly. "That's clear enough! And why the devil should he be here when the island's being flooded and there's not a living soul on it? How ridiculous! A stone's throw from home..."

I realised that nothing but pure chance could save us: either the water would suddenly stop rising, or we would find an abandoned boat. Most terrifying of all was the fact that we did not know why the water was rising so rapidly. It was hair-raising to think that only an hour ago there had been not the slightest sign of this night predicament of ours, and that we had walked into it ourselves.

"Let's follow the bank," I suggested. "We might come across a boat."

We groped our way along the bank, skirting the flooded places. Zuyev used his torch, but it was growing dim. Finally he turned it off to save it for an extreme emergency.

I stumbled against something dark and soft. It turned out to be a small haystack. Zuyev put a match to it. The stack blazed up in crimson, lurid flames. The fire lit up the turbid river, the now flooded meadows stretching ahead as far as the eye could see, and even the pine forest on the opposite bank. The forest was swaying and moaning indifferently.

We stood at the burning haystack staring into the fire. Disconnected thoughts flashed through my mind. At first I felt sorry that I had not done a tenth of what I had intended to do in life. Then I reflected that it was stupid to perish of one's own folly at a time when life promised many more days like this, bleak and autumnal perhaps, but fresh and dear to the heart, when the first snow has not yet fallen but everything already smells of snow—the air, the water, the trees, and even the cabbage leaves.

Zuyev must have been ruminating along the same lines. He slowly drew a crumpled pack of cigarettes from his coat pocket and held it out to me. We lit them from the burning hay.

"It'll go out in a moment," Zuyev said softly. "The water's at our feet already."

I did not say anything. I was listening. Above the moaning of the forest and the splashing of the water I could hear faint, intermittent sounds. They came nearer and nearer. I turned to the river and called out: "He-e-ey, you in the boat! This way! "

A boyish voice responded at once from the river:

"Co-o-ming! "

Zuyev quickly poked the hay. A column of flame burst forth, shooting sparks into the darkness. Zuyev began to laugh softly.

"Oars! " he said. "Those are oars creaking. How could we have suspected for a moment that we might perish in this dear spot of ours?"

I was particularly stirred by that responsive cry of "Coming". I'm coming to your aid! I'm coming through the darkness towards the smouldering light of the campfire! The call awakened memories of the ancient customs of brotherhood and aid, which had never died out among our people.

"Hey you, come down to the sand! This way! " a voice rang out from the river, and I suddenly realised that it was a woman's voice.

We hastened down to the water's edge. A boat suddenly drifted into the dim light of the fire and grounded its bow on the sand.

"Don't climb in yet, I've got to bail out some of this water," the voice said.

A woman jumped out of the boat and dragged it up on the bank. We could not see her face. She was wearing a padded jacket and boots, and her head was wrapped in a warm kerchief.

"What on earth are you doing here?" she asked brusquely, without looking at us, as she began to bail.

She listened rather indifferently to our tale and then said in the same brusque tone:

"Why didn't the beacon-keeper tell you? They opened the sluices on the river tonight. For the winter. The whole island will be flooded by morning."

"And what are you doing in the forest at night, dear lifesaver of ours?" Zuyev asked playfully.

"I was on my way to work," the woman answered somewhat reluctantly. "From Pustyn to Zaborye. I saw the fire and you people on this island here. So I guessed what had happened. The ferryman's been gone two days already; there was no reason for him to stay here any longer. It took me some time to find the oars. They were under the hay in his hut."

I sat down at the oars and rowed as hard as I could, but it seemed to me that the boat, far from moving ahead, was being carried along towards a black waterfall down which all this muddy water and the gloom and the whole night were falling.

At last we reached the other bank. We climbed up the slope and did not stop for a smoke until we had reached the forest. The forest was very still and warm, and smelled of rotting leaves. Way above us there was a steady, majestic roar—the only reminder of the gloomy night and our recent danger. Now the night seemed wonderful and beautiful. And the face of the young woman seemed to me very pleasant and familiar in the brief glimmer of the match as we lit up. Her grey eyes regarded us shyly. Wet strands of hair slipped out of her kerchief.

"Is that you, Dasha?" Zuyev suddenly asked in a very soft voice.

"Yes, Ivan Matveyevich." The woman burst into a light laugh, as though amused by something known to herself alone. "I recognised you at once. Only I didn't feel like telling you. We've been waiting for you all this time, ever since victory! We didn't want to believe that you wouldn't return to us."

"That's how it is! " said Zuyev. "I was at the front for four years and came close to death many a time. And now it is Dasha who actually saves me from death. She's my assistant," he told me. "She works in the forestry office. I taught her the job. She was a weak little thing, as slim as a stalk. And now look at what a beauty she's become. And she's grown strict, too."

"Oh, no! I'm not at all strict," Dasha replied. "It's just the suddenness of it all. Are you going to Vasilisa Ionovna's?" Dasha suddenly asked me, apparently to change the subject.

I answered yes, that I was going to Vasilisa Ionovna's, and invited the two of them to come along with me. We all wanted to dry ourselves and to rest in the warm old house.

Vasilisa Ionovna was not in the least surprised by our nocturnal arrival. She had reached the age when nothing surprised her any longer, and she gave her own interpretation to everything that happened. Now too, after hearing the story of our misadventure, she said:

"Great is the God of the land of Russia. And as for that Sofron, I always said he was a block-head. I just can't understand how you, a writer, didn't see through him! It only means that you have a blind spot for people too. Well," she said, turning to Dasha, "and I'm very glad for you. Your Ivan Matveyevich has finally come back."

Dasha reddened, jumped up, grabbed an empty bucket and ran out to the garden, forgetting to close the door behind her.

"Where are you going?" cried the startled Vasilisa Ionovna.

"To fetch water—for the samovar! " Dasha cried back.

"I can't understand the girls nowadays,"

said Vasilisa Ionovna, paying no heed to Zuyev, who somehow could not light his match. "You say something to them, and they blow up like fireworks. A wonderful girl, she is, though. In fact, she's my only comfort."

"Yes," agreed Zuyev, who had finally lit his match. "She's a wonderful girl."

Of course, Dasha dropped the bucket down the well. I know how to extract buckets from that well—with a pole. Dasha helped me. Her hands were ice-cold with agitation, and she kept repeating:

"Oh, how could Vasilisa Ionovna! How could she! "

The wind had blown away the storm clouds, and a starry sky was now flickering over the black garden. I pulled up the bucket. Dasha began to drink straight from it, her wet teeth gleaming in the darkness.

"Oh, goodness me," she said, "how can I go back now?"

"It's quite all right, come along."

We went back in. The lamps had already been lit and a clean cloth laid on the table. From his black frame on the wall Turgenev gazed down tranquilly upon the scene. A rare portrait, engraved on steel with the finest needle. It was Vasilisa Ionovna's pride and joy.

1946

IN THE HEART OF RUSSIA

Once in a while every writer feels like writing a story without bothering about any of the "iron" or "golden" rules set out in handbooks on composition. These rules are excellent, of course. They channel the writer's hazy ideas into a current of precise thought and guide them along to their final conclusion, the completion of a book, just as a river carries its waters to the broad mouth.

Obviously not all the laws governing literature have been neatly tabulated. There are many effective ways and means of expressing ideas which have not yet been formulated.

An experimental film about rain appeared some twenty years ago in Moscow. It was shown exclusively to people connected with the film industry because it was felt that the ordinary public would be bored by such a picture and leave the cinema wondering what it was all about.

The film showed rain from every imaginable sort of angle. Rain on the black asphalt of the town, in the leaves, during the daytime and at night, heavy rain, rain pelting down, drizzling rain, rain with the sun out, rain on a river and rain on the sea, air bubbles in puddles, wet trains through the fields, a host of different rain clouds, and a great deal more as well, which I will not go into here.

This film remained fresh in my mind for a long time and made me much more acutely aware of the poetry of ordinary rain than I had been before. Like many other people I had noticed the fresh smell of a dusty road after a fall of rain, but I had never listened carefully to the sound of rain nor perceived the dull, pastel colours of rainy air.

What could be better for a writer, and every writer must always be a poet as well, than the discovery of new fields of poetry right beside him enriching his perception, understanding and memory of things?

All this is simply a way of justifying myself for departing from the strict demands imposed on me by the subject of this story.

The morning on which this story opens was cloudy but warm. The broad meadows were drenched with night rain, so that there was a glistening drop of water on each corolla, and the whole great host of plants and bushes gave off a sharp, bracing odour.

I was walking over the meadows to a rather mysterious little lake. To the rational eye there was nothing at all mysterious about it, but it always left people with a feeling of something enigmatic. Try as I did, I could not put my finger on the reason for this.

For me the air of mystery lay in the fact that the water in the lake was crystal clear but at the same time had the colour of wet tar with a faint greenish tinge. According to the accounts of ancient, garrulous old men, carp the size "of a samovar tray" lived in this watery blackness. Nobody had ever succeeded in catching them, but occasionally there would be a flash of bronze disappearing with a flick of the tail deep down in the lake.

A sense of mystery comes from expecting something unknown and out of the ordinary. And, indeed, the height and denseness of the vegetation round the little lake made you think that there must be something unusual concealed in them: a dragonfly with red wings, a blue ladybird with white spots, or the poisonous flower of the oleaster with a juicy stalk as thick as a man's arm.

And all this really was there, including huge yellow irises with sword-like leaves. They were reflected in the water and, for some reason, their reflection was always surrounded by shoals of minnow like pins drawn to a magnet.

The meadows were completely empty. There were still two weeks to go before haymaking. In the distance I saw a small boy in a faded, artilleryman's cap obviously too large for him. He was holding a bay horse by the bridle and shouting. The horse was jerking its head and lashing its coarse tail at the boy trying to shake him off like a horsefly.

"Hey, Uncle! " cried the boy. "Uncle! Come here! "

It was an insistent call for help. I turned off the path and went over to the boy.

"Uncle," he said, gazing at me boldly with an imploring glance. "Give me a hand onto the gelding. I can't make it on my own."

"Who do you belong to?" I asked.

"The chemist," he replied.

I knew that the village chemist, Dmitri Sergeyevich, had no children and was somewhat surprised at the boy's reply.

I lifted him up, at which the gelding immediately took fright and began to shy away from me with mincing steps trying to keep an arm's length between us.

"Ee, yer wicked devil! " said the boy reproachfully. "Bundle o' nerves. Let me grab hold of the reins and then give me a lift up. He'll never let you like that."

The boy grasped the reins and the horse calmed down immediately, almost as if it had snoozed off. I lifted the boy onto its back, and it just went on standing, head bowed, looking as though it intended to remain on the same spot all day. It even gave a faint snore. Then the boy gave it a sharp kick in its bloated, dusty flanks with his bare heels. The gelding hiccuped with surprise and broke into a lazy, swinging gallop in the direction of the sandhills beyond the Beaver stream.

The boy kept on bobbing up and down, waving his elbows and digging his heels into the gelding's flanks. I realised that all this hard work was obviously the only way of keeping the gelding on the go.

A green, silt shadow lay on the lake, tucked away in the steep banks, and in this shadow the broom, itself silver, sparkled with silvery dew.

A small grey bird in a red jacket and yellow tie sat on a branch of broom making a short, pleasant rattling sound without opening its beak. I stood for a while marveling at this bird and its enjoyable pastime, then made my way down to the water.

A town girl called Masha who was very fond of plants had come to stay with us from Moscow after her school exams, and I had decided to pick her a bunch of nice flowers. But since there are no nasty flowers I was faced with the difficult task of choosing which ones to give her. In the end I decided to take one flower and one branch from each plant in the dense, sweet-smelling, dew-covered thickets round the lake.

I looked around me. The meadowsweet was already blooming in fragile, yellowish clusters. Its flowers smelt like mimosa. It was almost impossible to carry them all the way home, especially in windy weather, but I cut a branch all the same and lay it under a bush to keep it from wilting quickly.

Then I cut some swordlike leaves of sweet flag which gave off a strong, spicy smell. I remembered that in the Ukraine the women strew sweet flag over the floor before big holidays and its pungent aroma lingers in their homes almost until winter.

The first green cones had appeared on the arrowhead covered all over with soft needles. I took a branch of this as well.

Then I managed, with some difficulty, to hook a strand of frog's-bit out of the water with a dry branch. The petals of its white flowers with reddish centres were as thin as cigarette paper and wilted at once, so I had to throw them away. Using the same branch I hooked some flowering water buckwheat. Its pink panicles stood above the water like little round thickets.

I could not manage to reach the white lilies and did not fancy undressing and wading into the lake, because your legs sank into its silty bed up to the knees. Instead I decided to take a flower on the bank with the somewhat crude sounding name of *susak,* whose flowers were like tiny umbrellas blown inside out by the wind.

Large patches of innocent blue-eyed forget-me-nots peeped out from the banks of mint. Further on behind the hanging loops of brambles, a wild young mountain ash with tight clusters of yellow blossom was blooming on a slope. Tall red clover mingled with cow vetch and bedstraw, and above this happy union of flowers rose a giant thistle. It stood firmly up to its waist in grass looking like a knight in armour with thorny plates at the elbows and knees.

The warm air vibrated and swayed over the

flowers, nearly all of which revealed the striped belly of a wasp or bee buried in their petals. Butterflies fluttered about like obliquely falling white and lemon-coloured leaves.

Further still was a dense wall of hawthorn and eglantine. They were so closely twined together that it looked as though the bright red flowers of the eglantine and the white, almond-smelling blossoms of the hawthorn were miraculously growing on the same bush.

The eglantine stood proudly, arrayed in its best attire and covered with a large number of sharp buds. Its blooming coincided with the shortest nights—our Russian, northern-like nights, when the nightingale sings in the dew all night long, a greenish glow never leaves the horizon, and at the darkest time of all it is so light that you can see the craggy tops of the clouds clearly in the sky. Here and there on their snowy steepness glimmer flecks of pink from the sun. And a silver aeroplane flying at a great height sparkles above the night like a slowly flying star, because at that height the sun is already shining.

When I arrived home scratched to death by eglantine and stung all over by nettles, Masha was pinning a piece of paper to the gate, on which was written in printed letters:

> *Oh, there's dust along the roadside*
> *And there's dust along the way.*
> *If you wish to come inside now*
> *Kindly wipe your feet first, pray.*

"Ho ho! " I said. "So you've been to the chemist's shop and seen that notice on his door?"

"Ooh, what lovely flowers! " Masha exclaimed. "Really smashing! Yes, I did go to the chemist's. And I met someone really nice there. His name is Ivan Stepanovich Kryshkin."

"Who's he?"

"A boy. Really different from the rest."

I grinned. If there's anyone I know inside out it's the local village boys. I can confidently say, after many years of experience, that these noisy, restless compatriots of ours all possess one really unusual feature. A physicist might define it as "all-penetrability". These boys are "all-penetrating", or in archaic, highfalutin language "omnipresent".

In the most god-forsaken corner of a forest, lake or marsh I would always find these boys engaged in the most multifarious and sometimes startling activities.

This is to say nothing of the time when I met them on a freezing, misty September morning at sunrise, shivering with cold in the wet alder thickets on the bank of a remote lake twenty kilometres from the nearest house. They were sitting, concealed in the bushes with their home-made fishing rods, and the only thing that betrayed their presence was the familiar sound of snuffling noses. Sometimes they hid so well that I did not notice them at all and would give a start when I suddenly heard a hoarse, pleading whisper behind me:

"Give us a worm, Uncle! "

The boys' inexhaustible imagination and curiosity brought them to all these remote parts where, as the writers of adventure stories like to put it, "man's foot has rarely trod".

I am quite certain that if I arrived at the North Pole or, say, the Magnetic Pole, I would be sure to find a young lad with a fishing rod sitting there by a hole in the ice, snuffling and watching for a cod to appear, or hacking a piece of magnet out of the ground with a broken knife.

As this was the only remarkable feature of theirs with which I was acquainted I asked Masha:

"What's so really different about your Ivan Stepanovich Kryshkin?"

"He's eight," she answered, "but he goes around collecting all sorts of medicinal plants for the chemist. Valerian, for instance."

From the rest of her account it transpired that Ivan Stepanovich Kryshkin bore a remarkable resemblance to the boy I had helped onto the old gelding. Any remaining doubts of this point disappeared when I heard that the said Kryshkin had appeared outside the chemist's with a bay gelding and that, on being fastened to the fence, this gelding had promptly fallen fast asleep. But Ivan Stepanovich Kryshkin had gone into the chemist's and handed him a sack of valerian picked beyond the Beaver stream.

The only point which remained obscure was

how Ivan Stepanovich Kryshkin had managed to pick the valerian without getting off the gelding. But then I discovered that he had arrived leading the horse by the reins, and realised that he had ridden as far as the valerian and returned on foot.

It is now high time for me to turn to the subject of my story, the chemist Dmitri Sergeyevich or, perhaps, not so much to him as to the subject of a person's attitude towards his work, which has been occupying my mind for some time.

Dmitri Sergeyevich was entirely devoted to pharmacy. Talking to him convinced me that the popular assumption that certain occupations are uninteresting is a prejudice born of ignorance. After that I began to find pleasure in everything in the village chemist shop, from the clean smell of the freshly scrubbed floor boards and the juniper to the misted bottles of fizzy Borzhom mineral water and the white pots on the shelves, bearing the label *venena*—poison!

According to Dmitri Sergeyevich nearly all plants contain either medicinal or poisonous juices. The problem was to extract these juices, determine their properties and the use to which they can be put.

A great deal, of course, had been discovered a long time ago, for instance, the action on the heart of infusions obtained from lilies of the valley or foxgloves and such like. But there were still thousands of plants which had not been studied and Dmitri Sergeyevich saw this task as the most fascinating occupation in the world.

That summer he was engaged in extracting vitamins from young pine needles. He would make all of us drink a scalding green infusion prepared from them and although we grimaced and protested we were compelled to admit that it was most effective.

One day Dmitri Sergeyevich brought me a heavy tome to read—pharmacopoeia. I cannot remember its exact name. This book was as absorbing as the most brilliantly written novel. It contained a description of the properties of a multitude of plants—not only herbs and trees, but moss, lichen and mushrooms—which were at times really amazing and unexpected. It also gave detailed instructions on preparing medicines from these plants.

Each week Dmitri Sergeyevich contributed a short article to the local district newspaper on the medicinal properties of plants, such as some perfectly ordinary plantain or mushroom. These articles, which he referred to for some reason as essays, were printed under the general heading "In the World of Friends". I used to see them cut out of the newspaper and pinned up on the wall in people's houses and was able to recognise from them the specific ailment which an inhabitant of that particular house was suffering from.

There was always a crowd of little boys in the chemist's shop. They were Dmitri Sergeyevich's main suppliers of herbs. They spared no effort,

going off to the most remote parts, such as
Khvoshchi bog, for instance, or even beyond the
distant Kazyonnaya stream where hardly anyone
ever went, and those who did returned with
tales of waste ground covered with shallow
silted lakes and tall thickets of sorrel.

The boys asked nothing in return for gathering the herbs except babies' rubber dummies,
which they would blow up, straining hard and
going red in the face, and then tie with a piece
of tape so that they looked like "flying bubble"
balloons. The "balloons" did not fly, of course,
but the boys carried them around all the time,
sometimes tying them to their fingers with
pieces of string, then spinning them so that
they made a sinister buzzing noise, or simply
bonking each other on the head with them,
enjoying the delightful popping sound which
accompanied this pastime.

It would not be fair to think that the boys
spent most of the day idling around enjoying
themselves. It was only in the summer holidays,
and even then by no means every day, that they
were free to play around. Most of the time they
spent helping the grown-ups graze the calves,
gather brushwood, cut willow, bank up potatoes
and mend fences, and keeping an eye on the
younger children when the grown-ups were not
at home. The worst of it was that the little ones
could barely walk and you had to carry them
everywhere on your back.

The two people whom the village boys loved
most of all were Dmitri Sergeyevich and an old

man nicknamed Scrap.

Scrap used to appear in the village once a month, sometimes even less frequently. He would shuffle along lazily in a dusty loose overalls beside his old horse and cart, trailing a rope whip on the sandy ground and crying mournfully:

"Bring out your rags, bottles and bones! "

On the front of Scrap's cart there was a magic box made of ordinary plywood, with the lid hanging open. Suspended from nails on the lid there were lots of brightly coloured toys — whistles, yo-yos, celluloid dolls, transfers and skeins of bright embroidery cotton.

As soon as Scrap appeared in the village little boys and girls would rush out from all the houses, jostling each other and tripping over, like young chicks about to be fed, dragging along their younger brothers and sisters, with old sacks, worn-out homemade slippers, broken cow's horns and all sorts of old junk.

In return for the rags and horns Scrap would hand out new toys, the paint on them still fresh, and would conduct long conversations and sometimes arguments about them with his young suppliers.

Grown-ups never brought anything out for Scrap — this was the exclusive privilege of the children.

Dealing with children clearly develops many good qualities in people. Scrap had a severe, even frightening appearance with his shaggy head, bristly cheeks and purple nose peeling from sun and wind. His voice was loud and coarse. But in spite of these menacing features he never sent the children away empty-handed. Only once did he refuse to take two completely decrepit tops from a pair of boots belonging to her father which were brought to him by a little girl in a faded red sarafan.

The girl seemed to shrink up, her head receding into her shoulders, and walked slowly away from Scrap's cart to her house as if she had been beaten. The children, gathered round Scrap, suddenly fell silent, wrinkling their brows and some of them began to snuffle.

Scrap rolled himself a thick cigarette, appearing not to notice the weeping girl or the children who were stunned by his cruel action. He licked down the edge of the paper slowly, lit the cigarette and spat. The children remained silent.

"What's the matter with you?" said Scrap angrily. "Don't you understand? I'm doin' a job for the state. Don't you go bringin' me a load o' rubbish. I need stuff that can be used on the production line. Get me?"

The children said nothing. Scrap took a deep drag on his cigarette and said, without looking at them:

"Bring her back, then. Off you go. Starin' at me as if I was a monster! "

The children flew off like a flock of frightened sparrows to the house of the girl in the red sarafan. She was dragged back flushed and embarrassed, her eyes still brimming with tears. Scrap examined the boot tops ostentatiously, threw them on the cart and handed the girl the best, brightest doll with plump crimson cheeks, rapturously round, deep blue eyes and chubby outstretched fingers.

The girl took the doll shyly, hugged it to her thin chest and laughed. Scrap shook the reins, the old horse flattened back its ears, settling into the shafts, and the cart creaked its way on along the sandy road. Scrap walked beside it, looking as severe and coarse as ever, not saying a word. Only after he had passed a good twenty houses did he cough and start his long drawn-out cry:

"Bring out your rags, bottles and bones! "

Gazing after him I reflected that there were few less attractive occupations than being a rag-and-bone man, but this person had managed to turn it into a source of delight for the peasant children.

Another interesting fact was that Scrap went about his work with a certain inspiration, inventiveness and concern for his boisterous young suppliers. He managed to get a fresh batch of toys from his superiors for each trip round the villages. Scrap's assortment of toys was varied and fascinating.

It was a great event in the village when Scrap, at the request of Dmitri Sergeyevich, brought bronze fishing hooks as a form of payment for those boys who collected medicinal herbs for the chemist, ticking them off on a special sheet of quarto paper. Ivan Stepanovich Kryshkin received ten hooks for services rendered.

The hooks were distributed in reverent silence. As if in response to some silent command the boys took off their caps that had all seen better days and began to stick the hooks into the lining with tremendous care and concentration. This was the most reliable hiding place for all their treasures.

In Russia we have all grown accustomed to the idea that a person of unassuming, modest appearance may prove to be quite outstanding and unusual. The writer Leskov was particularly aware of this, due to the fact that he knew his country inside out and loved it with every fibre of his being, having travelled its length and breadth and been the bosom friend and confidant of hundreds of ordinary people.

Dmitri Sergeyevich's modest appearance which, to put it humorously, was striking for its lack of anything remarkable, concealed an indefatigable explorer in his field, a truly humane person who made high demands on himself and those around him.

Beneath Scrap's unprepossessing exterior beat a warm, kind heart. Moreover he was a person of imagination who applied it to his seemingly trifling occupation.

While I was reflecting on this I remembered an amusing incident which happened in these parts to me and a friend.

We had gone to fish on Staraya Kanava, which is a narrow forest stream with swift-flowing brown water. This stream is buried deep in the forest, far from human habitation, and reaching it is quite a difficult business. First you travel forty kilometres on the narrow-gauge railway, and then it is another thirty kilometres or so by foot. There are large ide in the eddying pools on Staraya Kanava, and this was what we were after.

We returned the following day reaching the station in the quiet forest twilight. There was a strong smell of turpentine, sawdust and cloves. It was August, and yellow leaves had begun to appear here and there on the birch trees. These leaves now lit up in turn with the rays of the dying sun.

The small train arrived with lots of empty goods trucks. We got into the truck with the most people—women with baskets of cowberries and mushrooms, and two tatty, unshaven hunters sitting by the open doors of the truck, dangling their legs and smoking. At first the women chatted about village affairs, but soon the magical charm of the forest dusk invaded the carriage and they fell silent with a sigh. The train emerged into the meadows and the quiet sunset became visible in all its glory. The sun sank into the grass, mist and dew, and not even the noise of the train could drown the chirping and warbling of the birds in the bushes along the track.

Then the youngest woman began to sing gazing at the sunset with eyes of burnished gold. She sang a simple Ryazan folksong and some of the other women joined in. When they had finished the scruffy hunter with puttees made out of an old army greatcoat said in a low voice to his companion:

"How about us singing, eh, Vanya?"

"Why not," answered his companion.

The two scruffy men began to sing. One of them had a rich light bass. All of us were stunned by the ease and power of his remarkable voice.

The women listened to the singers shaking their heads with amazement. The youngest one began to weep quietly, but nobody even turned in her direction because hers were tears of intense admiration, not of pain or grief.

When the singers stopped the women began to bless them and wish them long life and happiness for the rare pleasure which they had given.

We asked the singer who he was and he replied that he was book-keeper on a collective farm. Then we tried to persuade him to come to Moscow so that famous singers and professors from the Conservatoire could hear him sing. "It's a crime to hide yourself away with a voice like that, letting your talent go to waste," we told him. But the hunter simply smiled shyly and persistently refused.

"Give over! How could I sing opera with my untrained voice! Besides I've passed the age to go gallivanting around taking risks like that. I've got my house and garden in the village and a wife with two children at school. Go to Moscow, indeed. Are you joking? I was there three years ago and all the hullabaloo made my head ache from morning to night. I just couldn't wait to get back home to the Oka."

The small engine gave a shrill whistle—we were approaching our station.

"Listen," my friend said firmly to the hunter. "We've got to get out now, but I'll give you my Moscow address and telephone number. You must be sure to come. I'll introduce you to all the right people."

He tore a leaf out of his diary and rapidly scribbled down his address. The train had already stopped at the station and was now puffing hard preparing to resume its journey.

The hunter read what was written on the paper in the fading light and asked:

"You're a writer, aren't you?"

"Yes, I am."

"Of course. I've read your work. Delighted to make your acquaintance. But allow me to introduce myself—Pirogov, soloist at the Bolshoi. Please don't take offence at my little joke. The only thing I can plead in defence of it is that this is a fortunate country indeed when people are so kind and solicitous to one another."

He laughed.

"I'm referring, of course, to your eagerness to help a collective-farm book-keeper become an opera singer. And I'm sure that if I had really been a book-keeper you would have stopped me from wasting my voice. Thank you! "

He shook our hands warmly. The train moved off, and we were left perplexed on the wooden platform. It was only then that we remembered Dmitri Sergeyevich saying that the singer Pirogov came back every summer to his large native village on the Oka, not far from us.

But now it's time for me to finish this story. I can see that I have caught the habit of "going on" from the local old men, and got carried away like the ferryman Vasili. Whenever he starts to tell a story it always reminds him of another one which leads on to a third and then a fourth. There's really no end to it.

My aim was a simple one: to relate a few ordinary incidents that reveal the talent and warmth of the Russian character. And we will talk about the outstanding incidents another time.

1950

THE SWEETBRIAR *

A fog came down on the river in the night. The steamer could not go further; neither buoys nor lights were visible ahead.

The steamer nosed up to the steep bank and was silent. The only sound was the rhythmic creaking of the gangway as the sailors took the line down to the bank and lashed it round an old willow.

Masha Klimova woke up in the night. It was so quiet all round that she could hear a passenger snoring in a distant cabin.

Masha sat up on her bunk. Fresh air was streaming through the open window, bringing the sweetish smell of willow leaves.

Bushes, blurred in the mist, hung over the deck. It seemed to Masha that the steamer, in some incomprehensible way, had ended up on land in a clump of bushes. Then she heard the faint gurgling of water and guessed that the steamer must have stopped close to the bank.

*English translation © Raduga Publishers 1986

Something clicked and was silent again in the bushes. Then there was another click. And another silence. As if someone was clicking, then listening to measure the sound against the silence and responsiveness of the night. The clicking soon became a long trill and ended in a brief whistle. The whistle was answered by dozens of other bird voices, and a sudden tumult of nightingale song was borne over the clumps of bushes.

"Can you hear that, Egorov?" asked someone up above, presumably on the captain's bridge.

"There was never a battle of nightingales like that even on the Sheksna," replied a husky voice from below.

Masha smiled and stretched her arms out in front of her. They seemed very dark in the turbid light and only her fingernails gleamed whitely.

"Why am I so sad? I don't understand," said Masha to herself in an undertone. "Am I waiting for something? But even I don't know what it is."

She remembered her grandmother saying how there is an incomprehensible maiden sadness on this earth, and she had protested:

"Nonsense! What maiden sadness? It's just that my life's beginning. That's why I'm a little bit frightened."

Masha had long since graduated from the forestry institute and was now on her way from Leningrad to the Lower Volga where she was to do a job, planting forests for a collective farm.

Masha was, of course, fibbing when she said

that she was a little bit scared. She was terrified.
She imagined arriving at the forest sector and
the chief—inevitably a dusty, morose individual
in a black jacket with bulging pockets and in
boots stained with lumps of clay—would look
at her and her grey eyes that were "just like
saucers" (which was what Masha herself thought
of them), and at her braids, and would think:
"Charming! Haven't we got enough of these
girls in pigtails? You can bet they all recite their
textbooks by rote. But we can't be bothered
with them here! When the dry Astrakhan wind
sets in, your textbooks, my dear, won't be much
use to you here..."

During the long journey, Masha had become
used to the idea of the morose chief in a black
jacket and she was no longer afraid of him. But
her sadness would not go away.

Masha did not know that it was not sadness
at all, but a feeling for which there is perhaps
no exact name—the sinking of the heart before
the unknown future, before the simple beauty
of earth with its rivers, mists, deep nights and
the murmurs of white willows on the shore.

Sleep would not come. Masha got dressed and
went out on deck. Everything was covered with
dew—the rail, the wire mesh along the sides and
the wicker armchairs.

There was a muted conversation in progress
on the foredeck. "So I says to him," a young
sailor continued, " 'Grandad, Grandad, leave
me something to smoke.' He gives me his fag-end.
I take a pull and I ask, 'What are you doing here

at night in the meadows, Grandad?' 'I'm watching the dawn,' says he. And he laughs. 'Maybe it's the last dawn I'll ever see. You won't understand that,' says he. 'You're only a youngster.' "

The sailors fell silent. The nightingales began clicking in the bushes again.

Masha rested her elbows on the rail. Faraway in the mist, the cocks began crowing together. There was evidently a village somewhere over yonder.

"Was that the first crow of the cock, or the second?.."

Masha didn't know when the first cocks crowed and when the second cocks followed suit. She had read about it dozens of times in books, but she didn't know.

Her grandmother, a river captain's wife, had advised her to go by steamer, Masha was glad she had taken this advice. The steamer went along the blue-black Neva, then crossed Lake Ladoga. For the first time, Masha saw its grey waters and the stone beacons on the low capes. She saw the bubbling Svir, the sluice-gates of the Mariinsky Canal, the horsetail-covered bank, the inevitable small boys on the jetties, concentratedly angling with curved fishing rods.

Her fellow-passengers changed, but they all seemed interesting to Masha. At Byelozersk, the steamer was boarded by a still young pilot with white temples. He was on holiday, probably in Byelozersk, staying with his mother, a thin little woman in a grey gingham dress. She was weeping softly on the jetty as she saw her son off, and the pilot was saying to her from the deck:

"Don't forget the fish I caught, Mum, I hung them in the cellar, behind the ladder. Give Vaska one of the perch."

"I won't forget, Pasha, I certainly won't forget," the old woman nodded, wiping her eyes with a hankie screwed up into a ball.

The pilot smiled, joked, but never took his eyes off the old lady. His cheek was trembling.

Then the players boarded the steamer. They made a lot of noise, larked about and immediately got to know all the passengers. In the saloon, the piano, damp with river mists, was hardly ever silent now.

One elderly actor, sharp-faced and quick-moving, sang more often than the others. Masha listened to his songs with amazement; she had never heard anything like them before. The actor was particularly fond of singing a Polish song about a robber in love. He had failed to steal a star from the night sky for his sweetheart and the girl had sent him packing.

Each time the actor finished this song, he banged the piano-lid shut and said:

"The moral of this song is plain to see. Be kind to people who love. No objections, please. Conversation over."

He would adjust his black bow-tie, sit down at a table and order beer and dried Caspian carp.

Several students from an architectural institute joined the boat at Cherepovets. They were returning to Moscow from St. Cyril Monastery in Byelozersk. They had gone there on a field trip to take measurements and draw sketches of the old buildings.

All the way, the students argued about stone carvings, vaults, Andrei Rublev and the high-rise buildings in Moscow. As she listened to them, Masha could only blush at her own ignorance.

When the students boarded the steamer, the elderly actor quietened down somewhat, stopped singing the song about the robber and sat all the time on deck reading Stanislavsky's *My Life in Art.* He wore spectacles when he was reading. This made his face look kindly and old. It became clear to Masha that all the pompous actor's declamations were an obsolete habit and that the man was much nicer than he wanted to seem.

The passengers were now all asleep—the pilot, the actor and the students. Masha stood alone on deck and listened, trying to decypher the sounds of the night.

Faraway, a roar rose in the sky and slowly died down again. It must have been a night plane flying over the fog. A fish plopped near the bank, and then a shepherd's horn sounded somewhere in the distance. It was so far away that at first Masha could not understand what those sustained and agreeable sounds could be.

Someone struck a match behind Masha. She looked round. The pilot was lighting a cigarette. He threw the burning match into the water. It fell slowly through the fog. A rainbow steam formed round the flame.

"Can't sleep for the nightingales," said the pilot, and without being able to see him, Masha guessed that he was smiling in the dark. "Just as in the song: 'Nightingales, nightingales, not so much noise, Don't keep disturbing our soldier boys'..."

"I've never heard such nightingales before," said Masha.

"Travel round the Soviet Union and you'll hear plenty," replied the pilot. "You don't always even dream about a place like this."

"That's because you're an airman," commented Masha, "and the ground keeps changing under your wing all the time."

"I don't think so," replied the pilot, and he was silent for a long time. "It's getting light," he said at last. "It's turning blue over there in the east... Where are you going?"

"Kamyshin."

"There's a small town of that name on the Volga. Heat-waves, water-melons, tomatoes..."

"And where are you going?"

"Further."

The pilot leaned his elbows on the rail and watched the dawn blazing up. The shepherd's horn was sounding much nearer. A breeze sprang up. The mist stirred. Scraps of it were borne over the river. Wet bushes became visible and, among them, a hut of woven willow branches. A fire was burning nearby.

Masha also watched the dawn. The last star was glistening like a drop of silvery water on the rim of the sky, which was already turning gold.

"From today on," thought Masha, "I'm going to live a different life. I never noticed what I should have noticed before. But now I'm going to see everything, and remember it, and keep it close to my heart."

The pilot looked round at Masha.

"You've gone thoughtful, girl," he murmured, and turned away, but looked round at her again.

He had remembered a passage from a novel he had read a long time ago: there is nothing finer on earth than the eyes of children and girls in the mornings; in them, the night is still dark, but the light of morning has already begun to shine.

"Maybe it was not put so badly after all," thought the pilot.

The weather-beaten captain's mate ran down from the bridge in a canvas cape.

"Aren't you asleep?" he called cheerfully to Masha. "We're casting off in an hour. You can go ashore for a stroll."

"I think I will," said Masha to the pilot. "I'll pick some flowers too."

"All right," agreed the pilot. "Let's go."

They went down the gangway and on to the shore. An old man emerged from the hut; he was probably the one who had been watching the dawn in the night. At that moment, the sun rose over the mist.

The grasses all round were dark green, like deep waters. They still breathed the sharp chill of night.

"What do you do here, Grandad?" asked the pilot.

"I'm a basket-weaver," he replied and smiled apologetically. "I do a bit of weaving. Baskets for fish, baskets for potato picking, baskets for shopping... And you? Interested in the meadows?"

"We just want to see them."

"You're fast people! " laughed the old man. "I've been living here for seventy years and I still haven't managed to see everything. Take that path over there as far as the black poplar. Don't go any further. After that, the grass is higher than your head, you'll get drenched in dew and you won't dry on for the rest of the day. You can collect the dew there in the jar and drink it."

"Have you ever drunk it?"

"I certainly have. It's good for you."

Masha and the pilot slowly went off along the path. Masha walked several paces to the point where the path skirted a tall poplar and stopped.

On either side of the path there were steep walls of sweetbriar and it was blooming with such a crimson and moist fire that even the early sunshine falling on the leaves seemed cold and pale compared with the flowers. It was as if they had forever detached themselves from their thorny branches and were hanging in mid-air like bright little flames. Hornets, black with gold stripes on their backs, were buzzing busily in the clumps of briar.

"Knights of St. George," commented the pilot.

Indeed, the hornets looked like the short ribbons of St. George's medals. And they were behaving fearlessly, like old warriors, paying no attention to the human beings and even getting angry with them.

In some places, the clumps of briar parted, and the graceful candles of dark-blue, almost black delphiniums flowered in the gap. Behind it, all kinds of grasses, in incredible profusion, rose up shimmering and dappled in the sun: red and white clover, goosegrass, snow-white oxeye daisy, wild mallow with pink petals translucent in the sun and hundreds of other flowers whose names neither Masha nor the pilot knew.

A quail shot out from under their feet clucking. Hidden in the damp driftwood, a corncrake creaked, jeering at everybody. Skylarks soared trembling into the air, but their singing somehow didn't coincide with the place where they were weaving about in the sky — the sound seemed to be coming from the river. The steamer coughed and hooted, summoning Masha and the pilot back on board.

"What's that," asked Masha distractedly looking at the flowers. "What's that?"

She was hastily gathering armfuls of flowers. The steamer hooted again, peremptorily and angrily this time.

"What's that?" said Masha, annoyed, and she turned to the place where the smoke from the funnel was streaming over the bushes. "Just a moment! We're coming! "

They set off quickly for the steamer. Masha's

dress was wet and was whipping her feet. Her braids, tied up on the crown of her head in a knot, had come undone and had fallen down. The pilot walked behind her. On the way, he had managed to cut off with a knife several flowering branches of sweetbriar.

The sailors, who were waiting for them so that they could pull in the gangway, glanced casually at the armfuls of flowers and said:

"That's the stuff! They've pulled up all the meadows. Come on, Semyon, heave away! "

The captain's mate said from the bridge:

"Take the flowers into the saloon. For all the passengers! " And he shouted into the megaphone: "Slow speed ahead."

The wheels turned heavily, the blades churned the water, the bank floated away and the bushes made a rushing noise.

Masha felt sorry to part with the shore, the meadows, the hut and the old basket-maker. Everything had become like home to her, as if she had grown up here and Grandpa had been her guide and mentor.

"It's amazing," thought Masha, going up the companionway into the saloon. "I don't even know what region and district this is, or the name of the nearest town."

The saloon was clean and cold. The sun had not yet warmed the polished wooden walls, the little tables and the walnut-wood piano.

Masha began sorting out the flowers and arranging them in vases. The pilot brought some fresh water from below in a bucket.

"My mother," said the pilot, helping Masha to set out the flowers, "has a little garden in Byelozersk. Masses of flowers. Especially marigold."

"Did you have a nice holiday in Byelozersk?" asked Masha.

"Not bad. I read, put my life in order. But there's nothing else to do in Byelozersk."

"What d'you mean, 'order' "? asked Masha in astonishment.

"I wrote down everything I saw, did and thought. Then I sorted out whether I was living right, where I'd gone wrong, and I calculated what life had given me recently."

"Well?"

"Everything behind me is clear now. I can carry on living with a fresh mind."

"I didn't even know that such things existed," said Masha, and she looked intently at the pilot.

"You just try," advised the pilot with a smile. "You'll be amazed how full your life will become."

"Bravo! " said a familiar voice behind Masha. She looked round.

The actor was standing in the doorway with a Turkish towel over his shoulder. He was wearing blue pyjamas with brown cuffs.

"Bravo! " he repeated. "I love matutinal conversations. In the morning, our thoughts are as pure as freshly washed hands."

"Stop that," said the pilot, annoyed.

"Yes, it's all nonsense! " agreed the actor. "Don't be angry, I couldn't help overhearing your conversation and I want to add one particularity. One irrefutable truth. I arrived at it at the end of my life, so to speak."

"What is this great truth?" asked the pilot.

"I do not like that irony of yours," said the actor, mimicking the fruity voice of a bad poetry reader, and then he laughed. "A simple truth. In each day of our life, there is always something good. Sometimes even poetic. And when you put your life in order, as you express it, you involuntarily remember this poetic and rational content. This is magnificent. And amazing. Everything around us is full of poetry. Seek for it. That is my old man's farewell message for all times to come. No objections, please. The conversation is over."

The actor went away, laughing, and Masha thought how everything round her was indeed very simple and unusual. In Leningrad, at the institute, it had not been as noticeable as now, on the journey. Perhaps it was the portion of poetry, hidden before and now revealed to her, that is contained in every day of our lives.

There had been a wind on the Volga every day. Aetherial blue waves shimmered over the surface of the river and past the sides of the steamer. To Masha, it was as if the wind was playfully bearing all those summer days ahead of her, one after another.

The wind died down by evening. The river bore its waters out of darkness into darkness. Only the steamer lights wrested a small circle of illuminated water from the blackness.

Masha felt fine, but sad at times. She could not believe that her new life, after beginning so well, could ever become different.

Masha went ashore at Kamyshin. The wind swept a yellow murk over the Volga.

The pilot and the actor went down on to the jetty to see Masha off.

Masha was slightly agitated as she took her leave of the pilot. The pilot, not knowing what to do, went back on board the steamer and watched the actor saying goodbye to her.

The actor took off his hat, held Masha's hands and looked into her face with quizzical, laughing eyes.

"You're going to be happy," he said. "But my happiness is greater than yours. Because I am an old man."

"What are you talking about?" asked Masha.

"You cannot understand the happiness that is given to the elderly! " said the actor pompously. "The happiness of seeing tears in the eyes of Desdemona in love with her man."

He released Masha's hands and, hat in hand, withdrew to the gangway. The steamer sounded its siren for the third time and cast off.

The wind blowing into her face was redolent of oil. A stunted little man with a white moustache hovered round Masha and kept saying in an undertone, "Carry your bags, Miss?" Masha neither heard him nor replied. Then the little old man sat down apart on a wooden seat and lit a cigarette, waiting for Masha to compose herself.

A day later, Masha was already living a long way from Kamyshin, in a trailer in the steppe, near a pond with bare, clayey banks. It served as accommodation for the workers of the state farm's forest plantations.

The head of the section turned out to be far from dust-covered and gloomy; on the contrary, he was a very lively and amusing man. But the atmosphere in the section from the very first day of Masha's arrival was troubled. All were upset about the new acorns sent for planting. Would they grow? They were worried about the dry wind approaching from the south-east— over there, beyond the Volga, a glassy murk had already settled on the horizon. The term *"solon-chak"* was on everyone's lips. These patches of salty soil were the most persistent and dangerous foes of a young forest—they meant dead lichen in the middle of the steppe, they meant yellow clay, with the white gleam of salt in the cracks.

Once, Masha reviewed her life as the pilot had advised her to do, and discovered that it was divided into three distinct parts—life in Leningrad, the trip on the steamer, and work in the Volga steppes. Each such portion of life had its good content and its poetry, as the old actor had said.

In Leningrad, there had been the room from which she could see the sunset over Lakhta, there had been friends, the institute, books, theatres and gardens. During the river trip, Masha had understood for the first time the charm of passing but deeply affecting encounters and the charm of the open river landscapes of Russia.

Here, in the steppe, she understood the great meaning and scope of her work.

But somewhere deep down in her heart, she could not forget the pilot and how shyly he had smiled as he complained about the nightingales, and how he had looked at her from the side of the steamer at Kamyshin, and his cheek had quivered, as back in Byelozersk. Now he had passed her by, and it was a great pity.

Masha remembered her recent trip so often that she even dreamed about it once. She dreamed about the luxuriant sweetbriar in the dew. It was dusk. The young, tender moon, like a silver sickle forgotten by a reaper, lay on the dark blue curtain of night. And she felt such peace and lightness in her heart that she even laughed in her sleep...

The young forest plantations, like a shallow greenish river, streamed over the hills and receded into the dry steppes, where a reddish dust fumed over the roads.

There was a great deal of work to be done. They had to hoe the soil between the young oak saplings and plant acacias. Masha did this with special care and with tenderness for the baby trees.

Masha acquired a tan. Her braids were bleached in the sun. She looked like a girl of the steppes. Her dress, hands and everything around her was fragrant with wormwood. A scent of wormwood even came from Narzan, the shaggy black dog who used to guard the trailer when all the staff went off into the steppe to work.

The trailer was guarded by Narzan and a little boy aged seven, Styopa, son of the section head.

They sat together all day in the shade of the trailer and listened to the gophers whistling and the noise of the wind in the gnarled wild pear-tree. It rang as loudly as if it were of cast bronze.

Towards the end of the summer, the gerbils descended on the plantations. They dug holes near the saplings and rolled about in the dust to get rid of the fleas.

A plane had been sent from Stalingrad to scatter poisoned oats on the plantation.

One evening, when Styopa was sitting on the trailer steps and peeling potatoes, Narzan lifted up his head and began snarling. Low over the steppe from the direction of the setting sun flew a little aeroplane, its engine chuntering idly.

It flew over the trailer, turned steeply, touched down on the dry grass and, after taxying a few more paces, came to a stop.

The pilot climbed out of the cabin, took off his helmet and walked over to the trailer. He was still a young man, but his temples were grey. Styopa saw two medal ribbons on his jacket.

Instead of barking at the pilot, Narzan crawled under the trailer and began growling softly.

"Hello, laddie! " said the pilot, sitting down next to Styopa on the steps and lighting a cigarette. "Is this section number fifteen?"

"Yes," replied Styopa shyly. "Have you come to see us?"

"I have. I'm going to poison the gerbils."

"Look at you with all your medals," said

Styopa after a moment's thought, "and you poison gerbils. We thought they'd send us a learner pilot."

"I applied to come here, laddie," replied the pilot, and he was silent for a moment. "Does Masha Klimova work here?"

"She does," replied Styopa, and he frowned. "Why?"

"Where is she?"

"Over there, in the forest." Styopa waved his hand towards the plantations.

"A real forest! " laughed the pilot. He stood up and, without looking back, walked off towards the plantations.

Styopa watched him go. It had already turned darker, and visibility was bad over there. But Styopa could still see Masha coming out of the steppe. The pilot walked quickly to meet her, but Masha did not go as far as the pilot; she stopped and covered her face with her hands.

It was now quite dark. A wandering star of the steppes hung over the pond, looking into the dark waters from its great height.

"Why did Masha cover her face with her hands?" wondered Styopa, and he repeated the words that his father had often said in jest about Masha.

"She's an oddball here! "

Narzan growled all night from under the trailer at the plane as it dozed peacefully on the dry, warm ground.

1951

A BASKET OF FIR CONES

The composer Grieg was spending the autumn in the forest around Bergen.

All forests are beautiful with their rustling leaves and scent of mushrooms, but those that stretch down mountain slopes to the sea have a particular charm. They ring with the sound of waves breaking on the shore. Mist is constantly rising from the sea and the abundant moisture encourages the exuberant growth of moss. It even hangs down from the branches in green braids that touch the ground.

These forests are also inhabited by a lilting echo, like a mockingbird, that lies in wait to catch the slightest sound and send it cascading down the cliffs.

One day Grieg met the woodman's daughter, a little girl with pigtails and a basket, collecting fir cones in the forest.

It was autumn and if you could have collected all the gold and copper in the world and fashioned it into thousands of fragile leaves they would still be only a tiny fraction of the burnished splendour that lay on the slopes, and would look crude beside the real leaves, particularly those of the aspen. A bird's song is enough to make aspen leaves quiver.

"What's your name, little girl?" Grieg asked.

"Dagni Pedersen," she replied in a low voice.

It was shyness not fear that made her speak quietly. She could not be afraid of someone with such friendly twinkling eyes.

"What a pity," said Grieg. "I haven't got anything to give you—not a single doll, ribbon or velvet rabbit."

"I've got my mother's old doll," the little girl replied. "Once she used to close her eyes like this."

She closed her eyes slowly and as she opened them again Grieg noticed a flash of leaves in her greenish pupils.

"But now she sleeps with her eyes open," said Dagni sadly. "Old people always sleep badly. Grandad groans all night as well."

"You know what, Dagni," said Grieg. "I'll give you something interesting. But not just yet—in about ten years' time."

Dagni threw up her hands.

"That's an awfully long time! "

"The thing is, I've got to make it first."

"What is it?"

"You'll find out."

"Do you mean to say that you can't make more than five or six toys in your whole life?"

Her voice was very stern and Grieg felt embarrassed.

"No, it's not that," he replied somewhat at a loss. "I can probably make it in a few days, but it's not the right sort of thing for little children. I make presents for grown-ups."

"I won't break it, I promise," pleaded Dagni clutching at his sleeve. "Grandad's got a glass boat that I dust and I've never once even chipped it."

"Dagni has put me in a tizzy," thought Grieg, and then said what grown-ups always say when they find themselves in a difficult position with children.

"You're still very young and there are lots of things you don't understand yet. Just be patient. Now let me carry that basket. It's much too heavy for you. I'll see you home and we'll talk about something else."

Dagni handed over the basket with a sigh. It really was heavy. Fir cones weigh much more than pine cones because they have a lot of resin.

When the woodman's house appeared between the trees, Grieg said to the little girl:

"You can manage on your own now, Dagni Pedersen. There are lots of little girls with your name in Norway. What's your father's name?"

"Hageroop," she replied, then frowned and asked:

"Won't you come in for a minute? We've got an embroidered tablecloth and a ginger cat and the glass boat. I know Grandad will let you pick it up."

"Thank you, Dagni, but I haven't got time now. Goodbye."

Grieg patted the little girl on the head, then turned and walked off towards the sea. Dagni watched him go, pouting. She had tipped her basket and the fir cones were falling out of it.

"I'll write a piece of music," Grieg decided. "And on the title page I'll ask them to print the words: 'To Dagni Pedersen, daughter of Hageroop Pedersen, the woodcutter, on the occasion of her eighteenth birthday'."

* * *

Everything in Bergen was just as it had always been. Grieg had got rid of anything that could muffle sound—carpets, door-curtains and upholstered furniture—a long time ago. Now there was nothing left but the divan. It could seat up to ten guests and Grieg did not dare throw it out. His friends said that his house looked like a woodman's cabin. The only decoration was the grand piano. A person with imagination could hear the most magical sounds within these white walls, from the roar of the Arctic gathering up its breakers in the darkness and the wind whistling its wild saga over them, to a little girl singing her rag doll to sleep with a lullaby.

The piano could sing about love, about people's urge to do great things, about everything under the sun. Rippling under Grieg's powerful fingers the black and white keys would pour out a torrent of yearning, laughter, passion and anger, and then suddenly subside.

A single faint note echoed on in the silence like Cinderella crying because her sisters had been nasty to her.

Leaning back, Grieg would listen to this last note until it died away in the kitchen where a cricket had taken up residence some time ago. Then he began to hear the water dripping from the tap, counting off the seconds with the precision of a metronome. It was saying that time waits for no man and that you must hurry to do everything you have planned.

Grieg spent more than a month writing the music for Dagni Pedersen.

Winter had come and the town was tightly furled in mist. Rusting boats would arrive from other countries and doze by the wooden quaysides, puffing quietly.

Soon the snow came and Grieg would watch it drive past the window and cling to the treetops.

It is impossible to put music into words however rich our language may be.

Grieg was writing about happiness and the delight of being a young girl. As he wrote he saw a girl with shining green eyes rushing towards him breathless with joy. She put her arms round his neck and pressed her warm cheek against his grey, unshaven one.

"Thank you," she said, not knowing yet what she was thanking him for.

"You're like the sun," Grieg would tell her. "Like a gentle breeze and early morning. A white flower has bloomed in your heart and filled the whole of your being with the fragrance of spring. I have seen life. Whatever people may tell you always remember that it is amazingly beautiful. I'm an old man now, but I have given my life, work and talent to the young. I have given away everything and perhaps this has even made me happier than you, Dagni.

"You are a White Night with its mysterious light. You are happiness itself. You are the first glimmer of dawn. Your voice makes the heart leap and tremble.

"May everything that surrounds you be blessed, everything that touches or is touched by you, everything that gives you joy and cause for meditation."

Grieg put all these thoughts into his music. He had the feeling that others were listening to his playing and tried to guess who they were—the bluetits on the tree outside, the carousing sailors from the port, the washerwoman next door, the cricket, the snow falling from the low sky and Cinderella in her patched dress.

All of them were listening in their own way.

The bluetits were excited, but no matter how they fidgeted and twittered, they could not drown the playing. The carousing sailors sat on the steps below, listening with tears in their eyes. The washerwoman straightened her back, wiped her red eyes and shook her head. And the cricket crept out of the crack in the tiled

stove and peered at Grieg through a chink in the
wall.

The falling snow would hang suspended in the
air to catch the rippling strains of music. Smiling
Cinderella looked down at the floor where a
pair of glass slippers stood by her bare feet.
The slippers were jerking and tapping
against each other in time with the music wafting out of Grieg's room.

They were all dearer to Grieg than the polite, smartly dressed concert audiences.

* * *

Dagni left school when she was eighteen and
her father decided that she should go and visit
his sister Magda in Christiania. Let the girl (her
father still thought of her as a girl, although
Dagni was now a slim young woman with heavy
fair plaits), let the girl have a look at the world
and enjoy herself a bit. Who could say what the
future held for her? Perhaps a husband, upright
and devoted, but also mean, close-fisted and
dull? Or a job as shop assistant in the village
store? Or work in one of the many shipping
offices in Bergen?

Magda made costumes at the same theatre
where her husband Niels worked as a wigmaker.
They lived in a tiny attic in the theatre with
a view of Ibsen's statue and the brightly coloured flags of the ships in the fjord.

All day long the boats hooted through the
open windows. Uncle Niels had studied them so

carefully that he maintained he could recognise all their voices — the *Norderner* from Copenhagen, the *Scottish Minstrel* from Glasgow or the *Jeanne d'Arc* from Bordeaux.

Aunt Magda's room was full of bits and pieces for costumes: brocades, silk, tulle, ribbons, lace, old-fashioned felt hats with black ostrich feathers, gypsy shawls, grey wigs, jackboots with bronze spurs, swords, fans and creased silver shoes. All these had to be sewn, mended, cleaned and ironed.

The walls were covered with cuttings from books and magazines: cavaliers from the age of Louis XIV, beautiful ladies in crinolines, knights, Russian women in sarafans, sailors, and Vikings with oak wreaths on their heads.

A narrow staircase led up to the room which always smelt of fresh paint and gilt lacquer.

* * *

Dagni was fascinated by the theatre and used to go there frequently, but she found it difficult to get to sleep after seeing a play and sometimes even cried lying in bed.

This worried Aunt Magda who used to try and comfort Dagni by telling her that she must not believe everything she saw on the stage. On hearing this Uncle Niels would call Magda a "broody old hen" and say that on the contrary you should believe everything in the theatre, otherwise people would not need theatres at all.

And Dagni went on believing.

Nevertheless Aunt Magda insisted that Dagni should go to a concert for a change.

Niels did not object to this. "Music is the mirror of genius," he said.

Niels was fond of making obscure, high-flown statements. He said that Dagni was like the opening chords of an overture and that Magda had a magical power over people, because she made theatrical costumes. Everyone knows that when a person puts on new clothes he changes completely. This explains how the actor who was a foul murderer yesterday can be an ardent lover today, a court jester tomorrow and a popular hero the day after.

"Don't listen to all that awful rubbish, Dagni," Aunt Magda would exclaim on these occasions. "He doesn't know what he's talking about, that garret philosopher! "

It was a warm day in June, the time of the White Nights, and open-air concerts were being held in the City Park.

Dagni set off for the concert with Magda and Niels. She had wanted to put on her only white dress, but Niels had said that a beautiful girl should always dress in contrast to her surroundings. His long lecture on this subject boiled down to the fact that it was essential to wear black on White Nights and, conversely, appear in dazzling white on dark nights.

It was impossible to argue with Niels, so Dagni agreed to wear a black dress of soft silky velvet which Magda had borrowed from the theatre wardrobe. As soon as she put it on Magda had to agree that Niels was probably right—nothing could have set off the young girl's pale face and long plaits flecked with tints of old gold better than this mysterious velvet.

"Look, Magda," said Niels quietly. "Dagni is as lovely as if she were going to her first rendezvous."

"Quite true. Only I don't remember meeting any dashingly handsome young man when we had our first rendezvous, you old chatterbox! "said Aunt Magda and kissed him on the forehead.

The concert started after the traditional firing of the old cannon in the port at sunset.

Although it was evening neither the conductor nor the players switched on the small lamps over their music stands. It was still so light that the lamps in the lime trees had clearly been lit for effect rather than illumination.

This was the first time that Dagni had heard a symphony and it had a strange effect on her. The transitions and crescendoes conjured up a host of dream-like images.

Suddenly she started and looked up. It had sounded as if the thin man in tails who was announcing the items had mentioned her name.

"Did you call me, Niels?" she asked her uncle, looking puzzled as she saw the expression on his face. He was staring at her with a mixture of wonder and delight. So was Aunt Magda who had her handkerchief raised to her lips.

"What's the matter?" asked Dagni.

Magda clutched her arm and whispered:

"Listen! "

Dagni heard the man in tails announce the following:

"Ladies and gentlemen! Some members of the audience sitting at the back have requested me to repeat my announcement. The next item in our programme is a song by the celebrated composer Edvard Grieg dedicated to Dagni Pedersen, daughter of Hageroop Pedersen, the woodcutter, on the occasion of her eighteenth birthday."

Dagni sighed so deeply that it hurt her chest. She was trying to hold back the tears which were welling up, but it was no good. She leaned forward and covered her face with her hands.

At first she could hear nothing because of the turmoil inside her. Then she finally heard a shepherd's horn ringing out in the early morning and the quivering reply of a host of strings. The tune swelled, rose, raged like the wind sweeping over the treetops, tearing off the leaves, whipping up the grass and casting cool spray into the face. Dagni felt the wave of fresh air surging from the music and forced herself to calm down.

Yes, it was her forest, her own native land with its mountains, the sound of horns and the murmuring sea.

Glass boats foamed the water with the wind whistling in their rigging. Then this sound gave way to the tinkling of bluebells, the trill of birds somersaulting in the air, children's halloos, and the song of a girl whose lover has thrown a hand-

ful of sand at her window. Dagni had heard
this song in her native mountains.

So that grey-haired old man who had helped
her carry the basket of fir cones home had been
Grieg, the great musician. And she had re-
proached him for not being able to work quickly.

And this was the present he had promised
to give her in ten years' time!

Dagni wept without attempting to conceal
her tears of gratitude. The music now seemed to
fill all the space beween the earth and the clouds
over the city. Its waves sent a faint ripple over
the clouds revealing the stars.

The music was now a call. It was calling Dagni
to follow it into that realm where sorrow can
never quench love, where no one will destroy
another's happiness, and where the sun shines
like a crown on the head of a fairy godmother.

Suddenly a familiar voice rang out in the
flood of sound: "You are happiness itself. You
are the first light of dawn."

The music died away and the applause began,
slowly at first, and then rising to a great cre-
scendo.

Dagni got up and made her way rapidly
to the exit from the park. Everyone was looking
round at her. Perhaps some of the audience had
guessed that this young woman was the Dagni
Pedersen to whom Grieg had dedicated his im-
mortal work.

"He's dead," she thought. "Why?" If only
she could see him! If only he would suddenly
appear here! How her heart would beat as she

rushed towards him, put her arms round his neck and pressed her moist cheek against his, whispering: "Thank you! " "What for?" he would ask. "I don't know," she would reply. "Thank you for not forgetting me, for your generosity, for showing me the beautiful things that give meaning to our lives."

Dagni walked through the deserted streets, not noticing that Niels was following her trying to keep out of sight. He had been sent by Magda and was reeling like a drunken man, muttering something about the miracle which had happened in their ordinary lives.

Nocturnal dusk still hung over the city, but the northern dawn was touching the window-panes with a faint gold.

Dagni went down to the sea which was slumbering peacefully without the slightest splash of foam.

She clutched her hands and let out a cry at the overwhelming sense of the beauty of this world which possessed her and which she herself did not fully understand.

"I love you, life," she said quietly.

Then she laughed looking with wide eyes at the lights of the boats rocking gently in the translucent grey water.

Niels, who was standing a little way off, heard her laughter and went off home. He was no longer worried about Dagni. He knew that her life would not be wasted.

1953

GOOD FORTUNE FLOWER

One day last summer I was on my way back to the village from Borovoye Lake. The path ran along a cutting in a pine wood. Everything was covered with wild grass fragrant with summer dryness.

Eared grass and wild flowers grew in profusion round the old stumps. At the slightest touch of your foot these rotten stumps would fall to pieces, sending up dark clouds of brown dust like finely ground coffee, and from the maze of secret passages drilled inside the stump by bark beetles there was a sudden scuttling of winged ants, horned beetles and black flat-backed beetles with red stripes like regimental bandsmen.

A sleepy black-and-gold bumblebee crawled out of a hole under the stump and flew up droning like an aeroplane and taking aim to give the intruder a good bang on the forehead.

The sky was a mass of cumulus. The dazzling

white blankets of the clouds looked firm enough to lie on and gaze down at the friendly earth with its forests, cuttings, glades, ripening rye, still, glinting water and herds of grazing cattle.

In a clearing near the edge of the forest I saw some blue flowers nestling together in clumps like small lakes of deep, blue water.

I picked a large bunch of them, and when I shook it, the dry seeds rattled lightly. I had never seen these flowers before. They looked like bluebells except that their dry cups stood erect, not bending down like those of the bluebell.

The path ran out of the wood into the open fields. High above the rye some invisible larks immediately burst into song. It seemed as if they were tossing a string of crystals back and forth, letting it fall only to swoop down and catch it instantly in flight; their tremulous ringing never ceased for one second.

Two country lasses appeared walking towards me along the path over the fields. They must have come a far way. Their dusty shoes tied together by the laces were hanging over their shoulders. They were laughing and chatting about something, but fell silent as soon as they saw me, hastily smoothing their fair hair under their head scarves and pursing their lips primly.

One always feels a bit hurt when sunburnt girls with their smiling grey eyes turn stiff and stern at the sight of you. And even more hurt when you hear their smothered giggles behind your back after they have passed.

I was just about to take offence when the girls stopped as they drew level with me and both gave me such a shy, sweet smile that I felt quite at a loss. Nothing could be more delightful than an unexpected smile from a young lass on a quiet country path, when a moist affectionate sparkle appears in the deep blue of her eyes and you stand amazed as if a bush of fragrant, dewy honeysuckle or hawthorn had suddenly burst into blossom before your eyes.

"Thank you," they said to me.

"What for?"

"For crossing our path with those flowers."

The girls suddenly ran off, looking round several times, laughing and repeating warmly:

"Thank you! Thank you! "

I decided that they must have been teasing me in a burst of high spirits. Nevertheless there was something strange and puzzling about that little episode which I could not understand.

On the edge of the village I met a lively, trim old woman with a smoke-coloured goat on a rope. She took one look at me, stopped short, throwing up her hands and letting go of the goat and cried:

"Ee love! What a piece of luck you crossing my path. I just don't know how to thank you."

"Thank me for what, grandma?" I asked.

"No good pretendin' now," she answered with an artful shake of the head. "As if you didn't know! I can't tell you because you're not allowed to tell. You just keep going slowly, so as to meet as many folk as possible."

The mystery was not solved until I got to the village. It was explained to me by the chairman of the village Soviet, Ivan Karpovich, a severe, business-like man with surprising interest in local lore and historical research "within the boundaries of my district" as he put it.

"You've found a rare flower," he told me. "It is called Good Fortune. There's a popular belief—I don't really know whether I ought to give it away—that this flower brings young girls true love and old people a peaceful old age. And happiness in general."

He gave a laugh.

"And now you've crossed my path with the Good Fortune flower. Maybe it will bring me success in my work. Perhaps we'll finish building the main road from the regional centre to the village this year. And harvest our first crop of millet. It's never been grown here before."

He paused and smiled at a thought that had occurred to him, adding:

"I'm happy for the girls. They're good lassies—our best vegetable growers."

1953

THE OLD MAN
IN THE WORN GREATCOAT*

There are thousands of villages lost amid the fields and woods of Russia. Thousands of villages as inconspicuous as the grey sky or as the flaxen-haired peasant children. When they meet a stranger, these children always stand with their heads bowed, but if they suddenly raise their eyes, there is sometimes such trustfulness in them that the heart is touched.

Very rarely among the countless Sosnovki, Nikolskiye and Gorelye Dvoriki did you come across a village with a remarkable and even unusual name, such as Cape of Good Hope in Tambov Region or Kolybelki somewhere near Ostrogozhsk.

Villages with such surprising names invariably seemed to have acquired them as a result of some interesting or unusual occurrence.

I used to think so too, when I knew little of the Russian countryside. But later, with the years, when I came to know the land better, I became convinced that there isn't such a thing as a village, even the most unromantic, which doesn't have its own remarkable stories and people.

Take, for instance, the environs of the little town of Efremov in what is now Tula region—the Efremov that, according to Chekhov, was the most out-of-the-way of all the district towns in Russia. What obscure villages ought to have surrounded that little town!

At first glance, this was indeed so. But only at first glance.

In 1924 I spent the whole summer near Efremov in the village of Bogovo. It was the seventh year of the revolution, but so far there were few signs of external change.

The same old, balding oat-fields, billowing in wind, rustled drily outside the village fences. The same babies in dirty bonnets lay plastered with flies in their cradles. On market days, wagons rumbled along the highroad and peasant women in foot-wrappers were jolted about on them and sang rollicking songs in squeaky and unnaturally cheerful voices. And a little river, the Krasivaya Mecha (the locals called it the Krasivaya Mech) murmured drowsily by the mouldering dam.

After I had been living in Bogovo for a short time, I learned that not far from Efremov was the estate of Lermontov's father where, in the neglected old house, a dusty campaign surcoat that once belonged to the poet hangs on the wall. They said that Lermontov stayed with his father on his way through to the Caucasus, into exile. I learned that Ivan Sergeyevich Turgenev used to go hunting on the banks of the Krasivaya Mecha; and Chekhov and Bunin both visited Efremov.

But this was all part of the past. I was looking for signs of the present; I wanted to find people connected with the new times.

As if by design in Bogovo, there was no one at all who had fought in the Civil War or who had been a witness of the recent events. And also, as if by design, there was a retired colonel living in the village, a lonely and taciturn man, to judge by the stories. No one could explain to me why he had settled in Bogovo.

"He just lives here," said the peasants. "He doesn't do anyone any harm. He's rented a hut, he cooks his own potatoes, and he sits from dawn till dusk with rod and line on the river. What use is he? He's very old."

"Why does he live here?"

"Goodness knows. He came last year and stayed on. It's quiet round these parts. Of course, it means less trouble for him, seeing as he's an ex-officer. You know yourself, an officer nowadays is poison. Everybody tries to steer clear of him."

I met this retired colonel on the Krasivaya Mecha near the mill-dam.

It was a bleak, chilly day such as occurs sometimes in the middle of the summer. Fragmented clouds were crawling over the earth and shedding reluctant drops of rain. Then the shower eased off.

I went to the mill-race to catch fish. On a beam near the dam sat a gaunt old man with a long white beard; he was wearing an officer's greatcoat and a grey peaked cap. Instead of the gilt uniform buttons, ordinary black ones had been sewn on to his greatcoat.

The old man was smoking a short pipe made out of a gas-pipe joint. It was, of course, very heavy. When the old man knocked it out on the beam, it was as if he were driving in nails. He was fishing with one rod and paid no attention to me at first.

I was fishing with three rods, and so the fish kept giving me the slip. While I was changing the worm on one line, I would get a bite on the other, as if the fish wanted to spite me. I would snatch it up, but it was already too late and I would only pull the remains of a worm out of the water. The old man, however, casually landed big, leaden-coloured undermouths and fat roaches from time to time.

He coughed disapprovingly every time he glanced at my performance with the rods. It was obviously irritating him. Finally, he couldn't stand it any longer and said:

"You should fish with one rod, young man. For your mental balance. You're only ruining your nerves that way."

I took his advice, reeled in two lines and began fishing with one. I immediately landed a big perch. The old man grinned.

"You see! " he said. "You shouldn't fire simultaneously at three targets with three rifles;

you'll only miss. And you're missing so badly, it's painful to watch you."

We went back to Bogovo from the river in the late dusk. The old man walked slowly, looking down at his feet and never once raising his head. And so we reached the village when it was already damp and uncomfortably dark.

All the way, the old man told me how to boil peas as bait for undermouths, so I didn't have a convenient chance to ask him who he was and why he had settled in Bogovo. Here, as I knew, he had no one close to him at all.

The purple clouds in the west were slowly dying out. A bittern called out dismally. Again the cold raindrops began pattering heavily on the burdocks. And this gloom of the evening somehow transmitted itself to my thoughts about lonely old age and about the man in the worn greatcoat who was walking along beside me.

Only once during our conversation did he mention himself, saying that before the First World War he had been commandant of the Fort Osowiecz in Poland. And what undermouths he had caught there, in the River Bobr!

The summer continued. The old man was stubbornly silent about his past and I felt truly shy of asking him about it. I once tried to find out from him if he didn't need help in any way, but the old man merely grinned at my words and did not answer.

The whole business of this old man became

more baffling every day. Especially when I learned that each month he received some kind of notification from Efremov, went to town and returned very tired, but contented. Each time, he brought presents for the village children and for his neighbour Nastya, a woman with many children, who was still young but had been abandoned by her husband. The children got sticky boiled sweets and Nastya was given a packet of tea or a reel of cotton thread.

I never met a more timid creature than Nastya. Her every word and movement betrayed helplessness and good nature. She was always smiling guiltily, hastily straightening her hair under her kerchief, and her hands would tremble. She looked distraught, and I was simply too shy to go into her home—she would promptly rush to wipe the bench and the table clean with her skirt, chase the hen and its brood out into the passage, blushing almost to tears and all the time struggling to light the battered, greenish samovar.

Finally, autumn came and I decided to go to Moscow in a few days.

You leave some places, always thinking that you'll come back one day. This is easier than leaving with the knowledge that you're going away forever. Moreover, you invariably have the bitter feeling that you're leaving a piece of your heart there.

However dismal and unfriendly the place

you have left may be, however much you may
have been oppressed by your stay, there is always
a trace of regret left in the soul and perhaps even
of love.

So, perhaps, the mother loves her ailing child
as it plays with piece of a rotten wood. She
loves it to groans, to tears—helplessly, although it is condemned to loneliness among the
other healthy, jeering children.

I thought about the child probably because
Nastya had a sickly, quiet little boy of her own.
His name was Petya.

He was already turned six, but he could hardly talk. He sat all day on the road, pouring dust
from the palm of one hand into the other,
and he never spoke a word.

I once went up to him, squatted down and
talked to him. He looked at me in terror, his
face puckered, and he began shaking soundlessly; then he hid his face behind his sleeve and
burst into tears.

"What's the matter?" I asked in confusion
and touched his bony shoulder, it was trembling
under the much-laundered shirt.

I couldn't understand it. I could see only
the enormous, dumb, obscure grief of this little
being who was choking on his own tears.

"What's the matter?" I repeated, and I was
suddenly stabbed by the thought, as if by a
knife: "Could it be that he understands what's
wrong with him?"

Nastya ran out of the house, snatched up the
little boy in her arms and, smiling guiltily as

always, said:

"He's not well, he's a little bit touched, poor little mite. Don't be angry. If you're nice to him, it always makes him cry."

Suddenly Nastya's eyes darkened and she said in a bitter voice:

"I'd strangle them with my bare hands, those monsters, those brutes! All they want out of life is to guzzle vodka by the bucketful and swear. They beget children like this, and then your heart bleeds. He's my little boy! And he hasn't got anyone to stand up for him!"

As soon as I decided to leave, I immediately wanted to stay. I suddenly saw everything in a new light—the people, the pastures, all that autumnal landscape.

It was rainy and the heavy, overcast days were like dawns; it became damp and cold in the hut. Only the multitude of falling leaves lit up the ground with their chill yellow fire.

Before departing, I went fishing for the last time with the old man, whose name was Pyotr Stepanovich. The rains were over by then, but a mist hung over the ground for days. It did not even disperse by noon.

I asked the old man if he needed anything from Moscow.

"No, thank you," he replied. "I shan't see Moscow again. I'm going to end my days here. There's nowhere for me to go, and nothing to go for. I'm an old bachelor—I've no wife or children.

And there's no sense in talking about friends. Some have died, and the others have long been scattered all over the country. But I must confess, even in the old army I didn't have that many friends. One or two, and that was it."

"Why?" I asked.

"I'm a soldier's son. My father was a sergeant. As they used to say in the old days, I'm of humble origin, from the common people. Low class. If it weren't for that, they'd hardly have retired me from the old army with the rank of colonel. The commandant of a fort like Oso-wiecz should be a general. But they only put up with me because I was conscientious and knew my gunnery. I wasn't a bad artilleryman."

"Why didn't you get married?"

"Now, of course, it's hurtful," replied the old man and he stopped to regain his breath. Lean, tall, stooping slightly, he somehow reminded me of the woebegone image of Don Quixote. The old man's eyes were moist with tears. He pulled out a red check hankie and wiped his eyes.

"I regret it now," he said, when he had recovered his breath. "And not so much because I never had a wife—God be with her, that wife, I saw enough of those officers' wives—so much as because I never had a son or a daughter. And if you've no one to care for, then it's an empty sort of existence. A cold existence. So there you are, fussing over other people's children."

I finally brought myself to ask him:

"How did you end up in Bogovo?"

"That, my dear friend, is a long story. You

wouldn't believe me if I told you. A simply fantastic thing that happened to me in my old age. To be frank, I just came here. I heard about the Krasivaya Mecha, about the attraction of these parts, so I decided to end my days here. But before I made up my mind, there was this rather amazing event. I'm still astounded whenever I think of it."

"What event?"

"You're a nervous lot! " said the old man reproachfully. "I like a solid conversation. But you people make too much fuss and there's nothing there! No mental balance."

"Very well, Pyotr Stepanovich," I said guiltily. "I shan't interrupt you again."

"Very good! The revolution came, and at that time I was living in retirement at Kalyazin. Well, of course, I lost my pension. I pulled off my shoulder tabs and my brass buttons, but I couldn't get a civilian overcoat. I couldn't cope. And I realised I'd got to leave Kalyazin for a place where no one knew me. But in Kalyazin I felt as if I was on a hill-top. I knew I must lose myself among people. And what could be more populous than Moscow? I went to Moscow and rented a room from an old widow in Petrovsky Park. The money I had left from my pension was practically nothing. But I somehow managed to keep going. The old woman, my landlady, was frail and fairly kind-hearted, probably because of her illness — she had heart trouble. And she had her daughter living with her, a Young Communist. The girl somehow didn't ever seem to notice I was there. I still don't know whether she really didn't notice me or whether she was just pretending. To tell the truth I was always obliging, and especially at that time, if you remember my unenviable predicament. People like me had the same motto: sit quiet and don't stick your nose out unless you have good reason. The tsar's army gave the people's neck a rough time in its horsecollar. I always understood that. And you have to pay for everything in life.

"Yes, I was poor, poorer than you could ever imagine, until my last rubles ran out. No one wants to die, and anyway I felt ashamed before my landlady. I couldn't sleep for two nights, I kept thinking and thinking, and I couldn't think of any way out but to go and ask for alms, collect money, become a real beggar."

The old man stopped and looked at me as if in bewilderment.

"Just imagine—become an actual beggar! That's not life, that's just rotting in the grave. You hate yourself and you look at yourself with loathing. All the time, I was thinking during those days: 'Let God send me any kind of death as soon as possible, even the vilest, than let me live in such degradation.' Some people get used to it, but I couldn't. Begging is an art too; it takes skill, experience, acting talent. I had none of these things.

"I went begging in Petrovsky Park, but didn't go any further. I was afraid. I asked for alms as near the house as possible. I'd stand on the corner without raising my eyes because I was too ashamed to look passers-by in the face. I'd stand there leaning on a stick and muttering something, and it makes me sick even to think of it now: 'Give a homeless old man something for a crust of bread.' They gave badly, I'll tell you that straight. Everybody was put off by my officer's greatcoat. And they used to insult me so that my head went cold with rage. But what could I do? I held myself in check.

"In the evening I'd go back to my den, count my coppers—and I couldn't see anything. Everything was in a mist. Believe me, many's the time I thought of doing myself in. And I would have, too, if it hadn't been for one incident. I wouldn't have waited long otherwise."

The old man and I reached the mill pool and sat down on a damp beam, Pyotr Stepanovich's usual place.

"It feels a bit cold," he complained, and he turned up his coat collar. The inside was a fresh, blue-gray colour, but the facing was faded and yellowed.

It had indeed turned chilly, although there was no wind. A grey, almost wintry tinge had appeared on the clouds, as always in such weather.

"Yes," said the old man, lighting his pipe, "once in summer I came home earlier than usual with takings the like of which you'll never believe. A little boy gave me a five-kopek piece. And that was all! For the whole day. He'd probably been playing at heads and tails with that coin—it was so battered and damaged. They wouldn't have taken it on a tram, to say nothing of the Invalidny Market.

"At that time, my feet were beginning to swell. I was going to put an end to this agony in the night, I just couldn't fight for life any more. What was the point? Who needed me, a retired foot slogger? And, strangely, I thought that even so I ought to say goodbye to my native land, the clear sky, the sun (it was already setting), the birds and the trees.

"I went out into the street and sat on the bench at the gates. At that time the streets in Petrovsky Park were like village ones; they were overgrown with grass, and the old Moscow lime-trees used to rustle over them in the breeze.

"I was sitting there without a thought in my head. Diagonally, opposite our little house, there was an airmen's hostel. Wild youths, troublemakers. No one could shake them off, especially me. As soon as they saw me, they hung out of the windows and started shouting: 'Old gaffer! Museum piece!' But I'd walk past as if I was deaf.

"So I was sitting on the bench and I saw a man of medium height coming along on our side in a black suit and a peaked cap. He was in no hurry, he'd put his hands behind his back under his jacket, and he was obviously thinking something over. He stopped and looked at the limes, as if trying to find something in them, and then carried on. He drew level with me, stopped and said quickly and comically-like:

" 'Will you permit me to sit with you?'

"'Do, please," I said. 'No one gets into trouble for sitting here. Only keep a bit further away from me.'

"He knitted his brows, stopped smiling and looked at me very sharply.

" 'Why's that?' he asked.

"I said nothing, so he repeated it.

" 'Why's that?'

"'Can't you see for yourself,' I said a bit nastily, 'that I'm a beggar?'

"He looked at me again and said as if to himself:

" 'Yes, I can see. You're having a hard time.'

"'Couldn't be worse. I've only got human pity to keep me going. I go begging in the streets.'

" 'Are you an ex-officer?'

"'Officer,' I replied. 'A dog! A marked man, that's all there is to it! '

"He suddenly smiled, and so good-naturedly that I was even a bit taken aback.

" 'Wait,' he said, 'don't get upset. Officers were of all kinds too.'

"'That's just it—they were different, but they all carry the same can. I was once commandant of Osowiecz, and I was very tough with all those bullies that terrorise the soldiers. I hounded them as hard as I could. The Russian soldier is sacred. Just you remember that. All our history has been accomplished by the hands of the Russian soldier, yes, and that revolution of yours too, by the way.'

"He leaned back at that and laughed so heartily that I felt myself smiling in reply. He began questioning me about the old army, about Osowiecz and about the last war. I explained everything in detail. I said, amongst other things, that we army people had long known from the secret orders that war was being prepared. He was particularly interested in this for some reason, and kept saying 'Just so! Well, well! And then what?' And he asked me point-blank:

"'And what d'you think of the Bolsheviks? Are they coping or aren't they?'

" 'They certainly are! ' said I. 'Fancy asking, my dear sir! Can't you see for yourself! It's all very well, but they must watch that the people don't lose their moral values.'

"He looked at me again kind of quizzically and said:

" 'I fully agree with you. But to live like you is wrong. Very wrong. I'll write you a note for a certain place. Take that note with you and they'll be sure to help you.'

"He took out a notepad, wrote something quickly on it and gave it to me. I took it, folded it up and put it in my pocket. What use was his note to me? Who was going to help an officer? But, of course, I thanked him for his kindness and he went away. I called after him.

" 'Out for a stroll round here, are you?'

" 'Yes,' says he, 'I've been ill, and the doctors have ordered me to take a daily walk.'

"He went away. I felt easier after that meeting. 'There you are,' I thought, 'there're still decent and considerate people in this world. That gentleman wasn't ashamed of meeting me, he talked to a beggar, an ex-officer.'

"I sat there thinking. Then I saw the air cadets running towards me. I didn't know why, but they were all tousled and even pale. They ran up and they asked, 'D'you know who were you talking to?' But I felt so bitter about those air cadets, I was still boiling inwardly over 'old gaffer' and 'museum piece', that I was shaking all over. 'I know,' I said. 'Get the hell out of here. All you want to do is make a fool of an old man.'

"They promptly looked downcast and went away. But in the evening they sent a little boy with a packet of tea and a whole pound of sugar. 'What's that for?' I wondered. 'I chased them off, so it must be their conscience.'

"I'm very fond of young people. If there weren't any young people, there'd be nothing left to live for. It would be hellishly boring. So these air cadets didn't matter.

"Yes, I went begging again. What else could I do? I forgot about the note. I put it in an old book by Danilevsky *Moscow Burned,* my only property, and, imagine, I forgot it. But in the middle of the winter I was so done in, I thought I'd collapse in the street somewhere and peg out. Only then did I remember the note. I dug it out, and it was all crumpled, as if somebody had been chewing it.

"There was an address written on the note:

some kind of organisation — I couldn't read it. And I didn't want to get to the department because the note looked so crumpled. Yes, and it was a long way to the city centre. I'd never been there in the whole of my begging life. I went just the same. I made up my mind. The landlady simply made me go. 'You, Pyotr Stepanovich,' she said, 'are a boy, not a retired colonel. You're wool-gathering. It amazes me you were ever made commandant of a fort. You ought to have been teaching the humanities, not firing guns.'

"I walked along, and I didn't raise my eyes. Since my begging days, I've had that habit of not looking people in the eyes. It made things easier. I still can't shake off the habit. You've probably noticed it yourself. An old man's habits are very persistent and stubborn.

"Anyway, I got there. The department was a big one, but quiet. Big carpets everywhere. The doorman or the porter—I don't know what they call them now—said to me rather firmly, 'You'll have to take off your greatcoat, citizen.' How was I to take it off? I hardly had anything on underneath. 'Respect an old man,' I said. 'I've come with this note.' I showed it to him, he had a look, made quite a fuss, pushed up a chair for me and said, 'Sit there a while, Dad. I'll announce you in a sec.' He went away and came straight back again. After him came a middle-aged man in spectacles; he had a stern face but a friendly smile. He took me by the arm and led me after him. I walked along,

and the melted snow was dripping in whole
lumps from my old shoes. As if I hadn't suffered enough to last me the rest of my life.

"This man took me into the office, sat me
down in a leather armchair and asked if I had
any documents. I gave him all I had. Thought
I was done for. He went out, and the time
passed. Half an hour I sat there alone and not
happy that I'd got mixed up in this business. I
was even thinking of going, but I couldn't
without my documents. But at the moment the
man came back—evidently some sort of big
cheese—and handed me a pension book and a
ration book for food and clothing and for
something else—firewood, or treatment in a
clinic. He made me sign my name and gave me a
wad of money. 'That's on account of your first
pension. You must have starved.'

"I couldn't believe my eyes. He calmed me
down: 'Why are you upset, Pyotr Stepanovich?
We appreciate hard work, especially when it's
been done by an expert at his job and honest
man like you. You've been rewarded according
to your merits.' 'Who told you about my services?' He laughed. 'We got it from your dossier,'
he said. 'From your service records.' Good
Lord. All that from my officer's records! Fancy
that!

"We said goodbye like old friends. I went
out and wandered back home to Petrovsky Park
without raising my head; there were tears in
my eyes, and I couldn't shake off the old habit.

"I got as far as Tverskaya Street. It was already dark, and the street-lamps were on. And the shop-windows were lit up. 'I'll buy some bread and some sausage, not too expensive, and I'll treat the landlady,' I thought.

"It was the first time I'd looked up, and it was as if I'd been struck by lightning. There was a portrait on show in the shop-window. I looked, and it was him! The small gentleman who gave me the note. And there was an inscription under the portrait: *V. I. Lenin (Ulyanov)*. And in the next window, him again! Lord, Thy will be done!

"So I didn't buy anything after all and hastened home. Everything inside me was trembling, and, believe me, I was ready to shed my last drop of blood for that man. He freed me from spiritual bondage. I'm greatly indebted to him and only complain about one thing, that I've no way of expressing my gratitude. I haven't the strength any more, or the health, or the time ahead of me.

"I went home—you might say I ran—and rushed to the landlady's daughter, the Young Communist. 'Get me a portrait of Lenin. I want to check something.' She went into her little room and brought out a newspaper. It was called *The Poor*. And in the paper was his portait. Here he is, I'll show you.''

With uncompliant fingers, the old man unbuttoned his greatcoat and took out an old wallet bound with a piece of cord. He untied the knot and took out of the wallet a very frayed photograph of Lenin cut from a newspaper.

"Since that day, I've always carried him next to my heart," he said in a hollow, quavering voice. "He was a real man! "

The old man's head began shaking. The tears ran down his yellow, wrinkled cheeks, but he didn't wipe them away.

We sat for a long time in silence.

The mist was getting thicker, trickling in big drops from the yellowing willows. Somewhere far beyond the ends of the earth a railway engine shrieked. A faint odour of smoke and rye bread came drifting over from Bogovo. On the road beyond the Krasivaya Mecha, a wagon rumbled and a girl's voice started singing:

> *Where the tall summer corn is a-swaying,*
> *Our poor village is vanished from sight...*

"You see what it's like, our Russia," said the old man after a pause. "I'm a bit tired, my friend. Old age! Let's go! "

Ten years later I happened to go past Efremov on the railway branch-line from Tula to Elets.

It was autumn again. The hard carriage thundered as if made of tin. The electric lamps glowed dully. The tired passengers snored. Opposite me on the upper bunk lay a clean-shaven old man in high hunting boots. We got talking. It turned out that he was on his way to Efremov. He kept glancing my way, then said:

"Seem to know you. Can't recall where I met you. Must have been in Bogovo."

It turned out that he was the blacksmith from Bogovo. He remembered me, but I hadn't recognised him. He told me that the retired colonel had died six years ago.

"He was a harmless fellow," said the smith. "He was drawing a pension from our government. For something he'd done, no one ever knew what. He never said anything about it himself. Lived frugally, seemed to be saving up. The rumour got round that meanness had got the better of him. It's true, a man gets meaner as he grows older. But when it came to the acid test, it turned out different. When he felt death was near, the old man donated all his money to our school. So that the people shouldn't lose their moral values. And Nastya—remember?—he left her a tidy sum. He suffered for her little boy, Petya. But Petya died the year before last. He hadn't long to go in this world! He hadn't long to go! I reckon it was for the best."

The blacksmith alighted at Efremov. I went on to the platform to get a breath of fresh air after the stiffness of the compartment. The train was sleeping. It gave off an oily warmth.

There, in the night, where according to my estimate Bogovo lay and there also ought to be impenetrable darkness, there was a faint blue glimmer of light.

For a long time I wondered what that light

was in Bogovo, but I never found the answer. And there was nobody to ask.

This is a true story. I wrote down the retired colonel's narrative from memory. The only thing that has slipped my mind is his surname. I won't swear to it, but I think it was Gavrilov.

1956

ILYINSKY WATERS

People are constantly plagued with regrets of some kind or other—over big things, small things, serious or ridiculous things. As for me, I frequently regret that I did not become a botanist and do not know all the plants in Central Russia. There are absolutely masses of them, of course, more than a thousand at a rough estimate. But just imagine how interesting it would be to know all these trees, shrubs and flowers and their different properties!

Time rushes past with such unjustifiable haste that this must be our greatest regret of all. Before you know where you are, summer is fading, that "irretrievable" summer which is associated in nearly everyone's mind with memories of childhood.

In a flash youth has passed, old age is creeping on and you have still not seen the tiniest fraction of the enchantment that life has cast around you.

Each day, sometimes each hour, brings with it regrets. They waken in the morning, but do not always subside at night. On the contrary, they sometimes flare up at night and there is no sedative that will quieten them. Together with the strongest regret of all about the rapid flight of time, there is another one, as sticky as pine resin. This is the feeling that one has not been able and perhaps never will be able, to see the world in all its amazing and mysterious variety.

What am I saying, the world, when time and health do not even permit you to get to know your own country. For instance, I have never seen Baikal, the island of Valaam, Lermontov's estate in Tarkhany or the flat, broad waters of the Ob near its mouth by the small town of Salekhard which used to be called Obdorsk.

Going over the places which I have seen convinces me that I have seen very little. But if you think of these places in terms of their quality, their essence, and not in terms of quantity, the picture is more encouraging. You can see a lot of marvellous things even if you spend your whole life sitting on the same spot. It is just a matter of having a keen, searching eye. We all know that the tiniest drop of water can reflect a kaleidoscope of light and colour, right down to a multitude of completely different shades of green in the foliage of the elder or the bird cherry, the lime and the alder. Incidentally, alder leaves are like the palms of young children's hands with their plumpness between the thin veins.

A mere ten kilometres from the log house where I live each summer there is one of the greatest, though little-known spots in the whole of Russia. In my opinion the word "great" is just as relevant to some of these places in our country as it is to events and people. We obviously dislike exalted feelings because we do not know how to express them, and put up with dry officialese to avoid the accusation of being sentimental. In spite of this many people, myself included, feel like saying "the great fields of Borodino" not simply the "fields of Borodino", just as people were not afraid of saying in the old days "the great sun of Austerlitz".

Great events naturally leave their mark on the countryside. We are aware of a special solemnity in nature in the fields of Borodino and hear its vibrant silence. It returned here after the bloody battles of the last war and since then no one has disturbed it.

The place I want to tell you about has a simple name, like many other magnificent spots in Russia. It is called Ilyinsky Waters, and to me this name is just inexpressibly attractive. It is not associated with any historical events or famous people, but simply expresses the true nature of the Russian countryside. Thus it is "typical", even "classical" as people like to put it.

Places such as these have an incredibly powerful effect on one's emotions. It is only fear of being accused of sentimentality that stops me from adding that these places are serene, soothing and have a holy quality about them. Pushkin was right when he spoke of the "holy twilight" in the gardens of Tsarskoye Selo. Not because they were consecrated to any events from "Holy Writ" but because they were holy to him.

Such places fill our hearts with joy and reverence for the beauty of our native land, the Russian countryside.

You have to climb down a slope to reach Ilyinsky Waters. No matter how much of a hurry you may be in to reach the waterside, you cannot help stopping several times on the way down to glance at the vast expanses on the other side of the river. I have seen many broad vistas in different parts of the world, but the view over Ilyinsky Waters is something which I never expect to find anywhere else.

This spot with all its charm and the unassuming beauty of common field flowers fills one with a sense of profound peace and the strange thought that if you have to die, let it be here, in this patch of mild sunlight, among the tall grass. The flowers and herbs—chicory, clover, forget-me-nots and meadowsweet—seem to welcome you, a passerby, with a warm smile, nodding under the weight of heavy bees.

But the main charm of these spots was not in their herbs and flowers, or in their stout elms and rustling broom. It was in the magnificent view that opened up, tier upon tier, before one's eyes. Each tier, I counted six of them in all, had its particular blend of colour, light and air,

as an artist might put it. It was as if a magician
had taken all the colours of Central Russia and
set them out in a broad panorama shimmering in
the warm air.

Dry meadowland, *sukhodol,* in a riot of
green and flowers lay in the foreground. Here
and there in the thick grass sorrel rose up in
long thin torches, the colour of deep red wine.

Closer to the river there were water meadows
overgrown with pale pink meadowsweet. It had
already faded sending up swirls of dry petals
over the quiet dark patches of still water.

The second tier was made up of ancient willow and broom bathed in intense heat and resembling clouds of greyish green mist. The leaves
hung lethargically until the odd breeze blowing
up from nowhere turned their undersides to
the sun. And then the whole riverside kingdom
of willow and broom became a seething torrent
of foliage.

There were many rocky shallows in the river.
The water streamed over the stony bed with
a glinting murmur, sending out concentric ripples of river freshness.

Forests stretched up to the high horizon
in the third tier. At this distance they seemed
completely impenetrable and resembled mounds
of fresh grass piled up by giants. By looking
carefully at the shadows and the different
shades of colour you could make out where
the cuttings, tracks and the big dell were. The
dell naturally concealed an enchanted lake
with dark olive-green water.

Kites wheeled persistently over the trees. And the day sweltered in expectation of a storm.

Here and there the forest gave way to fields of waving rye, buckwheat and corn. They lay like patchwork quilts stretching out smoothly to the very ends of the earth and fading into the haze—the constant companion of remote expanses. The fields of grain shone through the haze like copper. It had ripened and a dry rustle, the endless whisper of the ears, rippled constantly from one vast stretch to the next like the majestic music of harvest.

Beyond the fields nestled hundreds of small villages stretching right up to our western border. You seemed to be able to smell newly baked rye bread, that enchanting, age-old smell of Russian villages. A dove-grey haze hung over the last tier, stretching above the horizon low over the earth. Something would flare up in it, like thin slivers of mica bursting into flame and dying away. The haze glinted and trembled with these slivers and in the sky above, blanched with the intense heat, solemn swanlike clouds sailed in a shining procession.

One summer I lived in the steppe beyond Voronezh. I spent all the day either in an overgrown lime park or in a windmill on a dry hillock. The mill was surrounded by coarse violet immortelle. Half of its plank roof had been torn away by blast at the time of the German advance on Voronezh. You could see the sky through this opening. I used to lie on the warm clay floor of the mill reading novels by Ertel or simply looking up at the sky through the hole in the roof, where I could see bank upon bank of billowing white clouds trail past slowly northwards.

The clouds cast their gleaming light down to earth, it crept over my face, making me close my eyes to protect them from the brightness. I rubbed some thyme flowers between my fingers and savoured their dry, healthy, southern fragrance. Then I had the strange feeling that the sea was just beyond the windmill and that the aroma of thyme was coming from its smooth sands, not from the open steppe.

Sometimes I would doze off by the millstones of pink sandstone and they would carry me back to the days of Ancient Greece.

A few years later I saw the famous head of the Egyptian Queen Nefertiti made out of the same stone and was astonished at the feminine grace expressed with such crude material. The brilliant sculptor had turned the stone into the beautiful head of a vibrant, gentle young woman and presented it to future generations, to us his distant descendants, as tireless as he in our search for eternal beauty.

Two years later in Provence I saw the famous windmill of the French writer Alphonse Daudet where he actually lived for a time.

Life in a windmill smelling of flour and old herbs must have been absolutely delightful. Particularly in our Voronezh windmill, since Alphonse Daudet lived in a stone mill, not a wooden one full of the delicious smell of resin, bread and convolvulus, full of fresh steppe breezes, the light of the clouds, the trilling of the larks and the twittering of small birds— yellow buntings or kinglets.

Unfortunately Ilyinsky Waters had neither a windmill nor a watermill. That was a great pity because nothing suits the Russian countryside better than these mills, as a colourful silk shawl on a Russian peasant girl makes her eyes darker, her lips brighter and her voice intimate and gentle.

In the far distance between the dim waves of oats and rye stood a knotted elm, its dark leaves murmuring from the gusts of wind.

I had the feeling that the elm was not simply standing amid these hot fields, but that it was guarding some secret as ancient as the human skull washed up by a heavy downpour in the neighbouring gully. The skull was a dark brown. It had been cleft from forehead to crown by the stroke of a sword and must have been lying in the ground since the time of the Mongol invasion. It must have heard the calling of the wood sprites, foxes yelping at the blood-red setting sun and the wheels of Scythian chariots creaking slowly over the steppe.

As well as going to the mill I often spent a lot of time sitting in the shade of this elm tree. Patches of shy short-stemmed clover were growing on the border between the fields. An angry old bumble-bee made a threatening dive at me

in an effort to banish man from its unfrequented
realm. I sat in the shade of the elm, lazily picking flowers and grasses with a deep affection
welling up inside me for each blade and petal.
I was thinking of my silent friends, all these
trusting stems and blades, and of the joy and
peace of mind which I got from seeing them
each day and living with them in this quiet
steppe under the open sky.

You could see the green wall across Ilyinsky
Waters. It was the forest on the right bank of
the Oka and beyond it nestled the Bogimovo
estate with its old park and terraced manor
house with Venetian windows. Chekhov once
spent the summer here and wrote *Sakhalin
Island* and *The House with the Mansard,* that
incredibly sad love story about the sweet young
girl Missie. Missie left these parts never to return,
but Chekhov's sadness remained. It dwells in
the dampish avenues and the empty rooms of
the large house where moths sleep on the
dusty windowpanes. Touch a moth and you
will find that it is dead.

The pond is covered with an enormous green
carpet of duckweed. Carp champ away quietly
at the waterweed turning first one side of dark
liquid gold and then the other to the sun. These
carp are the descendants of those for which
Chekhov used to fish here.

But Chekhov is no more. I was twelve the
year when he died and remember how my fa-

ther's shoulders hunched up and his head shook
when he learnt of Chekhov's death. And how
he turned abruptly and went off to grieve over
this irreparable, hopeless loss in private. None
of the Russian writers, apart from Pushkin and
Tolstoi, were mourned as deeply as Chekhov,
for he was not only a great writer but a person
whom we admired and loved. He knew the way
to human dignity and happiness and mapped it
out for us.

It is difficult to say how habits grow up, particularly unexpected ones. Every time I was
about to set off on a long journey I went to have
a last look at Ilyinsky Waters. I simply could not
leave without saying good-bye to the Waters,
the white willow and the rolling Russian plains.
I used to say to myself: "You'll suddenly remember this thistle when you are flying over the
Mediterranean. If you get there, that is. And
you'll think of that last blushing ray of sun lost
in the vast heavens when you are somewhere
near Paris. If you get there too, that is."
And I did. There I was flying over the Tyrrhe-
nian Sea. Through the small round window I
saw the yellow outline of an island looking like
a thistle appear in the fathomless blue depths.
It was Corsica. Later I learned that seen from
above islands take on fantastic shapes just
like cumuli. These shapes are the product of
our imagination of course.
The jagged coast of Corsica lashed by the cen-

turies and baked by the intense heat, its castles protecting the islands like spiky thorns, patches of bright red shrubs, a torrent of deep blue Mediterranean light bursting through the invisible weir of the heavens and cascading in all its might onto the island—all this could not distract my thoughts from a small damp hollow on Ilyinsky Waters smelling of hemlock with a solitary thistle that grew up to your head—impregnable, bristling with prickles, its sharp cubitieres and visors.

On the western shore of the island was a small town resembling a handful of carelessly scattered dice. It emerged from the wing of the plane like a honeycomb. This was Napoleon's birthplace, Ajaccio.

"All conquerors are mad," said my neighbour, a fat, jovial Italian in sun-glasses, glancing down at Ajaccio. "How on earth a person who was born and grew up in such beauty could become a mass murderer is completely beyond me!"

He opened his newspaper noisily, looked at a page and then threw it aside, announcing to all and sundry:

"Ho ho. De Gaulle's not a bad Catholic, it seems."

Rome was shining in the distance with the bright reflection of the sun on the glass of new, multi-storey blocks. The loudspeaker at the airport kept repeating agitatedly that Signor Parelli's car was waiting for him at the main entrance.

And I suddenly felt an intense yearning to

be back in my simple log house, on the Oka, on Ilyinsky Waters where the willows, the misty Russian sunsets on the plains and my friends were waiting faithfully for me.

As for the blushing ray of sun I saw that as well a few days later in the small town of Ermenonville near Paris where Jean Jacques Rousseau spent the last weeks of his life on an old estate.

The concierge opened the iron gate for us, took our entrance fee in silence and indicated with an angry wave of the hand where we should begin our tour round the park. Then in an equally angry manner she told us that the house was closed and all we could do was look at the park.

The park was deserted. We did not meet a single soul in it. If the ghost of Rousseau had been in the park, no one would have prevented us from communing with it. Yellow plane leaves rustled beneath our feet. They had covered the surface of the misty ponds as well as all the ground. I had never seen such enormous plane trees. Their leaves were falling fast baring the gigantic treetops. The trees seemed to have been cast in light bronze by some great sculptor. Their tops were enveloped in mist and this gave them a somewhat eery appearance.

Everything around was immersed in a grey silence. The park was enveloped in mist. Now and then transparent icy drops would fall off the branches onto our arms. The yellow, spreading

leaves fell constantly, their light rustle following
on our heels.

A slate-grey sky stretched overhead, but it
was a light, radiant Paris grey all the same.
Rousseau's tomb stood gleaming on an island
in the middle of a pond. The only way of reaching it was by boat and there were no boats on
the pond. Nor were Rousseau's remains on
the island. They had been removed to the
Pantheon a long time ago.

Then the rosy light of the sun began to break
through the shrouds of mist and the plane trees
suddenly seemed to come to life, transformed
into burnished copper. I remembered a similar
rosy evening on Ilyinsky Waters and was suddenly overwhelmed by the familiar feeling of home-
sickness, longing for our country, for the sunsets, the plantain and the gentle rustle of the
fallen leaves.

Beautiful France was magnificent, of course,
but indifferent to us. We were homesick for
Russia. That day I began to long to get home to
the Oka where everything was so familiar, so dear
and so open-hearted. My heart sank at the very
thought that my return home might be delayed
for some reason even by a few days.

I fell in love with France long ago, intellec-
tually at first and then really seriously. But I
could not sacrifice even such a small thing
as a saffron beam of morning sunlight on the
log wall of an old *izba* for her. You could follow
the movement of the sunbeam over the wall,
listen to the saucy shrieks of the village cocks

and the old familiar words would spring to your lips:

> *The cocks are crowing over Holy Russia —*
> *Over Holy Russia it will soon be day...*

Now and then the leaves drifted down from the plane trees. The gardens of Ermenonville, those sacred gardens imbued with the memory of Rousseau, nestled in the darkling autumn day as short and melancholy as a Russian autumn. Something very close and dear beckoned to us in this silent mist above the pond and in the hush of approaching night.

No! A Man's country is his very life-blood. He cannot live without it.

1964